For my friends Russ
and Wendy!
Sandy Graham
8/1/2012

Delbert Pillage

BY

SANDY GRAHAM

Copyright © 2012 by Sandy Graham

ISBN 978-0-7414-7278-6 Paperback
ISBN 978-0-7414-7279-3 eBook
Library of Congress Control Number: 2012931031

Printed in the United States of America

Published February 2012

INFINITY PUBLISHING
1094 New DeHaven Street, Suite 100
West Conshohocken, PA 19428-2713
Toll-free (877) BUY BOOK
Local Phone (610) 941-9999
Fax (610) 941-9959
Info@buybooksontheweb.com
www.buybooksontheweb.com

Dedicated to the Canadian education system, may its standards never waver, and to Mum, who instilled similar standards in me and from time to time intimated a hope that one day the writing bug might strike.

I wish to thank Paul Novak, whose teachings and partial edit of this book significantly increased my knowledge of the craft. Also, to thank Jim, Sheila, Karen and Laura Graham for acting as sounding boards and providing constructive suggestions through the book's evolution.

American readers will find an odd "u" cropping up in unexpected places, sometimes an "er" reversing itself, etc. This is a Canadian story. It deserves the Canadian spelling variations.

CHAPTER ONE

"Hey Delbert. That mop almost covers your ears."

"Look, one of them slipped down."

"Delbert, why's one ear lower than the other?"

"He hears high notes with the right and low notes with the left."

Each barb got a laugh from the bullies. They didn't care how it hurt the scrawny little kid. His shaggy black mop hid an oversized forehead. Ears protruded through it and in fact, the left did appear half an inch lower than the right. His worn pants ended in boots scuffed to an indistinguishable color and held on by laces knotted in half a dozen places.

"Shine your boots with clear polish, Delbert?"

"Look at all the fancy knots."

A strong chin and well-proportioned nose supported a pair of dark brown eyes that gazed rather than looked, missed nothing, and when they settled on you seemed able to read your thoughts. Perhaps that triggered the bullies' mean streak. Frail, shy and poor made him an easy target for incessant taunts.

Why pick on me, he wondered. I'm smarter than Tommy, Brett and Brian, but never show them up. What does it take to get them off my back? And why do so many in the

1

class side with the bullies? Are they afraid they might be the next punching bag? They don't need to join in like they do. Will it ever stop?

Only Sylvia Cairns stays out of it. Perhaps because she's shy. She turns away or hides in a book when they badger me. It bothers her. I'd like to thank her for showing sympathy but can't. It might turn them against her too. She's sure pretty.

Whenever their third grade teacher walked in on the harassment, she put a stop to it. She liked to toss out questions in a way that invited rapid response. The same two children always vied to be first.

"Not you two again. How about you, Delbert?"

"What was the question?"

"Oh, Delbert, pay attention. How do you spell receive?"

"I don't know."

"Try."

"I don't know how."

"Dumbert don't know how," Brett mimicked.

"Alright, Brett, then you spell it."

"R e s e e v e." Delbert suppressed a laugh.

"No, can anyone spell receive?" and then, with a resigned sigh, "OK, Jimmy."

In this way, Delbert plodded through the school year. He played dumb and seldom participated yet in the end exhibited enough to let the teacher pass him on with a clear conscience.

~~~

Words bottled up in school burst out at home, though not in his father's presence.

"Mum, why do kids at school make fun of my clothes, my boots, my ears?"

"Doesn't your teacher stop them?"

"It happens when she's not in the room."

"Do you want me to talk to the principal?"

"No! That would make it worse. They might beat me up."

"Then be strong dear, eventually they'll see you for the wonderful person you are."

"I'm not strong. If I was strong, I could fight them."

~~~

While still eight years old, she caught him one day with Charles Dickens' *Great Expectations*, part of her collection of Dickens' works, a wedding present from her mother and one of her few treasures.

"Delbert, what are you doing with that book? You shouldn't play with it. You know how much it means to me."

"I was just reading it. I won't hurt it."

"Reading it? You're too young to understand it."

"I want to see how Pip turns out. Right now he tries to impress people but he's phony. I want to see if he grows out of it. Usually people in these books end up good."

Taken aback, "What do you mean books? Have you looked at others?"

Sheepishly he confessed, "Some. I love them."

"But I never see you read. You don't even look at your school books."

"I've read them."

Teresa Pillage was slightly flabbergasted, if flabbergasting permits slightness. Has he actually read them or does he just thumb through the pages? It sounds like he knows what they're about. He seems brighter than his grades indicate. Wish I could figure him out.

"Be careful with it. Why aren't you outside in the fresh air on such a nice day?"

"I'll put it away in a few seconds."

Ten minutes later, Delbert was in the back yard batting rocks. With a board the size of a small baseball bat, he hit rocks picked up in the yard out over the bank down towards the creek that ran behind their house.

Still at it when his father got home, "That kid's out there hittin' them rocks agin. Sometimes I think he's auteristic."

"Autistic, dear, and I'm sure he's not. Today I caught him reading *Great Expectations*."

"What the dickens is that?"

"A novel by Charles Dickens."

"Well, I got no great expectations fer that kid."

"At least he rids the yard of rocks."

"As long as they're not goin' inta the garden. Doubt if he has enough meat on his bones to reach it anyway."

What seemed like endless repetition rock after rock was anything but to Delbert. In his imagination, he laid out an elaborate ballpark. The flight of every rock meant something. Not just foul or fair balls but also singles, doubles, triples, homers, sacrifice flies, bunts, fly ball outs, ground outs, double plays, all based on how the rock flew, where it ended up and the game situation. Carefully chosen zones matched probabilities found in baseball.

He played full baseball games with players on real teams. His schedule copied the National League although he narrowed it down to contenders. He created his own season complete with a pennant race and continued it through the World Series.

Each day, he read the box scores in the paper to compare his players' performance with the real ones. He tried a little harder on behalf of the better hitters and fine tuned his ballpark zones to improve the correlation. This complexity, of course, hid in his head.

To his parents he mindlessly batted rocks hour after hour. His father, Phil, stuck his head out the door, irritated enough to yell, "Delbert quit hittin' them rocks. Get in here an' wash up fer dinner."

CHAPTER TWO

Every spring, the creek behind the house flooded its banks and by summer dwindled back to a well behaved stream. When the warm weather arrived, Phil built a dam to raise the water level about three feet. A log the diameter of a telephone pole spanned from bank to bank. Planks were leaned against the log and driven into the mud to hold the dam in place. Sods dug from the bank were thrown in front of the planks.

The dam created a swimming hole and made the creek navigable for a quarter of a mile upstream. Delbert, his brother Paul and their neighbourhood friend Tony poled a little scow and paddled a leaky canoe up and down the creek for hours.

At the swimming hole they made a mud slide on the bank and plastered closed any mud wasp holes they found. Between the slide and the silt, the water in the swimming hole never stayed clear long. No girls ever played in the creek so the boys often shed their swim suits. The mud slide worked better with a naked bottom and the feeling was more erotic.

Alone in the swimming hole one day, his swim suit hung over a branch, Delbert went down the slide half a dozen times, then floated lazily in the water. He heard footsteps on the path and looked up to see Brett and two girls approach.

With no time to get away, he kicked up more silt to muddy the water and covered his crotch with his hands.

"Hi Delbert, whatcha doing?"

"A little swimming."

"Don't seem to be making much headway."

Please make them go, he prayed silently.

"You naked Delbert?"

"No, what makes you say something like that?"

"That swim suit on the branch over there."

Keep the water muddy. Please make them go. Instead, they sat down on the bank.

"We won't leave until you come out and get your swim suit, Pillboy."

Brett grinned and the girls giggled. He could see they meant it. Could he outlast them? It would get cold standing in the water. He summoned the courage to make a break for the branch. Brett beat him to it, scrunched up the swim suit and threw it to one of the girls.

"Give it to me," he shouted.

"Come and get it."

He ran from one to the other until finally the younger girl felt sorry for him and held it just long enough for him to snatch it away. He turned his back to the girls to put it on.

"Did you notice his head isn't the only thing bigger than normal?"

The girls snickered and started up the path. Brett gave Delbert a shove that sent him flying back into the pool, then followed the girls.

Delbert started to cry as he trudged up the path to the house. Why are they so mean? Until now Brett left me alone at home and on the school bus. I thought he joined in at school only to be part of the gang. Guess he had to show off in front of the girls. He's as bad as the others. Now I can't swim alone. Sobs racked his little body.

Near the house he stopped and took a number of deep breaths, then wiped the tears from his face. His father might be home already and he couldn't let him see he cried.

CHAPTER THREE

Saltspring Island is the largest of a series of small islands sprinkled along the southeast corner of Vancouver Island in British Columbia. Local literature calls it the Queen of the Gulf Islands. Half way up the thirty mile island, a long inlet aptly named Long Harbour almost divides it in two. Ganges, the only town, surrounds the head of this inlet.

Another slightly shorter inlet pierces the southern end of the island. Called Fulford Harbour, a village sprawls along its edge. More important, it has a ferry dock which is the main connection to Vancouver Island.

During Delbert's early school years in the 1940's, students were bused from all over the island to a single school in Ganges. Most came from families of modest income, some dirt poor, a few well off. Transistor radios were not yet invented, television unknown. On hearing a radio for the first time, a six-year-old girl screamed because she didn't know where the voice came from. Children made up their own entertainment.

A tradition developed that repeated every school day, year after year. The soccer game. It started in the morning when the first boy with a soccer ball arrived at school. The teams were always the same; Ganges against Fulford. The game paused when the bell rang, continued through morning recess, noon hour, afternoon recess and after school until the

9

boy with the ball left. The score at that time decided the day's winner.

Everyone knew which team they were on and there was no limit to the number of players. A bruising no-holds-barred facsimile of soccer with no discernable organization. To an observer it looked like a swarm of shin-hacking scramblers chasing the ball.

Still, buried in the madness existed an element of method. A few outriders often poised to make a breakaway with a clearing pass. They consisted of two types, those short of breath after a hard run and those too timid to join the flailing melee. Delbert fell in the second category. Yet, while others would run from the ball when it came their way, he didn't.

He would trap the ball, look around and pass it to an open team-mate before the mob could descend on him. Since a pass was not uppermost in the horde's mind, most thought him afraid to hang on to it. Sometimes one of his tormenters would bowl him over even though the ball had moved on.

"You put the pill in pillage, Delbert," Brian flung back at him.

His approach never changed, even as the years added firmness to his spindly legs. He still wandered along the fringes of the field and waited for the ball to arrive. However, a few of the better players came to realize the advantage of clearing the ball his way. They always managed to make it appear accidental. Sometimes threw up their hands in disgust while they hoped in secret for good things from his dilapidated boot.

~~~

Children brought their lunches from home and usually ate in the classroom. One day fat Tommy slouched by and noticed Delbert had a cookie. The teacher was out of the room so he snatched it.

"Look, I pillaged Pillage's lunch box," the slob said in a loud voice. Many laughed.

"Give it back."

"Make me." He took a big bite out of it.

Resigned to the loss, Delbert finished his half-eaten sandwich. He hid his inner turmoil behind a mask of forced calm.

Tommy snatched a cookie the next day too. This time Delbert grabbed his fat wrist. The bully shook his free fist in Delbert's face.

"Let go or you'll get this right in your ugly puss."

Delbert let go. That evening, he told Teresa not to give him a cookie anymore.

"Why not dear, I thought you liked them?"

"Tommy steals them."

"Why does the teacher let him?"

"He does it when she's out of the room."

"Why don't you tell her? Do you want me to call her?"

"No, don't do that."

Angered by the treatment he received, Teresa longed to strike back. How could she without endangering him? One possibility came to mind. She baked a small batch of cookies laced with a laxative.

"Let him take one of these, dear. It will make him run to the bathroom and maybe he'll eventually come to realize your cookies aren't worth stealing. Don't you or any of your friends eat it."

"What friends?"

The cookie thief appeared on schedule and Delbert made a show of resistance. Thirty-five minutes into the class after lunch, Tommy's hand shot up. Two fingers. The teacher nodded and he lumbered from the room. Twenty minutes later, two fingers again. The teacher looked quizzical but nodded again. He almost ran this time.

Delbert gazed at him, now with a calm inside to match the exterior version. Two fingers shot up a third time. The teacher let him stew for a few minutes. He began to squirm and wave his arm.

"Tommy, what's going on?"

"I really have to go."

"Well, go then."

The next day brought a repeat performance.

"You must've eaten something that doesn't agree with you," the teacher said exasperated.

He glanced at Delbert who gazed back unfazed. That night he told Teresa they better stop since Tommy started to suspect the cookie caused his problem. The next day Tommy noticed there was no cookie.

"Where's my cookie, Pill?"

"My mother sees no point in giving me one if you steal it every day."

"Well, you don't get one either then," he sneered.

CHAPTER FOUR

The Pillage family, though not the poorest on the island by a fair margin, fell far short of the richest. Phil worked odd jobs when he could find them. The rest of his time he tended their small farm, able to feed the family from what he grew if all else failed.

On the twenty farmable acres he kept a cow, a couple of pigs, a dozen sheep and a number of chickens. He grew vegetables and fruit in the rich soil beside the creek with one whole field devoted to potatoes. Although Phil handled most of the labour, he frequently conscripted the boys to help. He didn't expect much from Paul because of his age but hounded Delbert to do more.

"C'mon Delbert, put your back into it. We gotta get this whole field hoed today. Don't just scratch the soil. Dig the hoe in an' cut off them weeds."

Why can't I just play like other kids, the boy thought? It's not fair. He had no choice but to push his aching muscles until the field was finished. He fought back the tears that tried to form.

Their rocky relationship did have a few good moments. One occurred when Phil let him drive their old tractor. An antique before its time, its big steel rear wheels contained diagonal cleats and no brakes; gear and gas determined its speed uphill and down. To stop, one brought the gas lever back to idle, horsed the gearshift into neutral and let it grind to a halt.

Delbert worked the gas and choke while Phil cranked to get it started. When it fired up with a great belch of smoke and noise, Delbert madly pumped the gas lever to keep it alive until the engine warmed enough to idle on its own. As long as he kept it running he avoided Phil's wrath.

Phil and Delbert prepared the soil in Spring and harvested in Fall. This required Phil to walk or ride behind to operate the plow, harrows, mower or rake while Delbert drove the tractor. He loved to drive it from about age nine. After a full day, he came in spattered with black oil spots spit out by the ancient engine. They were a badge of honour. Even though Phil did the hard work, he appreciated Delbert's contribution and these times fostered a rare but tenuous camaraderie between them.

"Maybe the runt will amount to somethin' after all," he would confide to Teresa after a hard day's work. This positive atmosphere might survive until the next rock baseball game.

Perhaps the best and worst for Delbert came in the Fall harvest. It took most of a day on the tractor with Phil behind to mow the fields. Half that time to rake the hay into rows. About a week later, the heavy work began. They collected the hay into stacks by hand. Phil did most of the work, with Delbert badgered to help. It was back-breaking work and Delbert's soon screamed in agony. He kept at it though the pain brought tears to his eyes. He faced away from Phil to hide them.

When the hay dried, Delbert drove the tractor and trailer from stack to stack while Phil pitched the hay on. He pretended he was in a big truck and trailer rig and could hardly wait for a full load to haul back to the barn. He learned to back the trailer up to the barn door with precision.

Not an easy feat when the load of hay blocked his vision. It impressed even Phil.

So, although relatively poor, the farm allowed the Pillages to eat well and each year Delbert's scrawny limbs looked more able to support his head and body. By the time he reached his teens, they might look like a reasonable match if his development had not been interrupted.

CHAPTER FIVE

When Delbert was eleven, Tony, his swimming hole buddy, contracted polio. The worst kind, it attacked his throat and constricted his breathing. Doctors on the island in 1949 didn't know it could suffocate him if left unattended. He died that night.

It was traumatic to watch Tony's father wail uncontrolled at the funeral. As each day passed, Delbert became more resigned that Tony would never come back. The finality of death permeated his thoughts. He could see it as a release from his daily torment. Yet he saw it as too permanent a solution for what might some day fade away of its own accord. And he couldn't stand the thought of his mother crying at his funeral like Tony's father.

That December Delbert began to experience nightmares. Teresa noticed a tic in one of his eyes and he often coughed to clear his throat.

"There's something wrong, Phil. We need to get him to a doctor who specializes in nervous disorders."

"Sure won't find that on the island. Think we should get him over to a doc in Victoria?"

"I'll ask Doctor Franklin who he recommends. Hope he's not offended."

A week later, Phil had Delbert in a waiting room in Victoria. After a brief examination, the doctor asked, "Do you have nightmares?"

"No."

"Do you have to clear your throat often?"

"No."

"Yes, he does," Phil interrupted, "and he's developed a tic in his eye."

The doctor handed him a small jar, "Urinate in this. You can stand over there in the corner."

Immediately embarrassed, Delbert glanced at his father. "Pee in it, Delbert."

Delbert faced the corner, unbuttoned his fly and tried. He was too tense. When it finally broke loose, he barely got stopped in time to prevent overflow. He couldn't button up with one hand so he covered up as best he could. Sheepishly, he handed the full jar to the doctor, who put it on a counter for later analysis. While the doctor wiped the dribbles off his hands, Delbert buttoned his fly.

"Hold your hands out and stretch your fingers."

Delbert did and was surprised to see they wobbled up and down and would not stay still.

"That finger movement is where his problem gets its name," the doctor said to Phil, "it looks like he has Saint Vitus Dance."

The doctor told Delbert to go and sit in the waiting room while he talked to Phil. As Delbert sat alone, he sensed their secret conversation meant something serious. He began to tremble.

"Saint Vitus Dance is a form of rheumatic fever. No one has found a remedy for it so he will have to cure himself. It effects the heart, often leaves just a minor tick in the heart beat, sometimes more. It can recur later in life and during times of stress."

"What can we do, Doc?"

"I recommend complete bed rest for three months and he will probably recover on his own. I'll prescribe some pills which will sedate him at first and others which will make him relax later on. He should stay in bed in a dark room with no noise, no excitement, no radio, nothing for at least two weeks. After that, he can listen to a radio but the room should stay dark for another four weeks. Even then his eyes should not be exposed to direct sunlight. He needs to rest for three months before he leaves the house."

The doctor pulled a small roll of adhesive tape from a drawer and handed it to Phil.

"There's a sports store two blocks up the street. When you leave, go there and buy a pair of swim goggles for him. Tape them over but leave a small hole in the center of each lens for him to see through. That will protect his eyes until you get home."

Delbert stared at the goggles. "Do I have to wear them?"

"The Doc said you do. Put 'em on."

Two children they passed on the street pointed at him and laughed. It embarrassed him. He thought he looked like some giant insect with big white eyes. On the ferry, he stayed scrunched down in the truck so no one would see him.

When Phil relayed the outcome to Teresa, he couldn't resist a comment, "A stronger kid probably wouldn't have this problem."

"Oh Phil, it could happen to anyone. We need to put him close to the kitchen so I can keep an eye on him. Move his cot into the dining room. We'll eat at the kitchen table until he's better. I'll get a blanket for you to hang over the window. Don't be negative, we need to encourage him to get well."

Delbert slept through the first two weeks in darkness, awake only to eat a little food twice a day. He had to put on the goggles to go to the bathroom. He lost track of the days.

Teresa worried constantly about him. Would he recover unscathed or end up with a damaged heart? She knew some polio symptoms were quite similar to what he experienced. Did the doctor just give it a different name to not scare them? No, she had to believe the doctor. Still, she worried.

By 1950, the family owned a radio, considered small at the time though large beside transistor radios invented later. Delbert got the radio and discovered he could sometimes pick up a station that broadcast St Louis Cardinal baseball games played on the other side of the continent. He dreamed he shared the lineup with Stan Musial and Enos Slaughter though he could never decide which position he himself played.

Isolation from the world disturbed Delbert. He didn't remember the first two weeks. After that, he recalled why he was bedridden and it scared him. Now more conscious, the nightmares returned. Sometimes in the night he was a giant white-eyed insect attacked by a classroom of even bigger black-eyed ones. What if he didn't get better? What if he had to wear the goggles the rest of his life? Teresa found him in tears one morning.

"What is it dear?"

"Am I going to get well or die like Tony?"

"You're already getting better dear."

"Maybe better if I didn't."

"Don't even think that, Delbert. We all need you to live and rejoin us. We love you, Delbert."

"Even Dad?"

"Even Dad."

~~~

Three months without exercise or sunlight left him frail and pale. Muscles atrophied. When he returned to school, he discovered a few classmates felt sympathy for him. Not the bullies. When they learned he had Saint Vitus Dance, they hopped up and down from one foot to the other like an amateur's puppet doing a jig.

"Look, I've got the Vitus dance too. This how you do it, Pillboy?"

"Stop it!" Sylvia shouted at them.

Her outburst startled her as much as them. Brian started jigging toward her.

"Hey Silly-via, you want to do the Vitus Dance with me?"

Before he reached her, he remembered her older brother Barry and turned away. He didn't want a run-in with Barry.

Delbert's teacher thought the three month absence was sure to prevent him from passing to the next grade. He'll loaf in my class again next year. It was a pleasant shock when his test papers revealed acceptable marks. Oddly, it seemed he had learned material covered while absent. When she ran into Teresa in town, the teacher thanked her for tutoring Delbert during his illness.

"Oh, the doctor wouldn't let me do that. He insisted on complete rest the whole time."

CHAPTER SIX

Things took a turn for the worse for the Pillages that Fall. Phil developed a malignant tumor. It must be removed, the sooner the better. What little money they saved would be needed for the operation. Now more than ever the farm had to feed them.

"Delbert, I've talked to Ted next door and he's willin' ta milk the cow in the mornin'. He'll keep the mornin' milk. You milk her in the evenin' every day. We'll get by on half the milk. I'm sellin' the sheep and pigs. I'm countin' on you to keep the farm runnin' Delbert. You're the man of the house 'til I'm well agin."

So each afternoon, Delbert walked out to find the cow. He called "Cow Boss" every so often like Phil did, even though they named her Bunty. As the days shortened in November, a fog often settled in during the late afternoon. Delbert's vivid imagination conjured up all manner of beast lurking just out of sight. When Bunty appeared right on top of him out of the fog, it made his heart jump. Still it somehow comforted him to walk with the dumb animal back to the barn.

She stuck her head into the manger which Delbert had filled with hay. He locked her in and sat down on a three legged stool with the big bucket to milk. Bunty was young and cantankerous. Like all cows, she knew the difference between an experienced milker and a tentative beginner. She tired of Delbert about the time the hay ran out and kicked the bucket. Perhaps she took the "Cow Boss" honorific too literally.

As the Fall wore on, Delbert came to expect a kick from her long before he finished. In an effort to prevent it he talked softly to her, sung to her, stroked her, yelled at her, punched her in the ribs, tried to block her leg. Nothing worked. When she kicked he usually managed to hold onto the bucket and didn't spill milk because it contained so little. Settled down to finish the job, it wasn't long before another kick interrupted him. After the third kick, he often gave up. She became like the kids at school, another bully who tormented him daily.

Unfortunately, he began to anticipate the kicks and would jump back when he saw one begin. The final straw came when his reaction tumbled him backwards into a wet manure pile just outside the barn doorway. Milk spilled, bucket splattered and the back of his pants and shirt plastered to his skin, he swore at the cow and swung the bucket with all his might to whack her on the rear end.

This finally caught her attention. She bellowed, then stood still for him to start over. Poor Delbert had to go wash the bucket and return to face her again. She let him struggle away for about half an hour before her foot moved forward a couple of inches in a symbolic kick. So Delbert got the four inches or so of milk once more.

A few days after this tentative truce, Ted talked to Teresa. "Either that cow of yours gives an awful lot of milk or Delbert's having a problem. I get a full bucket every morning and there's still some left."

"Delbert comes in with about four inches in the pail. The cow kicks him. The other day he came in covered with manure and claimed she kicked him clear out of the barn."

Ted laughed. "I'll help him milk her in the evening for a while to get it balanced again."

"Thank you so much Ted. I'll tell Delbert to get the cow and clean out the barn. Maybe he can learn from you."

But Delbert never mastered the art. Perhaps his wrists were not strong enough. Ted showed him the correct technique and let him milk first each afternoon. When the cow started to rebel, Ted would take over. He never berated Delbert or scoffed at his effort. Delbert wished his Dad had half Ted's patience.

Delbert and Paul did what chores they could through this period when life became so hard for Teresa. Although she did her best to hide it, they knew she worried about Phil. What if he doesn't recover enough to work again? Similar thoughts haunted Delbert. Will I have to plant the garden and hoe all the potatoes? Do all the work Dad did while he drives the tractor? He was way too young to be a man of the house.

CHAPTER SEVEN

Phil recovered slowly. A lot of muscle went with the tumor. Unable to lift much, each day ended in pain. It was more difficult than ever to find work. The few jobs he got seemed like charity, which humiliated him to add to the pain. Evenings were hard for the whole family.

Phil and Teresa quickly discovered farm food alone couldn't sustain them. They needed money to buy necessities and Phil earned too little.

"Maybe I should find a job," Teresa suggested.

"It's bin years since you worked outside a the house. What would you do and who'd hire you here on the island?"

"I was a good legal secretary before we were married. I could be again."

"Damn it to hell, I can't even support my own family!"

"Phil, you'll get stronger. It would just be until then."

"I can't say no even though I want to. Lord, it galls me to be in this position!"

Her eyes welled up as he stomped out of the house to hide the tears in his eyes as well. His pride shattered, she knew only time would bring it back.

Bracewell's Real estate Agency in Ganges decided to replace a secretary who cost them three thousand dollars on a sale because of a typographical error. Teresa got the job. It paid only two-fifty an hour but that would be enough to tide them over.

Her job allowed Phil to spend most of his time on the farm for the next few months. He could work at a therapeutic pace without the pain he felt when forced to earn wages. Oddly, the milking which caused Delbert such agony did more to strengthen his wrists and arms than anything else. He even began to sing to the cow in his mellow baritone voice. Swept off her feet, Bunty responded periodically with a low moo, often in harmony with him.

Delbert smiled to himself as he shoveled the day's manure onto the pile he visited two months earlier. It delighted Teresa when he reported the singing. Her long hours became less strenuous. Delbert hoped it would be as beneficial for his Dad to hoe potatoes.

As Phil's strength returned, so did the jobs. Population growth led to new houses and increased services. An addition had to be built onto the school and a new hospital planned. More work than workers pushed up wages. Experience and his natural skill with tools allowed him to transition from labourer to carpenter.

Work on the farm was good for Delbert too. No longer spindly, his growing muscles and height ate into classmates' urge to harass him. And the relative prosperity meant new clothes and shoes. A new Delbert emerged, although he still showed little interest in classes and just managed to pass each test.

Sylvia secretly rejoiced in the transformation. She found Delbert more and more on her mind. The hormonal changes she experienced as she entered puberty played a role. If anything, her shyness increased. Once, after a glance at his crotch, she turned beet red and hoped no one noticed. No one did, except Delbert, who wondered why she blushed. He also noticed her developing breasts, thin waist and perfectly proportioned hips and legs. He dreamed about her.

Sylvia's shyness kept her out of the popular crowd. It would have mortified her to know half the boys mentally undressed her every day. The girls in her class would have fumed. Outside the in-crowd was something she and Delbert shared. That didn't bother her, however, she wished Delbert would talk to her or at least show some interest. For his part, Delbert anguished in silence. He hid his intense interest in her because he had no idea how to develop a relationship.

CHAPTER EIGHT

Occasionally, better-off parents threw a birthday party for their spoiled children. One of them, Tim Maple, lived with his mother, Tina. No one knew where his father had gone. Most of his class was invited to his fourteenth birthday party. At her insistence, this included Delbert, much to Tim's chagrin.

"Why invite him? He'll just sit in the corner and stare at us. It puts a damper on the party."

"There's something about him that intrigues me. I'll make him participate. Don't worry."

Tina created a game to break the ice. Cards with girls' names on them were placed in a bowl. One for each boy was put in a second bowl. A card picked from each bowl selected a couple that was sent to another room to dance.

Sylvia blushed when her card was drawn in the third round. Most of the boys prayed their card would be picked. There was an audible groan when Delbert got the nod. Tina led the pair into a room with subdued lighting and quiet music, Delbert awkward and Sylvia still embarrassed.

"I don't know how to dance," Delbert confessed after Tina left.

"It's easy to dance to this slow music, just move with the beat."

What started as a somewhat formal and stilted thing gradually transitioned into a thrill for both of them as she moved closer in his arms. His right hand marveled at the vee formed where waist ended and hips began. Her hair brushed his forehead at about the same time her breasts touched his chest. She pressed closer and they drifted to the music as a single body, her warm breath wafting over his ear. They never noticed when the music stopped.

~~~

For the next two weeks, Delbert warred with himself. Sylvia was on his mind constantly. He wanted to think she liked him but another side wondered why she would. Every boy in the class is attracted to her. What can she see in me? She never goes out with boys, she hardly even talks to them. Maybe it's because she's shy like me. I thought I'd died and gone to heaven when we danced. She's the only good thing that's happened to me. I've got to find a way to be with her—if she'll let me.

Delbert's grandmother lived alone in an old house on Rainbow Road, about a mile from the school and just past Sylvia's house. As the warmth of Spring arrived, Delbert decided to walk to his Grandma's twice a week to help her with chores around the house.

With careful timing he managed to be available to carry Sylvia's books. And she let him! Like the dance, conversation was awkward at first. Gradually they relaxed into small talk. Grandma knew exactly where his priorities lay when she saw him on the road with Sylvia. Still he could help her a great deal and she wasn't about to jeopardize that for the sake of teasing him.

Two afternoons a week together on Rainbow Road eventually exiled their shyness. Sylvia brightened his outlook on life and made the bullies' torments tolerable. She made him feel good about himself. Even the revelation and change about to sweep over them didn't dampen their deepening relationship.

One sunny afternoon, the teacher made Sylvia stay after school to go over a concept that baffled her. Delbert whittled on a stick while he waited in the school yard, turning it into a resemblance of Sylvia. Finally, he could wait no longer and still reach Grandma's to do some chores and get back in time for a ride home. He started off alone. When the teacher let her go, Sylvia rushed out the door and hurried after him. He came in sight about a quarter of a mile from her place. She called to him, he turned and waved, then threw the stick into the bushes.

"What was that you threw away?"

"Oh nothing, just something I whittled. Let me carry your books the rest of the way."

"Thanks."

CHAPTER NINE

Hal Lundquist, the ninth grade math teacher was noteworthy on two counts. First, a talented teacher, he motivated his students to master the subject so well his classes always scored high on provincial standardization tests. Second, he would show up at each school dance three sheets to the wind, walk up to the band, usurp a tenor sax and wail away with the band for about half an hour. He never looked at the music. Within a bar or two, he knew song and key and he was off. Occasionally he sang a chorus as well.

Each time, the Principal would reprimand him the next day. "Hal, you set a bad example for the students. This behavior must stop."

"Yes, Jack, you're right. It won't happen again."

They both knew it would, a small price to pay for his teaching excellence. In fact, students thought it funny and his humanity endeared him to them.

He was one of the few people who didn't get nervous when Delbert gazed at him. Delbert recognized in him a guileless individual with nothing to hide and complete integrity. He, on the other hand, found Delbert an enigma.

Hal liked to challenge the class. One day he said, "I'll bring in a classic Icelandic delicacy for the person who first solves this puzzle. A man has eight ball bearings, all exactly the same size. One of them is either heavier or lighter than the rest. All that's available to test them is a balancing scale—the kind used to weigh gold or chemicals. Your task is to identify the odd ball bearing and tell whether it's heavier or lighter using only three balances.

"You can spend the last fifteen minutes of this period on it. Label your ball bearings A through H so you can say which ones go on each side of the scale for each weighing."

Most of the class scribbled, erased, scribbled again. Delbert doodled away, lost in another world as usual. When the bell rang, Hal asked if anyone had solved the riddle. No one responded.

"Well, I'll extend the time until our next class. Perhaps it will come to you in your sleep."

After the class filed out, Hal erased the blackboard, put away his books and started for the door. He noticed Delbert had left his doodles on the desk again. Irritated, he picked up the sheet of paper and was about to crumple it when he saw below a sketch of a scale what looked like a logic tree. On inspection, he was shocked to see Delbert had somehow solved the riddle.

When they met again, Hal showed up with a covered dish which he placed on his desk. "Well, has anyone solved the puzzle?" No one moved.

"Well, in that case, the prize goes to Delbert since he left an interesting doodle on his desk last time. Here, Delbert," he passed the dish to him.

"What's this?"

"It's an Icelandic pâté. You eat it on those crackers."

"Do I have to?"

"Try it, Delbert, you'll like it."

Delbert thought it was meant to punish him for leaving the paper on his desk. He gingerly spread some of the odd smelling paste on a cracker. Resigned to his punishment, he bit into it. Surprised, it tasted good. After the third cracker, others became curious.

"You might share a little with your classmates, Delbert."

He embarrassed Sylvia with the first sample. As each new tester nodded their approval, the rest of the class wanted to join in. The dish emptied in no time and Hal smiled to himself at the success it enjoyed. At the end of the period, he asked Delbert to stay for a minute.

"Delbert, I saw your solution. It was perfect and it looked like you didn't have to erase anything and start over. You must have seen the riddle before?"

"No Sir."

"Hmmm. Why didn't you admit you solved it."

"I didn't want the class to laugh at me."

"If they were to make fun of you, it might be because they envied your ability. Perhaps they would think you were just lucky this time."

"No, I don't want them to know."

"But Delbert, even if they laugh at you, so what?"

"They would find a way to tease me about it, along with everything else."

"Well...I guess it must remain our secret then. You better get on to your next class."

"Yes Sir."

I wonder about that kid. Have we misjudged his ability? Does he show just enough to get through each year to avoid harassment? I need to challenge him to see what's in that shaggy head. It will have to be subtle if I'm to keep his secret safe.

CHAPTER TEN

From that point on, Hal included an extra difficult problem in each test he gave. It was seldom answered except by Delbert. He would leave a third of the questions blank but always answer the tough one. He can't resist the challenge, thought Hal. My God, he hides a brilliant mind. I can't blow his cover or he might avoid me and draw further into his shell. What a damn shame! The wasted talent ate at him more with each passing month.

~~~

The Department of Education subjected every tenth grade class in the province to a standardization test. With limited time allowed for each section, it addressed both aptitude and intelligence. The teacher's "Time's Up" came long before students could hope to answer all the questions.

Delbert had no way to determine how many answers would keep him near the bottom of the class. He liked the challenge of the test and decided there would be no repercussion if he did well. It was graded somewhere else and he thought individual marks were not passed back. So he rose to the challenge.

Within a week, Jack Farquhar, the Principal, got a phone call from Joe Smithson, head of the provincial department.

"Farquhar, what the hell you doing down there? You blew that standardization test. Someone leaked answers to one of your students."

"That's impossible. We don't have the answers. We just run the tests and send in the results."

"Someone leaked them. You know of anyone with connections to the department here in Victoria? Relative maybe?"

"Not that I know of."

"Well, I'm coming down on Monday and personally re-administer the test. I want to watch this kid answer them again from memory. And I'm going to throw in a few extra problems no one but me will know about. We'll catch the little bugger dead to rights."

"OK, which student is it? I'll have her ready."

"Him. Kid by the name of Pillage."

"WHAT? No, must be some mistake."

"Only mistake is the one he made."

Monday morning Delbert was called out of class and marched to a vacant room where a steely-eyed Smithson told him to sit down.

"What made you think you could cheat on the standardi-zation test?"

"I didn't cheat, Sir." Delbert trembled.

"In that case, you'll be able to repeat the feat while I watch. Here's a pencil and the first section. Start."

As Delbert worked through each section, the inquisitor checked answers for the previous one. What started out as irritation to find the same answers turned to surprise when he found Delbert answered even more questions than before. He seems to work out the answers, he thought, not just copy them from memory.

"OK. Now tackle these six problems. I'll give you thirty minutes to work on them."

It looked like the first one was solved within minutes. The next four seemed to take about five minutes each. As he peered over Delbert's shoulder, Smithson could see the answers looked correct. Now amazed, he thought the kid won't answer that last one. More information is needed to solve it. Delbert stared at the last problem until the thirty minutes were up.

"I see you didn't get anywhere with the last problem."

"No, Sir. I don't think it can be solved. If it could be assumed that the density can't be infinite, I think there is a solution. There just isn't anything in the problem statement that justifies that."

"Suppose we make that assumption. Show me the solution."

Now intrigued as Delbert worked through the provisional solution, he watched with a mixture of awe and excitement. All thought of cheating evaporated.

Later, he said to Farquhar after Delbert went back to his class, "That boy's mind performs at a level we seldom see. Why've you kept him hidden here?"

"We had no idea. He barely scrapes through tests each year. Every one of his teachers complains about him in class."

"You need to get in touch with your students," fired as a parting shot.

A few days later, the results came back. Delbert had scored far higher than anyone in the class. Both teachers and students knew there must be a mistake. The two top students each thought his papers were crossed with theirs.

An included note said Delbert Pillage's answers indicate a very high intelligence level although it would take considerably more work on the school's part to persuade him to put it to good use. A miffed Jack Farquhar brought this up at his next staff meeting.

"Well, we've got a genius hidden in a country hick skin. What irritates me more than not discovering it for ourselves is that they implied we should have done more to develop him."

"I had figured out that he has above average intelligence", Hal offered, "however, he was so sensitive about how his classmates might ridicule him I felt obliged to not blow his cover."

"Damn it Hal, what's more important—to develop the kid's potential or worry about classmate reaction?"

"I really don't know."

"Well, now it's out anyway. He'll have to live with the consequences."

And Delbert did. The bullies now made fun of his brains rather than deal with their inferiority.

"Now I see why your forehead's all swollen, Pillboy."

"Guess that's why your ears are pushed out so far."

Their jeers had a false ring to them as though they grasped at straws. Their class support slipped. To continue to feel superior they pushed him around or knocked him down whenever the opportunity arose. Most of his other classmates thought it strange that he could keep his intelligence a secret so long. They didn't feel threatened, just surprised.

At the first opportunity, Hal got Delbert aside.

"The cat's out of the bag Delbert. All these years you've hidden your talent and done just enough to get by. I confess it's bothered me a great deal this past year to keep your secret and see your ability wasted. You must be bored in class?"

"Sort of. Sometimes I make up games in my head or reread books in my mind."

"You can see printed pages in your mind?"

"No, not really. But I can recall what the pages say even though I can only see pieces of them."

"Is that why you never open a text book in class without being forced?"

"I read each year's textbooks in the first month or so. Then I don't need them anymore."

Hal was astounded. What a waste of talent! How can we put this right and help him reach his potential?

"I want to give you extra books to read to combat that boredom."

"You mean read in school? I can't do that. They make fun of anything about me that's different."

"I think you're worrying unnecessarily about them."

"No. No. It would be another chance for them to make my life miserable."

His distraught was obvious. "Well, how can I pass them to you?"

"My mother works at Bracewell's Real Estate. She could bring them home."

~~~

The next afternoon, Hal dropped in on Teresa. "I'm Hal Lundquist, one of Delbert's teachers."

"Oh yes Mr. Lundquist, Delbert has talked about you."

"Please call me Hal. Are you aware of the revelation we've experienced with regard to Delbert's abilities?"

"No, is something wrong?"

"No, no. We learned from a recent provincial test that he's far more intelligent than he made apparent with his work. I must confess he tipped his hand to me a number of months ago. When I confronted him, he said he didn't want his classmates to know he could do better than them because they would tease him even more. So we had an unwritten pact to keep his secret. It was very hard to reconcile the waste of his intelligence with the social pressure he felt."

"Oh!" pausing, "I should have realized he hides his ability. He's often shown flashes of brilliance but I'm afraid I overlooked them in view of the grades on his report cards."

"Well, now that we know, I would like to feed him extra books and assignments. He won't let me give them to him at school so may I drop them off with you?"

"Certainly."

Now Hal could challenge Delbert in earnest. Not just hard problems. He fed Delbert extra assignments designed to make him think ahead of the class. He passed advanced books on a variety of subjects through Teresa. Although Delbert understood just about everything in them and retained the content once read, it wasn't rote memorization. After he finished a book on aerodynamics, he said to Hal one day, "You know, Mr. Lundquist, people would sleep better than they do on a mattress if they used a rubber bladder filled with a viscous fluid."

"Why, Delbert?"

"Because the bladder would apply equal pressure to all parts of the body in contact with it. There would be no hard spots."

"And no broken coils to stick out", Hal chuckled.

"No. It would have to be a very viscous fluid so that it wouldn't slosh around and make people seasick. Actually, if there were baffles inside, the fluid could be lighter. Maybe even water would work."

"That's a good idea Delbert but I don't think people will take a chance on having a water bladder spring a leak and flood their carpets."

"Maybe not."

It would be many years before that chance was taken.

~~~

Sylvia was secretly proud of him, although she couldn't shake the concern that their difference in intelligence might undermine the possibility of a life together. Recently she dreamed of that, even though no discussion along that line took place.

For his part, intelligence had no bearing on how he felt for her. He cared only about her velvety voice, strength of character and unrivaled beauty. He worried that she might tire of him and turn to other boys. He knew some of them could entertain her more, even make her the most popular girl in the class. Where would that leave him? He couldn't compete with them.

Perhaps she sensed his inner conflict. She tried to say things that would bolster his confidence. They still walked the Rainbow Road twice a week but the coming winter conspired to decrease the frequency.

CHAPTER ELEVEN

Delbert soon outgrew what the school could teach him. Hal thought the answer might be to get him into university early. His mind turned to Dean Walter Calder, head of admissions at the University of British Columbia.

Dean Calder taught an advanced calculus class Hal attended one summer. He was inspirational and able to make even the most convoluted concepts easy to understand. With an incredible memory, he seemed able to recognize and name almost every student he ever met.

When Hal phoned, he gave his name to Dean Calder's secretary and asked for an appointment to talk to the dean about a very promising student. She gave him a time on the following Thursday. So Hal took two days vacation and headed to Vancouver.

When Hal entered his office, Dean Calder stood up and came around the desk with hand outstretched.

"Hal Lundquist! How's the best Math teacher in the province? Still wasting away on Saltspring Island?"

"Yes, Dean," shocked that the dean remembered this.

"With your talent you should be in a big city school."

"You flatter me but I like life on the island. I get my own way. It might be hard to adapt to the regulations of a big city school."

"S'pose you're right. Pity. Well, that's not why you're here. What about this bright student of yours?"

"His name's Delbert Pillage. He completely hid his brilliant mind from everyone until about a year ago to reduce teasing from classmates. He comes from a poor family. That, and his looks and shyness, made him an easy target for harassment.

"Then, last year he scored so high on one of those provincial IQ and aptitude tests, Joe Smithson thought he cheated and came over to the island to retest Delbert. He ended up raving about him. We've fed him extra work ever since and he eats it up. He's far ahead of the class and has surpassed what we can do for him. You're our best, perhaps only hope for continued growth."

"How old is he?"

"Sixteen."

"And you think he's already mastered high school?"

"Certainly in math and physics. He's run through differential and integral calculus, differential equations and more. In Physics he grasps quantum mechanics."

"My, my, that's impressive at sixteen. His family is poor, you say?"

"Yes. There's no way they could pay his way to university."

"Well Hal, I would like to meet Delbert. Any chance you could bring him over?"

"I'll talk to his parents and see. I appreciate your interest in this."

"Hal, this boy is lucky to have you go to bat for him."

Hal left elated· from both the positive reaction and the kind words said about him. His respect for the dean's stature as a man and educator was reinforced.

~~~

Back on the island, Hal began to worry about how to approach Delbert's parents. Would they resent his intrusion? Would they be reluctant to let Delbert go off to Vancouver on his own at seventeen? For that matter, would Delbert want to leave home and face university life? Only one way to find out. To broach the subject with Teresa first, he stopped in at the real estate office after school.

"Teresa, we've tried to keep Delbert challenged however he's outstripped what we can teach him. Hope it's not out of line, I've talked to the dean at UBC in charge of student admissions to see what could be done next. He would like to meet Delbert."

"Why would he want to meet Delbert? He's only sixteen. And," with a catch in her throat, "we can't afford to send him to university even when the time comes."

"Yes Teresa, I understand. But Dean Calder is a remarkable man and if anyone can find a way to give Delbert the latitude he needs to progress, Dean Calder can. If you see fit to let Delbert talk to him, I'll be happy to drive him over to Vancouver for the meeting."

"I don't know. This is all very sudden. I'll talk to my husband, although you should know he probably won't be very sympathetic."

"I understand. The purpose of the meeting would be to explore what might be possible in the future. Perhaps Dean Calder can find a way to finance Delbert's university education."

"That would be a dream come true for me, Hal. My husband might not feel the same. When do we have to decide on this meeting?"

"I would like to strike while the iron's hot. We should get back to Dean Calder within a week or so."

"I'll talk to Phil and get back to you."

"Thanks."

Teresa's thoughts were in turmoil. Wouldn't it be wonderful if they could find a way for Delbert to realize his potential? Is he really that smart? How can he go to university at sixteen or seventeen? He'll be harassed just like he was in school. What will Phil say? Oh Lord, I want to see that boy do well and be happy! I've got to find a way to approach Phil so that he's not immediately against it.

Later that evening, when Phil relaxed after dinner, Teresa broached the subject. "Phil, one of Delbert's teachers talked to me this afternoon."

"What's he done wrong now?"

"Nothing wrong. It seems that Delbert's far more intelligent than he's let on with his school work. He must take after your mother."

"What're you talkin' about? He ain't never got more than barely passin' grades. I seen his report cards."

"Yes but Mr. Lundquist said he did that on purpose to avoid teasing by his classmates. The intelligence and aptitude tests he took proved he has a very fine brain."

"Yer tellin' me he's not man enough to stand up to a little teasin' even tho' he's smarter than them. Don't make sense."

"Phil, it started way back in the lower grades. You know they were hard on him. So many times he came home beaten down it's no wonder he developed this defense mechanism."

Phil paused. "Well I must admit, there've bin times when he did seem to git things awful quick. Maybe yer right 'bout my Mum. She's a smart old cookie. But yer no slouch either, Teresa. He coulda just as easily got it from you."

"Well, it doesn't matter where he got it. The problem is he's now learned everything they can teach him in high school and Mr. Lundquist, the teacher, wants to have him meet a dean at UBC to see what can be done to get him into university."

"University! Hell, Teresa, you know we can't afford that. No way."

"I know, Phil. He seems to think Delbert's so exceptional they might find a way to finance it for us, like with scholarships."

"Come on, Teresa, be real. They ain't goin' to foot the bill for four or five years. An' whatever they do give, they'll expect back. We'd be indebted to them."

"Would it hurt to let him meet the dean just to find out what they might do?"

"Nah, yer dreamin'. He's too wet behind the ears to go off talkin' to some dean, whatever that is."

"Phil—"

"Nope."

Chapter Twelve

"Phil won't hear of Delbert going to Vancouver," Teresa reported back to Hal.

"Perhaps if I talked to him?"

"Don't think it would help. He's adamant."

Dismayed, Hal hated to go back to Dean Calder and tell him his interest in Delbert had been rebuffed by a cynical father. He wondered why it's so hard to help our most talented children? We go to all lengths to give disadvantaged children more education than they can absorb. Why can't we do more for the gifted ones who can improve all our lives? The next morning he called Dean Calder's office.

"Good morning, Hal. When are you and Delbert coming over?"

"Dean, I've got bad news. Delbert's father won't let him go to Vancouver. Says there's no point in it since there's no way they can pay for university. I'm sorry to have taken your time—and failed Delbert."

"Courage, Hal, we've only begun the battle. Let me talk to the father. If this boy is as talented as you think, we won't let it go to waste. What's his name?"

"Phil. He's a solid citizen but he hasn't had the benefit of much education. It's hard for him to appreciate its worth. His wife, Teresa, is a gem, smart, educated and on our side."

"What's their phone number?"

"Ganges 20X."

"OK, let me have a go at him."

Hal resigned himself to an anxious few days.

~~~

Dean Calder waited until evening to catch Phil at home. When he answered, the dean said, "Phil, this is Wally Calder. I'm with the university in Vancouver and I want to talk to you about your son Delbert."

"Don't think there's much to talk about. Can't afford to send him to university and can't afford to take on the debt if someone else pays for it. Simple as that."

"Phil, if your son's as brilliant as it appears, we can find a way to give him an education without you owing a red cent. The reason I want to meet Delbert is to see for myself if he deserves the help. We don't run a charity here. If he's what's claimed, he will pay off our investment with what he gives back to both the university and society in general."

"Seems to me that's charity and I don't like bein' beholdin' to others."

"Yeah Phil, I'm the same way. But like I said, it's not charity, it's an investment, like planting potatoes. You expect to get more back than you put in."

"Don't believe that. Besides, how can he go off by hisself to Vancouver, he's only sixteen? Too young to be on his own. Just put him in a position where the older kids start harrassin' him like they did back in grade school."

"That's one of the reasons I want to talk to Delbert. To see how mature he is and assess his character along with his intelligence. I understand your concern. I wouldn't let my son go off on his own at that age without someone to watch over him. There's a good family here on the university grounds, friends of mine, who might like to take Delbert under their wing for a few years. Can't promise anything right now. I need to meet Delbert first and assess the situation carefully."

"Nah, can't see the point of lookin' into this. We'd just be beholdin' to your friends an' the university. He can finish school an' get a job like ever'one else."

"Yes, he can but he won't be happy unless he can put his brains to good use. He needs more education to do that."

"Sorry, don't agree."

"Well, please think it over and call me if you can see fit to meet."

"Don't think things are goin' to change. Bye."

When he hung up, Teresa asked, "What did he say?"

"Oh, he went on about how they'd pay fer the education an' how the boy could live with his friends. Just leave us owin' more'n ever."

"I thought they were talking about scholarships. Did he say we would owe the university?"

"He claims we wouldn't but I think they'd come back at us, with a guilt trip if nuthin' else."

"I don't know why you jump to that conclusion. Don't you think we should at least find out the details."

"No need to."

"What's the harm in meeting with him?"

"Don't wanna be bothered."

"Phil, in eighteen years of marriage you've made good decisions and I've always gone along with you but not this time."

"Ter—"

"No, you listen to me! Delbert spent too many miserable years with his brain stifled. Now he's finally able to use it. He needs that education to spend the rest of his life happy and productive. You have no right to deny him that opportunity!"

"You're all het up, Teresa—"

"Damn right I'm het up! His whole life hangs in the balance!"

A long silence. Delbert and Paul could hear them through the walls, shocked at their mother's outburst.

"Well..."

"Well?"

Another pause. "Reckon there's no harm in meetin' with him."

"Thank you, dear, that's all I ask and to keep an open mind."

It surprised Phil to realize his heart agreed with her. He kept a gruff expression to hide that fact.

"It'll still take some convincin' fer me to let him go off."

Once she had Dean Calder's number, Teresa called back and put Phil on the line.

"Hello Phil. Have you thought more about it?"

"Yeah, after thinkin' it over, reckon there's no harm in meetin' to talk but I want you to know I'm not sayin' yes to his goin' to university."

"Sure, that's great, Phil. It's good of you to think twice about it."

"Well...you make a convincin' argument, Wally. Guess that's why they made you that dean. And maybe they should make Teresa one too fer the same reason. Lemme think...I'm workin' a hot job this week but maybe I could see fit to bring the kid over later next week, if you could see him then?"

"How about next Thursday? I can have my secretary arrange for a place for you to stay Wednesday and Thursday night."

"Well...OK."

"Fine. She'll call with details and I look forward to meeting you both Thursday morning, at ten o'clock say."

"OK."

"Great. See you then. Good-bye."

"Bye."

The next day, Dean Calder took time to let Hal know the outcome. A relieved Hal said he would bring Delbert over for the meeting.

"No, Phil wants to do it and I think that's great. In the long run, we have to convince him this is a deal he wants to participate in."

"Well great. You continue to amaze me, Dean Calder. I thought it a lost cause."

"Causes are never lost until we throw in the towel, Hal. Must admit though, the towel was in the air until he called back."

· No one thought to ask Delbert whether or not he wanted to jump to university.

CHAPTER THIRTEEN

Teresa broke the news to Delbert. He and his Dad would go over to Vancouver to meet a dean at UBC. The thought of university scared Delbert but at least it was way off in the future, if at all.

Wednesday morning the two of them drove to Ganges to catch the Princess Mary. This inter-island steamship, small by world standards, seemed like a liner to Delbert. With three decks to explore, he roamed all over the ship in the first half hour. Phil sat down in one of the lounge areas and waited. Eventually Delbert showed up and Phil suggested they get some lunch.

Everything was elegant, table cloths, silverware, crystal glasses, Delbert had never seen such luxury. The modest prices pleased Phil. After lunch, Delbert was back up on deck again. He loved to lean over the rail and watch the bow wave flow away in a vee. He decided the angle of the vee was determined by the speed of the ship. It was obvious water was displaced to make room for the hull to move forward. The wave's continuous change engrossed him until a seagull diverted his attention.

Seagulls swooped and drifted on air currents as they searched for scraps thrown overboard. They had to beat their wings to catch up with the ship. When they turned and floated towards the stern, they glided at a lightning rate. That led to vigorous flapping to get back. Strange, he thought, when they're close to the ship they seem able to coast along with it. The ship must create a draft that pulls them. Well it would have to displace air just like it does water. Some of the air must come back in an eddy.

Once, the crew threw out a bunch of scraps from the galley. Every seagull in the area pounced on them, squawking and screeching, to snatch them before they sank. For a number of minutes all was quiet other than the ship's propeller as it churned through the water. Then the first seagull beat its way back to the ship in search of the next handout.

When underway for almost two hours, Phil joined Delbert on deck.

"Yer goin' to see an interestin' sight, Delbert. We'll soon be goin' by Stanley Park and under the Lion's Gate Bridge."

"Under a bridge? How can a bridge be high enough to go under?"

"You'll see."

Delbert's excitement mounted as the Princess Mary rounded Stanley Park. There was the bridge straight ahead. No way would the ship fit under. Yet it steamed right at the center. Up to the last instant it looked like the mast would be knocked off. And then it swept under the bridge with feet to spare. You can't trust your eyes, Delbert concluded, you need numbers to get a true perspective.

The downtown area laid out in front interrupted his thoughts. He had never seen a city the size of Vancouver. Victoria seemed big when Phil took him to the doctor. It was nothing compared to this.

"We'll land over there," Phil said, as he pointed to an empty dock surrounded by ships tied up at piers. Other large freighters were anchored around the harbour. A feast for a country boy's eyes.

Absorbed with the logistics of docking, Delbert watched small ropes tossed to the wharf, men haul them in to pull heavy lines ashore, which they slipped over massive hawsers. Then the ship churned in reverse to pull itself in to the pier. Phil dragged him away to disembark with the other passengers.

They came out on the sidewalk at the foot of Granville Street where a line of taxis waited to gobble up fares. When they headed for the nearest one, a driver yelled at them to take the first in line. Chastened, Phil changed course. He gave the driver the address of their hotel. A short ride took them to a small but elegant old hotel on English Bay. The fare of a dollar thirty-five Phil rounded up to a dollar and a half, which caused the driver to shake his head as he fumbled with the few coins in his hand.

Concerned about money as always, Phil asked the desk clerk for the room rate as he checked in.

"The room's already paid for Sir. Will you need a wake-up call?"

"Hardly likely. I haven't slept past dawn in years."

"Right. Enjoy your stay Sir."

They had a third floor room which faced English Bay. Phil pointed across the water and told Delbert that's where they were going in the morning.

"What's this meeting all about, Dad? I'm nervous and don't know what I'm supposed to do or say."

"Don't know either. We're goin' to meet with some high-falutin' dean named Wally and he's goin' to ask you questions. Best thing is to not worry an' take 'er as she comes."

~~~

The next morning Phil got up with the sun just like he did on the island. By nine o'clock they were in a taxi to the university. The driver deposited them in Dean Calder's lobby by a quarter to ten. Sharp at ten, his secretary ushered them in.

"Hi Phil, good to meet you," Dean Calder said shaking hands. "Everything OK with the hotel?"

"Ever'thin's gone smoothly 'cept they're not lettin' me pay fer the room."

"It's standard practice for the university to foot the hotel bill when we request a guest to come to town. Sit down, please. Delbert, it's good to meet you too."

As he sat down, Delbert studied Dean Calder. For a few seconds the two sized each other up. Delbert liked what he saw in Dean Calder. Yet he remained nervous and intimidated. The dean sensed his tenseness and decided to break the silence.

"Let me go over what I have in mind for the day and see if it's OK with you, Phil. This morning I want to spend some time alone with Delbert so I've arranged for one of our people to give you a brief campus tour. Then, we'll have lunch. After that, if all goes well, I want to describe what kind of program might be possible and answer any questions you have. In fact, please ask questions whenever they come to mind. Then, if it looks like a university program makes sense, I've arranged to have you visit some friends here on campus who will consider taking Delbert into their house for the first two years at least. Does that seem like a reasonable action plan?"

"OK Wally, or should I be callin' you Dean Calder like it says on the door?"

"Call me Wally or I'll call you Mr. Pillage." That brought a laugh from them both. Phil felt a little more relaxed.

After Phil left on the tour, the dean turned to Delbert. "Well Delbert, are the things Hal Lundquist said about you true? Let's go over to my little blackboard. I want you to show me a few things. Hal tells me in addition to advanced mathematics, you've become familiar with quantum mechanics?"

"Some, Sir."

"How about Schrödinger's equation for a hydrogen atom?"

"Do you want me to write it on the board?"

"Sure, go ahead. Then we can talk about it a little."

Delbert wrote out the complicated equation, in itself a feat in the dean's mind.

"Well Delbert, what do you think about it?

"Do you mean about matter as a wave rather than particles?"

"Yes."

"I'm not sure. It seems like matter can't simply be thought of as particles or as energy. His equation looks like it makes sense on the surface but I don't think it's the complete story. From what I've read, it doesn't seem to accommodate relativity effects. Don't you think there are other forces at work, forces we can't detect?"

As they continued to talk, Dean Calder was impressed with Delbert's knowledge and perceptiveness. One mind in a thousand, he thought. After a brief assessment of his mathematics ability, he wanted to investigate the breadth of his interests.

"What's your favorite book or story?"

"I guess my favorite books are those written by Charles Dickens. His stories touch close to home for me. But I like dramatized history books too."

"Do you play a musical instrument?"

"No Sir. I've never had a musical instrument."

"Do you like music?"

"I guess so. Mozart's music is my favorite. It sounds right. I like Beethoven too, especially his Minuet in G and Eloise. I only get to hear them when my mother plays them on the gramophone. Popular music is OK."

"What do you like to do most, Delbert?"

He thought for a while, "I guess I like to create new things, new ideas, concepts, gadgets, sketches or even real things."

"You seem to have a variety of interests rather than a narrow focus on one thing, am I right?"

"Yes Sir. Everything interests me."

"Good for you. Come on, I want to show you the library and some of our physics labs before we meet your Dad for lunch."

They walked over to the library, which amazed Delbert with its thousands of books and dozens of carrels occupied by students who poured over the literature. In the Physics building, he saw amphitheatre lecture halls for the first time. These class-rooms intimidated him when he thought about the number of students it would take to fill them, all older and bigger than him. Then they passed through labs which displayed more equipment than Delbert thought possible to find anywhere.

After lunch, the dean took Phil and Delbert back to his office. He told Phil Delbert's ability impressed him and said he did appear ready for university.

"I would prefer Delbert spend another year in high school but I respect Hal Lundquist's opinion that there isn't enough left to teach him on the island.

"Consequently, I want to propose a plan for you to consider. Delbert should graduate from high school before he starts university. From what I've seen he could pass the grade eleven exams right now and probably grade twelve as well. I would like to have the school give him both sets of exams at the end of this year. Delbert, you would have four months to prepare. If you pass them, you will qualify for university fair and square.

"If that happens, I will arrange for a full scholarship for each year of university based on good grades each Spring. A scholarship is not a loan—no repayment is expected. You will owe nothing and you will have no obligations in future."

"I hear you, Wally. Reckon that's a challenge for Delbert and I dunno if he's up to it. You an' Lundquist seem to think he is an' you know better 'n me. There's still the issue of his age an' bein' away from home."

"Right, Phil. Give me a minute to make a phone call and see if we can visit the friend I told you about."

After the call, the dean said Dan Martin expected them. He took Phil and Delbert to an elegant old house about half a mile from the campus centre. Phil admired its architecture, both were awed by its size and its well-groomed flower gardens and lawns. A jovial man of about fifty opened the door.

"Hello Dan, here's the boy I told you about, Delbert Pillage, and his father Phil. Phil, this is Dan Martin. Dan's a professor and head of the electrical engineering department."

"Pleased to meet you Phil and Delbert. Come in."

"How do," said an uneasy Phil.

Once inside, they were introduced to Dan's wife, Samantha, a woman with a quick smile and warm demeanor that immediately sets people at ease. It even worked to some extent on Phil. Delbert intuitively liked them but his shyness left him nervous.

"Our son Charlie is off at a soccer game. I wish he were here to meet you, Delbert, he's seventeen so he's close to your age. He'll start university in the fall."

The dean said, "Phil quite rightly is concerned with sending Delbert off to university alone. The scholarship funds will be no problem, however, we need to provide a home environment which will guarantee Delbert is properly looked after."

"Phil, Samantha and I told Dean Calder about a year ago we would take in one or two exceptional students. Our two eldest have flown the coop. They left a couple of empty bedrooms and frankly we like to have teen-agers about— they keep us young. Naturally, we set standards and rules of behavior we expect, and will insist upon, to ensure the boys stay on track as they mature into young men. Not a prison environment, I assure you. We try to provide opportunities for our children to experience all the healthy aspects of life. If Delbert were to stay here, we would treat him the same way we treat our own children."

Samantha could see Delbert was shy and nervous. He seemed likeable and she had the impression he could fit into their family.

"How do you feel about university next year, Delbert?"

After he thought for a moment, "it frightens me. There's so many students and they're older and more worldly."

"True, although most of them felt the same way when they arrived here. At first, everyone's a stranger. Soon a number become acquaintances. Then the better ones grow into friends. By the time you graduate, you will cherish life-long friends."

"That makes it sound less scary."

She suspected they could help him transition to university life. After a glance at Dan and his imperceptible nod, she made the decision for both of them.

"We would like to have Delbert join us for the school year, if he wants to and you see fit to let him come. Let me show you the room he would have."

She led them upstairs to a large room with a bed, desk, table, bookshelves and an exceptional view over English Bay with snow capped mountains beyond. Phil felt humbled in their company and didn't want to say anything. He knew he would expose his lack of education with his first words. Wish Teresa were here, he thought, she could talk their language. Perhaps I wouldn't feel this way if someone had given me one of them educations. He knew he had to say something.

"We're indebted to you fer even offerin' to take him in. Do we have to give an answer now or can I talk it over with Teresa and get back to you."

"Of course, Phil. Take as much time as you need."

~~~

On the way back to Saltspring, Phil asked Delbert what he thought of the Martins.

"They're good people. We can trust them. The house and room are fantastic. Did you see the books in it?"

"Don't let them books an' things blind you. It'd take a lot of work to keep up with them older kids."

"I know, that scares me."

"Perhaps you should wait a year then."

"I don't know. It's the challenge of university versus another year of boredom in school. Even though I'm real nervous about it I think I can handle the jump."

"So you wanna take this on?"

"I think so."

"Remember, you'd have to pass them exams. Don't want you takin' all their favors and then flunkin' out."

"I know. I think I can pass them."

"Well I need to think on it—an' you do too. You better be sure you can pass 'em, before we'll let you go."

Delbert was in much more of a quandary than he let on. Separation from Sylvia bothered him more than the expected age difference. But boredom in school outweighed them both. He wondered what Sylvia thought.

CHAPTER FOURTEEN

Phil described the meetings to Teresa. He was still wary of the proposed action but Teresa could tell he no longer opposed it out of hand.

"It's like the kid says, challenge of university 'gainst boredom of school. He seems to think he can handle it."

"What did you think of the Martins? Can we trust them?"

"Yeah, we can trust them. They're solid folks."

"Well...I'll miss him if he goes but we'll have to face that sooner or later anyway. It's the chance of a lifetime for him. Guess I'm in favor of it. What do you think?"

"Goin' over there and meetin' them people, it's a different world from what I grew up in here on the island. And strange enough, I can see Delbert livin' in it. Reckon he aint made for hoein' potatoes or hammerin' nails."

"So you think we should let him go?"

"Yep, we should let him take a shot at it."

She felt an euphoric blend of relief and joy. Phil phoned Dean Calder with their decision and thanked him for his patience with them.

Classmates were surprised and in some cases envious when word leaked out he might skip Grade 12 and go straight to university next year. Sylvia feared she would lose him. Dreams of another year together and going to the senior prom with him were dashed. However, she had the fortitude to hide her disappointment and instill enthusiasm in him.

True to form, Delbert sensed her underlying regret and found it mirrored in his own feelings.

"I don't think I want to do it. It may be more than I can handle and I don't want to be so far away from you."

"You can handle it. You're smarter than everyone, here and there. I hate the thought of being apart but you need the challenge. That doesn't happen here." It hurt her to admit it.

"Do you think so? If I go I'll write to you and tell you all about it. Will you write back?"

"Yes, but there's no if."

"Sounds like you want to get rid of me."

Impulsively, she stepped forward and kissed him. Her soft lips and firm body took his breath away.

"I love you," she whispered.

"I love you too," he replied. With pounding hearts, the admission, long pent up by shyness, now gave both a tremendous release.

The school year passed too soon for them. He studied the extra books. Sylvia struggled to maintain concentration in class. It was too easy to slip into a daydream. With freedom born from their declared love, she confessed her difficulty with some classes and Delbert became an after-class tutor.

It didn't take long for classmates to notice the time they spent together. Now the boys had a second reason to be jealous. What does she see in that gangly guy? They could show her a much better time. The girls tended to write them both off as social misfits.

When Delbert finished the Grade 11 exams, Hal fed him the Grade 12 ones. It took almost an extra week. It irritated some teachers to see him take final exams without the benefit of their teaching prowess. Perhaps the reason became clearer as they marked his papers. Questions that had a right or wrong answer, he got right. On the subjective questions, like write a paragraph or essay on..., they had to admit he did a credible job, in some cases a good job. Sometimes he introduced aspects they hadn't thought of before. Being human, they took marks off here and there on these questions. Still he came through with high grades. A jubilant Hal called the Pillages with the results.

"Phil, Hal Lundquist here. Your boy easily passed both sets of exams."

"S'pose he's got somethin' special 'tween his ears like you bin sayin' all along. Well, if he's goin' to university in the Fall, I'll get him workin' with me this summer. See if he can make some spendin' money 'fore he goes."

"Good. You'll get a transcript in the mail with his marks. I'll mail off a copy to Dean Calder too so he can put together the scholarship funds and firm up the arrangement for Delbert with his friends."

"The Martin's."

"Yes, I hadn't heard their name before."

"I'll tell Delbert an' Teresa the news."

"Good. Bye now."

Teresa was excited. Delbert experienced a combination of excitement and apprehension. He felt like a fallen branch in a turbulent river, not at all sure where the current would take him. Paul oscillated between pride in what Delbert had done and impending loneliness when he contemplated home life without his brother next year.

True to his word, Phil got Delbert hired as a labourer. It paid $1.72 an hour, the current rate. The pay came in cash in a little brown envelope every other week.

"You can keep out five dollars from each a them to spend this summer. The rest goes in the bank."

Five dollars was enough to take Sylvia every other week to whatever movie played at the only theatre on the island and still have money left over to spend in a coffee shop.

As the movies started, Sylvia would slip her hand into his and lean against him. That's all it took to immediately excite him. It was a constant battle to keep track of the movie when he was so conscious of her warmth. As the movies wound down, Delbert had to move her hand away and concentrate ferociously on the ending to get things back to a presentable state before they left.

On non-movie weekends, Delbert spent half a day with his grandmother, the rest with Sylvia. The couple often walked down to Rainbow Beach and along it to a secluded little place where they could sit on a log and talk. Once, later in the summer when they did this, their eyes locked on each other. Her hands slid up around his neck as they came together in a kiss that left them both breathless.

With her head cupped in his neck, her left hand gently stroked his right arm.

"Delbert, we can't have sex," she said, almost in tears.

"I know. The time will come."

They hugged tightly. The warmth they both felt drove them mad.

"Oh Delbert," she whispered in his ear.

"We better stop before we lose control," he said.

They ended with another long kiss. Both had trouble with sleep that night. The rest of the summer continued this way, a constant struggle between desire and their ingrained compulsion to protect her virginity. On the last weekend before he headed to Vancouver, she could hold back tears no longer.

"I'm sorry," she said, "I was determined to not make a scene but I just can't help it. I'll miss you so much. I'm afraid you'll meet some beautiful, smart girl and forget all about me."

"I'll never forget you. There won't be anyone else. I'll come home at Christmas and we'll have next summer together. Heck, maybe you will be charmed away by some new guy. Every male is attracted to you. I'm the one who has to worry."

"Never, you're my only love."

"Then neither of us has to worry."

~~~

Phil bought Delbert a small suitcase and duffel bag. More than enough to hold his meagre belongings. Teresa bought some new clothes for him. Next day they drove to Ganges to put him on the Princess Mary.

Out on the dock, Phil said, "Well Delbert, you're goin' out on yer own at seventeen which is 'bout when I struck out too. Pay attention to what them Martins have to say. I want to hear only good things from them and Wally."

"You will Dad."

Teresa hugged him, "I'm proud of what you've already accomplished, dear, and know you'll do well in university." He wished he shared her confidence.

Paul gave him a perfunctory hug, "You take care of Mum and Dad now, Paul."

"Yeah, sure," and they all gave a halfhearted laugh.

Delbert carried his suitcase and duffel bag up the gangplank. He turned on deck, waved good-bye and took his bags inside to check them with the Purser. Afterward, he came back on deck and saw they had left. Then he noticed Sylvia on the sidewalk in front of Mouat's store. He waved. She gave a small wave back.

As the boat began to move, they continued to look at each other with a foreboding sense of extended separation. Both wondered how long? Four cheeks had a tear of their own as the boat slid past a rock outcrop that finally blocked their view.

CHAPTER FIFTEEN

The trip proved far different this time. Extreme loneliness that comes after parting settled on him like a cold morning dew. For most of the trip, he sat and stared at the sea, his mind back at Rainbow Beach. How can I be homesick one hour from home? Be honest, you're lovesick, not homesick. Pull yourself together, you'll see her again at Christmas. His thoughts turned to the months ahead. They frightened him. Could he handle the work? The crowds of students, all older than him? Would they treat him like a little kid and make fun of him? To distract himself, he went out on deck to watch the entrance to Vancouver once again.

As he hauled his bags through the crowd towards the taxi stand, he heard, "Delbert! Delbert! Over here." Dan Martin waved, a grin on his face.

"Mr. Martin, I didn't expect to see you here."

"Had a couple of free hours so thought I would save you the hassle of a taxi."

"Thank you, Sir."

"We'll see a lot of each other in the next few years, Delbert, I'd prefer you call me Dan. Mister makes me feel older and more decrepit than I like to think I am. This is Charlie."

"Hi Delbert."

"Hi Charlie. You had a soccer game last time."

"Yeah, you interested in soccer?"

"I played a very disorganized form of it so I can't claim to be any good and certainly don't know any of the fine points."

"We'll see. Let me take one of those bags."

"Thanks."

They piled into Dan's old Mercedes and headed for the university district. Amazed once again at how this other half lived, he marveled at how the big car glided over the streets. A far cry from Saltspring roads in a pickup.

"Well, Delbert, Dean Calder wants to meet with you at nine thirty Monday morning and Charlie plans to register on Tuesday. You might want to go with him and work through it together."

"I would appreciate that, if you don't mind?"

"Sounds good," Charlie responded.

At home, Samantha welcomed him back. Charlie helped him move into his room. "You travel pretty light, Del. Do you mind if I call you Del?"

"No, that's fine. I come from a poor family, especially compared to you. It doesn't take much to move me around." They both laughed.

"I was able to save up some money this summer to buy things I need as we go along."

"From what Dad thinks, your scholarship will cover everything. You can save your money for things they'd frown on."

They spent the weekend together. The Martins all came under Delbert's analytical scrutiny and like Hal Lundquist and Dean Calder, were not bothered by it. They know they can trust me to do everything possible to earn a place in their family. Samantha gave him a house key and told him he had the run of the house.

"You're one of us while you're here,"

On Sunday afternoon, Charlie showed Delbert around the campus. At one of the fields, a soccer team scrimmaged. Charlie borrowed a ball and they kicked it back and forth for a while. He noticed Delbert trap and kick the ball with either foot.

"You know Del, you should turn out for our team. You handle the ball well."

"I'm not in shape, doubt if I have the stamina needed and I'll be younger and probably smaller than everyone else."

"Age and size mean little in soccer. Join me on the exercise circuit over at Memorial Gym. That'll get you in shape."

"I don't know. Might just make a fool of myself."

"Nobody cares how you look at first, it's how you look after a couple of weeks that counts."

"It would be a good thing to do. Guess I'm just nervous."

"How about if we drop by and look it over tomorrow afternoon? Then you can decide."

"Well, OK. I'm sorry to be such a nuisance to you."

"You're not."

~~~

Nine-thirty Monday morning Delbert sat in Dean Calder's reception room. The Dean's secretary welcomed him back and told him to go on in.

"Delbert, good job on those exams! Not surprised. Fully expected you to do well. Sit down."

"Thank you, Sir."

"I've got a package put together for you," he laid a thick brown envelope on the desk. "It contains some literature on how things work with your scholarship. There's a cashier's cheque in there for eight thousand dollars." Delbert's jaw dropped. "It will cover tuition, books, lodging, et cetera. The Martins won't take a cent from you so that will give you some leeway. I wanted to cover the remote possibility that your stay with them might not work out. We prefer you not go out and buy a car, however," he laughed.

"That seems like a lot of money unless tuition is much higher than I imagined. And I saved six hundred and fifty dollars this summer."

"You'll work it out. Please budget it so you don't have to beg for more in the Spring. If you have money left over, you can turn it back in for some other needy student. Now, let's talk about what you intend to study. Have you given that some thought?"

"I'm interested in the sciences, especially physics and mathematics. Seems I should approach them from the engineering side rather than pure science."

"You need to read about both but I'm not surprised to hear that. Engineering offers a solid, practical education with almost as much theory as the pure sciences. You might take a look at the Engineering Physics curriculum. It's a fair blend of theory and practice. In either case, your first year will be the same since the engineering school requires a prerequisite year of general arts and science.

"Well, you've got your money. You might want to open a bank account this afternoon so you can write a cheque for tuition. You need to be registered by Friday afternoon, however, the sooner the better."

"Charlie invited me to go with him tomorrow."

"Fine. You're all set then. Delbert," he said standing up, "if you have any problems or need advice on anything, just give me a call. I'll check back with you from time to time."

"Thank you, Sir, I'm indebted to you for making this possible."

"Do us proud, son, and we'll be indebted to you."

~~~

Later he asked to open an account at a campus bank and presented his two cheques for deposit. The cashier raised her eyebrows when she saw the amount on the university one. She looked up at him, "This your first year at UBC?"

"Yes, Ma'am."

"Well, it looks like you're very well endowed." She blushed at how it came out. Delbert pretended not to notice.

"I'll need to write a cheque for my tuition tomorrow. Is that possible?"

"I'll give you six blank cheques. You can use them for anything you need in the next few days. Your cheque book will be sent to your address within a week."

"Thank you." He wondered again how anyone would need eight thousand a year. Did they really think he was worth that kind of investment? How could he possibly live up to their expectations? What would happen if he didn't? His father would be so ashamed of him.

~~~

Charlie helped him get into the swing of things. At the bookstore he found book after book he wanted to buy.

"Del, you're like a drunk in a liquor store. You can borrow all those extra books from the library. Only buy the ones you want for reference purposes."

"I guess you're right, I've never had money to spend on things like this."

Classes differed too. Except for English and Latin (his latest new language), they took place in the two hundred seat amphitheatres. Lectures had none of the give and take between teacher and student found in high school. At first nervous, he paid strict attention. Everyone around him furiously copied down everything the professor wrote on the board. He wondered why they didn't just watch and listen in order to understand what the lecture covered. To not look out of place, he wrote down a phrase or two every so often.

Once he read the course textbooks, he realized most professors simply worked through exercises in the book, with minor excursions to reinforce the topic covered. One even went verbatim through the textbook. Delbert noticed that he often made mistakes as he regurgitated it and chuckled when everyone religiously copied them down.

English literature was taught in a class of about thirty by a bearded man who arrived in a long black gown and looked a lot like Orson Welles. He dropped his books with a bang on the desk in front of the class and opened with, "Will the ladies in the front row please cross your legs. I hate the gates of hell staring me in the face all day."

A mixture of chuckles and blushes spread across the room. As it turned out, he was a master at class participation and treated Delbert to one of the few classes never to leave him bored.

After a few weeks, he realized lectures added little beyond what he already knew. Still he attended them, partly because of unscheduled tests, partly out of obligation for his scholarship, mainly out of fear of being caught absent. The lab sessions and English classes captured his attention. However, in amphitheatre lectures, he started to sit far back and read books borrowed from the library. For example, in Physics he read Einstein's Theory of Relativity while the class covered Newton's concept of gravity and motion.

With Charlie to goad him on, he endured grueling sessions on the circuit, a series of exercise stations that included running up and down the grandstands. His body soon hardened as a result. He could feel his stamina grow as the circuit got easier. Charlie persuaded him to practice with the soccer team and he turned into a competent left midfielder. His ability to receive the ball and pass it to an open man stood him in good stead. And since it was hard to find players with a strong left foot, he soon played the position regularly.

After two weeks, he described the new environment and scholarship in a letter home. The amount he received astounded Teresa and Phil. Although jealous, Phil hid it and told Teresa to warn him to handle it with care. There was no question about who would be the family letter writer.

His letter to Sylvia avoided the subject of money other than to say the university paid all his expenses. He talked about his classes with no mention of the gates of hell. He described life with the Martins, the exercise circuit and soccer. He asked how she was and told how he missed her.

Five days later he received a letter from his mother with a little island gossip, his father's admonishment and her own happiness that he enjoyed the new environment. A week later he received a short letter from Sylvia. She said she was glad everything was going well. School was the same as always only she missed the help he gave her last year. She had to study harder than ever. At least that helped take her mind off how she missed him.

His intention to write home deteriorated immediately to once a month. He had to admit that university life claimed more of his attention as time went by. Still, he wrote to Sylvia every other week, even if she hadn't responded to his previous letter. He confessed a budding concern that many classes lacked the challenge he anticipated.

CHAPTER SIXTEEN

One day in October, Dan asked if he wanted to fly over to Victoria on Sunday.

"I have a Cessna 182 and full instrument rating so we needn't worry about weather. Have to meet with a professor from Victoria College and an engineer from Orenda Engines for a couple of hours at most."

"Does Charlie want to go? I don't want to take the opportunity away from him."

"No, he doesn't."

"OK, if I won't be a nuisance to you."

Sunday morning they drove to the airport and Delbert followed Dan to the light airplane hangar.

"Thought we would fly over to just south of Comox, then down island to Victoria. Show you some grand scenery."

As Dan conducted a preflight walk-around, he described what he inspected. Satisfied, they climbed in and buckled up. Delbert noticed Dan referred to a plasticized list as he adjusted knobs and switches. I'm surprised he doesn't have these things memorized by now, he thought with some apprehension. Then Dan held open a little window in the door and yelled "Clear!" in a loud voice to no one in sight. What the devil? He was interrupted by the starter cranking the propeller and engine ignition.

"OK, we've got oil pressure. Beacon on. Carburetor heat on. Delbert here's your first job. This is a checklist. No matter how many times you fly and how well you think you have all steps memorized, you always go through the checklist to be sure you haven't forgotten something. I'll tell you which checklist I want and you read off each item and wait for my response. Tell me if I don't get it right. OK?"

"OK."

"Give me the before taxi checklist."

Delbert read each item and finished with, "That's it."

"Checklist complete, Delbert."

"Sorry. Checklist complete."

Dan requested clearance to taxi.

"Roger, Double O Romeo cleared to taxi to runway One Two, ATIS Tango," came back over the speaker and Dan revved the engine. The airplane started forward and he swung it around ninety degrees to head to the taxi-way. He brought the airplane to a halt just short of the runway, advanced the throttle, did some more checks.

"OK, before takeoff checklist." Delbert read off the items and got a response which seemed right for each of them. "Checklist complete."

"Double O...ROmeO cleared for takeoff."

Dan taxied onto the runway and as he turned in line with it, pushed the throttle all the way in and adjusted the pitch. Delbert watched intently, so excited he had to tell himself to breathe.

"OK, at sixty knots I pull the nose up and we're off— into the wild blue yonder!" he sang.

75

Dan leveled off at one thousand feet, banked into a gentle right turn that seemed to take forever to Delbert's heightened senses.

"Notice how the controllers call us Double **O**...**RO**me**O**. That comes from my call letters, which you saw painted on the plane, C two five zero zero R. To make them clearer to understand over the radio, every letter is given a name. C is Charlie, R is Romeo. The first time I contact them I give them the whole thing. After that they use the last bit to speed up communications. They love to call this airplane Double **O**...**RO**me**O** with that flair you just heard. Guess it relieves ·their boredom."

As they flew up the coast, Dan encouraged Delbert, still engrossed in instruments and dials, to look outside. He pointed out Sechelt as they flew by. Then explained the difference between communication and navigation radios. Showed him where on the map to find frequencies to tune and explained how VOR navigation worked. Delbert soaked up the information like a sponge.

"That's Texada Island up there a little left of dead ahead. See it on the map? See Comox beyond it?"

"Yes."

"The military fly big, fast, mean airplanes out of there. We don't want to tangle with them and certainly want to stay clear of their restricted airspace. After we cross Texada, we'll turn left to cross Denman Island and head back down the coast. But before that, I want you to take the controls. Just hold the wings level and maintain altitude."

"Are you sure?"

"Go ahead, hold the yoke in your right hand and the throttle in your left. Always do things gently, we're not in a dogfight."

Dan introduced him to altitude and speed control in level flight and through turns.

"Let me take over for a moment, Delbert. I want to show you a three sixty turn using forty-five degrees of bank. If I do a good job, I'll cross my own wake and we'll feel a bump."

Delbert watched the compass swing around and noticed the power and nose up pitch Dan used to maintain speed and altitude.

"There's the bump. The old man hasn't lost his touch yet. Now you do it. Remember to scan all the instruments, never fixate on one...and look outside too."

Delbert rolled the airplane smoothly into a forty-five degree bank and copied Dan's technique. It seemed to take forever for the compass to swing around. As the original heading approached, he smoothly brought the wings back to level, lowered the nose and backed off the throttle. And there was the bump!

This kid has talent, Dan thought. Charlie was all over the sky when he tried that—just before he got sick. Delbert was excited but willed himself to remain calm. His mind raced at a speed which made everything seem like slow motion. He had plenty of time to read each instrument and integrate the information into a whole picture of the airplane's situation.

"OK Delbert, we're crossing Texada. Give me a gentle turn to a heading of two three zero."

"Good. That's Comox air base off to the right. See it? Look, there's a jet fighter coming our way."

"Wow! He really moves!"

"He sure does, but don't forget you're still flying this little puddle jumper. After you cross Denman Island, we'll swing down the coast."

Delbert brought his focus back to Double O Romeo. A little later, Dan took over so Delbert could enjoy the scenery.

"We'll fly by Nanaimo off the coast and pass over the north end of Gabriola Island. Can you give me an approximate heading to take us from there over Fulford Harbour?"

Excited by this new prospect, Delbert struggled with the map. "How about one three zero?"

Dan chuckled to himself at how Delbert picked up the lingo. "We'll try it. You take over again and fly it."

As they went over the top of Gabriola, he turned to one three zero and hoped for the best. He wondered if he could pick out Sylvia's house. He hadn't heard from her since his last letter. The north end of Saltspring Island broke his reverie. Once he had his bearings, he brought the airplane slightly to the right to fly closer to Sylvia's house.

"I noticed that," Dan said with a chuckle, "Must be a house you're interested in."

Delbert blushed. He recognized Rainbow Beach and traced the road back to her house. If she was outside, she would look up and he could waggle the wings, but she wasn't. Within minutes, her house was behind them and Fulford Harbour came into view.

"There's our house." He pointed. "It's funny how small the island looks from up here and how big it used to seem down there."

"Airplanes change your perspective on a lot of things. Well, I better get on the radio to Victoria tower. Descend to fifteen hundred feet and follow the shoreline along Isabella Point."

The tower cleared them for a straight-in approach to runway zero eight, after rechristening them Double O...ROmeO. Dan gave Delbert instructions to get them lined up with the runway before he took control and landed. Delbert remained on cloud nine as they taxied to the light airplane area near the terminal and shut down.

"Good job, Delbert. I'll meet with these fellows in an office in the terminal building and I'm afraid I can't ask you to join us. Military secrets involved. Do you mind waiting in the terminal? You could grab some lunch and perhaps find something to read."

"Sure, I'll be fine."

An hour and a half later, Dan found Delbert engrossed in a book.

"Private Pilot's Study Guide, I see. That's the pilot's bible. A person has to know all that stuff in order to get a license. Well, let's get going. A front moved in so you're about to see a very different flight."

They made a dash to the airplane through a hard rain. With the engine start checklist complete, Dan again yelled "Clear" before he cranked the engine. As if anyone would be out in this weather, Delbert thought, but I understand the need for thoroughness. Diligence is the pilot's best friend the book said.

"We'll be in clouds to Vancouver. It's a short flight but the controller will vector us all the way. We do as he says. It could be bumpy so make sure your straps are tight."

"Romeo. Maintain heading zero eight zero, climb to four thousand feet, squawk five five zero zero," came over the radio.

Dan acknowledged the clearance.

"Why don't you fly this, Delbert?"

More than a little nervous, Delbert took the controls. "Remember, scan your instruments, especially attitude. It's easy to slip off into a spin if you ignore it. We're almost at four thousand."

Not long after, they were instructed to turn to heading three five five, which Delbert did. In spite of the rough air, he kept the airplane pretty well on altitude, speed and heading. His mind again raced at a pace which made things seem to happen in slow motion. If one could peer in through the windshield, they would see his eyes dart from instrument to instrument, but he felt like he moved from one to the next at a deliberate rate which permitted him to digest what each told him.

Fifteen minutes later they were told to proceed to the Vancouver VOR and hold until further notice. Dan talked Delbert through the process of entry and flight in the holding pattern. He explained how to compensate for crosswind to stay on path.

"This gets pretty tricky so anytime you want me to take over, just say the word."

Delbert wasn't about to say the word. It was too much fun. Dan couldn't believe his new prize student could pull this off but determined to let him go as far as possible. Delbert made three circuits before they were cleared to exit the pattern. Dan talked him through the exit and flight in to the Vancouver airport, including approach path and glide slope capture.

"Very good, Delbert. I've completed the descent check-list. Gear down."

"Gear down?"

"That's a joke. We've broken out of the clouds. There's the runway."

"Romeo, cleared to land runway zero eight."

"You've done such a great job, you could probably land too but I want to take over since there's a nasty wind out there."

"Thanks for letting me fly so much, Dan, It was fabulous."

"It's been quite an introduction."

As they rolled off the runway onto a taxiway, Dan switched to the ground control frequency and got clearance to taxi to the terminal. When parked, ground control came on again.

"Double O Romeo, your controller said that was a fine exhibition of precision air work. Most light aircraft in that holding pattern drift out to sea."

"Thank you. Good day."

"Well Delbert, you heard him. Doubt if many first time fliers have matched what you just did."

Delbert felt a pride new and foreign to him. As they walked back into the terminal, Dan asked if he would like to do this again and work toward a pilot's license.

"I'd love to but will Dean Calder think I should study instead?"

"Do you think you're falling behind?"

"No, I haven't had any trouble with classes."

"Then let's start and adjust the pace to suit your workload."

Dan made a quick stop in the flight supply store.

"This is your log book, Delbert. Since I have an instructor rating, I'll log the time you flew the airplane today, along with forty minutes of IFR. Very few students have IFR time logged on their first flight. You earned it."

The success boosted Delbert's self confidence in a way which would have met with Sylvia's approval. Still, he couldn't help worry about Dean Calder's reaction and more important, his father's.

CHAPTER SEVENTEEN

When Dan described their flight over dinner, Delbert glanced at Charlie, who kept his head down eating. Charlie felt a pang of jealousy and had to tell himself his stomach sorely wanted Del to take his place in the airplane.

Alone later, Delbert broached the subject.

"Guess Dan asked me to go since you weren't available. If I horn in on your flight time, just say the word and I'll be busy when he invites me."

Charlie laughed, "He only asks me so he'll have company and because he harbours an insane hope I'll learn to like it. I get airsick every time we go up. You do me a favor if you get him off my back."

"Great! I just love it."

He described the day's experience in a letter to his family, how he pointed out their house as he flew over and how Dan wanted to give him more lessons so he could get a pilot's license. And by the way, school's going fine. Phil responded to the news as one might expect.

"Better remind 'im he's there fer the schoolin'. Don't want 'im lettin' Wally down by flunkin' out cause of flyin' all day."

"I'll mention that dear."

In a second letter to Sylvia, he apologized for writing again before she had a chance to answer his last letter, which of course agitated her. Then he dove into the flight experience once again, this time he told how he flew over Rainbow Beach and her house. He hoped to see her but nobody was outside. He said it hurt to be so close and not talk to her. It brought home how much he missed her.

Sylvia wrote back after reading his letter. She thought she heard an airplane fly over on Sunday, maybe him. She asked him to be careful since those little airplanes must be dangerous. Still it sounded exciting to see everything from the sky. Maybe someday when he's a pilot, he could take her on a tour of the islands. She missed him terribly and apologized for not writing sooner, it just seemed like there wasn't much to report.

~~~

During the first three lectures that week, Delbert read the Private Pilot Study Guide. Unfortunately, the professor in the third class recognized it.

"You there, with the uneven ears," he pointed, "yes you. You seem to think learning to fly is more important than Physics so get out."

Shocked and frightened, Delbert didn't know what to do but he immediately closed the book.

"I said get out. I won't have students in my class who are not prepared to concentrate on Physics. Think about that before you come to the next lecture. If it happens again, you'll be banned for the rest of the term. Now leave."

Delbert rose and left in a state of shock. There wasn't a sound in the room. Outside, he started to tremble. What if Dan hears about this or worse, Dean Calder. He walked across to the Library and found a vacant carrel to sit and wait for his next class. He was still in shock when that class began but he paid close attention to the lecture.

From the professor's words, Delbert assumed he was allowed back in for the next Physics lecture. He arrived early and sat on the opposite side from before. The professor scanned the class until he found Delbert. He made it clear he intended to carry out his threat.

~~~

Although Delbert made sure he learned everything the classes offered, he began to live for weekend lessons. Dan did too. Delbert absorbed everything covered with little need for repetition. The Vancouver airport was far too busy for anything other than departure and return. So they flew to various small airports in the region for touch and goes or to more isolated areas for air work.

After one of their weekend sessions, Samantha questioned Dan alone.

"You two are spending a lot of time in the air. Is Delbert keeping up with his studies?"

"He claims he is. The boy's very smart and has an incredible memory which allows him to learn quickly and well."

"I just hope you don't lead him astray."

"Me too. We'll know when his grades come out. Sam, when he's in that airplane, he's a different boy. He gains a confidence in himself that's normally missing. Perhaps it's a piece of his life where he is in control rather than the other way around. And he's a talented pilot already. I think it's good for his self esteem."

"You're probably right. He does seem more sure of himself than when he arrived."

~~~

UBC follows a two term system. This means mid-term tests occur at the end of October and March. Although exams in December cover the first term in detail, finals in May can contain questions on the whole year's work. Students are encouraged to learn material thoroughly. Since Delbert felt no need to cram, it worked in his favor. Still mid-October found him reviewing textbooks in search of things he might have missed.

He went into the tests with a natural anxiety, which rapidly dissipated as he looked over the questions and realized they were easily answered.

~~~

By the first of November, Delbert logged over twenty-five flight hours. That Saturday they flew across to Abbotsford and performed two touch and goes. Then Dan told him to make a full stop and taxi to the terminal building.

There, he unstrapped, "Delbert, I want you to take off, fly around the circuit, make a touch and go, then a full stop on the second pass. Be sure to come back and pick me up. I don't want to hitch-hike home."

Delbert suffered an anxious moment when he realized he was about to solo. He told himself it's just the same as if Dan were in the airplane. I can do it. Still, his hands shook as he applied power to take off. Once airborne, he calmed down and the flight went without incident. As he taxied up to Dan, he felt an increased sense of confidence and pride.

Dan climbed back in, "Good job, Delbert. You're now cleared for pilot in command, however, the lessons are far from over. From now on, unless I say otherwise, you're in complete charge. Consider me a passenger. So let's do three more touch and goes, then take me home."

Determined not to screw up, Delbert took charge of radio communications, checklists and control of the aircraft. This is a pleasure to watch, Dan thought, although if I'm not careful it could eat into my flight time.

"I'll go with you on our next session. Then you're to take the airplane up alone for a few hours until you get comfortable. Then, we'll plan—I should say you'll plan a cross country flight and I'll come along as a passenger. After that, you'll plan and fly a solo cross country flight."

As they left the parked airplane, Dan called to a mechanic, "Jack, this is Delbert Pillage. There'll be times in the next while when he'll take Romeo up on his own. Just so you don't think he's high-jacking it."

"Fine. Howdy Delbert. Didn't think he'd ever let anyone else fly his pride and joy. He hates it when I take a check ride after engine maintenance."

"Jack, you're so rough I always have to do a walk-around with a fine tooth comb to be sure it's still in one piece."

"Talk like that and I'll set you up to practice a dead stick landing one of these days."

They all laughed. Delbert felt a warm glow of pilot camaraderie.

On the way home, Dan explained the ground rules to be followed. Delbert had to get his permission before each flight. He had to list everything he planned to practice. Flying was not to interfere with his studies in any way. He was not to skip any classes or lab sessions to fly. It was illegal to take anyone with him until he obtained a pilot's license and after that he still needed Dan's permission and Dan had to meet anyone he wanted to take up. With the prospect of more flight time, all conditions were accepted.

On two consecutive weekends, Delbert flew a cross country route from Vancouver to Powell River to Campbell

River and back to Vancouver, once with Dan and then alone. After that, they alternated instruction sessions with solo flights. More time was spent under the hood to simulate flight in clouds. They worked on mountain procedures, spin recovery and simulated engine failure. And all the while, the touch and go's accumulated.

By early December, Dan felt Delbert was ready to take the private pilot exam so he scheduled a session with a certified examiner he knew in Victoria. Delbert flew over to pick up what turned out to be a salty old bow-legged character in jeans and worn cowboy boots. He climbed in and set a paper cup of coffee on the glare shield, with the clear implication that he expected it to sit there without spills throughout the flight.

"Take it up," was all he said or more accurately, grunted. Delbert performed the smoothest taxi, takeoff and climb of his still modest career, with the coffee cup added to his scan pattern. Out over the water, he grunted Delbert through a series of maneuvers. For a landing configuration power-on stall, the examiner judiciously retrieved his coffee as the airplane stalled out and the nose plunged down.

Then he made Delbert put on the hood and close his eyes until he told him to open them. Delbert knew they climbed to a higher altitude and leveled off but could sense nothing else.

"OK, it's your airplane."

When he opened his eyes, he realized the airplane was in a spin. His automatic reaction was to level wings and push the nose down further to get the airplane flying again. He marveled at how the examiner was able to set up that situation without a clue. As he brought the airplane to level flight, the examiner grunted, "Take me home."

Delbert turned towards the Victoria airport, which showed he knew where he was after the spin. He was quite sure he had done well so far. Still with no feedback, he felt uneasy. The coffee cup was back on the glare shield, now less than half full. Just enough to make a mess in a hard landing. After a gentle touch down and taxi to the terminal, the examiner asked for his logbook, thumbed through it and scribbled a new entry.

He opened the door and threw out the last of his coffee, then handed back the logbook, "You're a pilot."

He climbed out and hobbled off across the apron. Delbert stared at him, chuckled, opened the logbook and saw the magic words "Private Pilot Certificate Issued" followed by the examiner's name and license number. In perhaps the only unnecessary words the examiner had used in years, that was followed by "Good job". A happy and excited pilot flew the airplane back to Vancouver. I wish the cookie thief could see me now, he thought.

CHAPTER EIGHTEEN

Sylvia found grade twelve difficult on three counts. Class work seemed harder than ever, she missed Delbert constantly and she had an increased loneliness brought on by her reluctance to participate in social functions. The more aggressive boys each tried to date her. But she rejected passes with a variety of excuses and longed for the Christmas holidays when Delbert would be home again.

The island population barely supported a classroom of students in each grade so there weren't many extracurricular social functions. However, there was a high school dance before Christmas and of course a senior prom in the spring. A quiet, yet attractive boy in her class named Sal Lightfoot screwed up his courage and asked her to the Christmas dance. On the verge of refusal, she hesitated. I really hate to miss this dance, she thought. He probably won't hound me for additional dates. Would it hurt to go with him?

His silent patience while she struggled with a decision was rewarded with an acceptance. His surprise turned to elation. Sal, a little shy himself, was unaware of his potential for success with most girls in their class. To avoid competition on a social level, he threw himself into school sports and excelled in them. This added to his unrecognized appeal.

Athleticism ran in his family. His older brother, Robin, graduated from high school five years earlier. Unlike Sal,

Robin managed to cut a sexual swath through most of the girls his age. Where Sal was shy, Robin was aggressive. Not long after graduation, he managed inadvertently to get a girl pregnant. Actually, that's too polite. She told him it was not a good time and the callous bastard forced her into intercourse anyway.

It came as a surprise to find he had to marry her or suffer the consequences of an unfriendly visit from her six foot six giant of a father. Now, four years later, she had given birth to two girls and his interest had moved on to other women on the island.

With Sal and Robin, it was hard to tell if old man Lightfoot's naming philosophy worked or not. He believed that feminine names would make them strong characters.

"They'll either develop into a lady's man or a man's lady an' I don't rightly care which," he liked to say.

While Robin went overboard in the "lady's man" direction, it wasn't clear which way Sal might head. But taking Sylvia to the dance convinced the old man he was simply a tamer version of Robin.

At the dance, jealousy spread like wildfire. It didn't take long for the sharks of both sexes to attack, prying them apart for dances. Sal repeatedly reclaimed her and both had fun that night. Back at her door, his shyness allowed her to thank him and say good night without the need to fend off an advance. All in all, a successful date from her viewpoint. He longed for more.

~~~

When Delbert arrived home the next week, she wanted to be the first to tell him about the dance and as soon as they were alone in Phil's pickup she started in on what sounded like a confession.

"Delbert, you said I should participate in school social life but I didn't want to without you. I turned down dates all fall but thought I should go to the Christmas dance and when Sal Lightfoot asked me, I said yes. I hope you don't mind. Nothing happened other than dancing and I haven't had any other dates."

"Did you have a good time?"

"I enjoyed the dance."

"Great! I'm glad you went. You shouldn't live the life of a social hermit. Sal's a good guy. He wouldn't force you into anything you don't want."

"I was worried you'd be mad when I told you."

"It's a small island, Sylvia. Paul told me last night. I confess I was a bit jealous at first but I realized you shouldn't live a nun's life just because I'm not around."

"I love you, Delbert," she said, as she slipped her arms around his neck and initiated a long, intense kiss. As their bodies merged, they felt the same immediate excitement so often felt last summer. As she leaned towards him, her blouse pulled out of her skirt. When he slid his arm around her he felt skin in place of cloth. She trembled as his hand moved slowly up her back. It stopped at her bra strap, not knowing what to do next. As they came out of the kiss, she pressed her cheek against his so that her hot breath caressed his ear.

With thrills pulsating through her body, she moved her right hand to his thigh, then crotch. He took that as permission to unsnap her bra. She pulled his shirt up and unfastened the buttons. He unfastened hers. His legs slid under her as she moved forward on top of him. Skin to skin from the waist up triggered feelings neither experienced before. For long minutes they held each other tight in an embrace.

"Oh Delbert," she whispered, "I love you!"

"I love you, Sylvia," he breathed in her ear. They kissed again and again.

Still committed to protect her virginity, sanity returned slowly as passion cooled. Somewhat self-conscious, they buttoned up and tucked in.

"Delbert, I'm sorry we can't go all the way. Is it hard on you?"

"Our time will come," he said evasively.

Events conspired to prevent a recurrence, although they spent a memorable New Year's Eve together. Too soon it was time to head back to Vancouver. She fought back the tears and bravely they both agreed it should only be a few months before they would be together again.

CHAPTER NINETEEN

Physics class on the first week back provided a new and different experience. The professor came into the front of the lecture hall with an armful of exam papers which he threw across the floor.

"That's what I think of your work! If you think you can get through this course with that kind of crap, you're wrong! Get back in your seats! You can find your garbage after I'm finished."

He waved a paper in the air "There was only one respectable paper in the whole class. You can't all be that stupid", as he pointed to the papers scattered across the floor. "So you must not pay attention. Too many of you are like slope ears there, reading a pilot manual or picking your nose or whatever else you do. How can I get you to perform like students?"

A stunned silence greeted this outburst. Finally, with no thought of consequences, Delbert spoke up, "Perhaps it would help if you talked to us more about the concepts rather than just copy down formulas and stuff from the textbook."

The class gasped as all eyes turned first to him, then back to the professor.

"Slope ears, the flyboy! You were too buried in your books to notice what I might be up to."

Another long pause.

"Well, looks like no one else has the balls to say anything." He glanced at the paper still in his hand, "out of one hundred and seventy-four papers, there was one decent score. Will Pillage please come and get it?"

His jaw dropped when Delbert stood up and walked down to retrieve his paper.

"Well, Pillage, maybe I shouldn't disparage your ears, apparently they work quite well." He turned and walked out.

As students scrambled around on the floor to find their papers, more than one glanced at Delbert. He didn't look like a leader but he certainly acted like one. A good score was one thing. Courage to stand up on their behalf counted far more.

The professor too gained their respect because he interacted more with the class. While he still reverted to the board, more time was spent in front of the class. He explained concepts, asked and fielded questions. The class was livelier, the students more responsive and the professor found he enjoyed lectures more than he would have thought possible a month earlier. He felt invigorated.

Delbert passed all exams with high marks. It didn't surprise him since they appeared straight-forward. Still he wrote home to tell his parents, as much to put Phil's mind at rest as to give Teresa the happiness he knew she would feel. Mid January, Dean Calder's secretary left a message with the Martins for him to call and schedule a meeting.

Back in the Dean's office a few days later, "Well Delbert, I see you didn't let us down in the first term. Good work!"

"Thank you Sir."

"Any problems with your classes?"

A little hesitant, "No Sir."

"Have you decided on your course of action for next year?"

"I've decided to go the Engineering Physics route."

"Good," pausing, "something bothering you, Delbert?"

"No Sir. Everyone's been very good to me."

"I sense something troubles you, Delbert. Out with it. We can't find a solution until we confront the problem."

"Well...It seems so ungrateful, I shouldn't mention it but I thought university would be an incredible challenge back in September. It's harder than high school yet I don't feel challenged by it. So much of it is just straight from a textbook. Sounds crazy but the course with the most challenge is English literature and that's only because the professor's so good. I'm sorry. This sounds like a complaint and that's wrong after all you've done for me."

"Don't give it a second thought, son, I want that kind of feedback. We don't want you to sink into a sea of mediocrity. Frankly, I'm not surprised. Your mind cries out for challenge. I should have anticipated this. It seemed like a good idea to let you get your feet wet with university routine before we push extra things your way. Although there wasn't any doubt that you could handle the workload, we had to be prudent and let you give us the proof."

"Thank you Sir," he said, relieved to have the problem out in the open.

"So where do we go from here? I'll talk to a few professors to see if you can join in their research. If they agree, I'll describe their projects to you to find out which pique your interest. You didn't hear it from me but students have been known to skip a few classes to work on research projects. Of course, it doesn't free you from the need to get the grades we expect. Does that interest you?"

"Definitely! Although professor's research sounds intimidating."

"No need to worry. Many professors use student assistants. By the way, Dan tells me you've become an excellent pilot. He thinks you would make a top notch test pilot, which is quite a complement."

"I love flying. It's great physical and mental exercise."

"I'm reluctant to say this but if your interest continues unabated you might want to look into the Air Force Reserve. They sometimes take on talented students and give them jet training during the summer months."

His heart skipped a beat. Jet training! Summer— Sylvia—maybe it wouldn't be all summer—is there harm in finding out?

"They must want more experience than I've got. I'll talk to Dan just to see what it's all about but I won't let it impact my school work."

"Fine. You're capable of much more than your studies. The trick will be to put that extra capacity to good use. But you're right, it's important to tick off the courses with good grades so that you leave this factory with a degree that opens the doors you desire. Along the way we can exploit your talents in extra things. Summer flying could be one of them. Anyway, let's add some challenge to your life now."

"Thank you Sir."

"I'll get back to you in a few days."

After dinner, Dan collared Delbert, "Have you talked to Dean Calder lately?"

"We talked this morning. He plans to ask some professors if they can use me in their research work. We both agreed that some additional challenge would be good."

"Guess I'm not surprised. Too many professors feel they have to cover all the prescribed material for each course so they don't have time to explore avenues outside the text book. That can get tedious for someone with your ability. In fact, that's one reason I encouraged flying last Fall."

"I can't thank you enough for that. I'm excited every time I climb in the airplane. By the way, Dean Calder mentioned the Air Force Reserve summer program. Are you familiar with that?"

"Sort of. They keep their eyes open for students who would make exceptional test pilot candidates. I told Wally that you might be one of them. Frankly, I wanted him to make the decision on whether or not to discuss it with you. Since he has, the program works like this.

"If you apply and they accept you, they send you back to Malton, Ontario for the summer. You go through the same ground school and flight training that regular Air Force pilots receive. Once a month during the school year, they want you to spend a weekend over at Comox for refresher training. That's to maintain your proficiency through the winter."

"Would they consider someone my age?"

"That's a good question. Really don't know. They may want you to get another year under your belt. Tell you what. I know the man who runs the program here at UBC. If you want, I could describe your situation to him and see what he thinks?"

"Guess I'd like to learn more about it, if you don't mind."

"Fine. I'll talk to him."

Just the thought of an opportunity to fly jets introduced an unexpected stress level. How can I pass up the chance? But can I disappoint Sylvia by robbing us of a summer together? How could she possibly understand what the opportunity means to me? Do I dare risk losing her? They probably won't even consider someone my age. Maybe I don't have what they want. Why worry about something that's not yet a problem? Still, he did.

CHAPTER TWENTY

Three days later there was a request from Dean Calder's office for Delbert to make another appointment.

"Delbert," he began straight in, "I've talked to professors in electronics engineering since they seem to have more appropriate projects. There are two possibilities."

"The first, Mike Medane, would let you help him on a project to develop a scanner which reads printed Braille for use by blind people. Braille books are expensive and hard to obtain because characters have to be embossed so they can be felt. The scanner would make it possible to print them on paper like any other book. It would produce a sound for each character which the reader could recognize. A simple concept but the devil is in the details and you would be introduced to some complicated issues along with solid state electronics design.

"The second is much closer to home. Dan is working on the thermodynamic design for a secret new jet engine. It involves a sophisticated and complex analysis, along with a lot of brute force calculations. I won't say he's stumped but he has run into some thorny problems which he thinks would benefit from a fresh pair of eyes. If you were any less gifted I would say forget it and he worries whether a collaboration almost within the family might pose problems. Also, he would have to get military approval before he can show you the data. Still, he thinks it might work and it would certainly provide mental challenge, so he'll take on the military if you're interested."

"Both of those sound good."

"Well, why don't you begin with Mike Medan and see what develops. It will take Dan some time to work your security clearance. In fact, it's unlikely you would be able to start with him before next Fall."

"OK."

"I'll tell Mike you want to help him and get my assistant to set up a meeting between the two of you."

"Thank you, Sir."

~~~

The meeting was set for 4:30 the following Monday afternoon. A knock on the office door produced a barely heard "Come in". He found Professor Medane hunched over his desk to mark a test paper. His hair was supposed to be combed straight back but flopped down towards his ears on both sides and he had the pasty look of a person who seldom sees sunshine.

"Sit down." He didn't look up.

Delbert sat in the only chair available in an office cluttered with books and papers. On a cabinet near the desk sat a box with a piano-like keyboard on top.

Eventually the professor raised his head to peer at his visitor.

"What I wish you could do is mark these damn papers. Calder would run me out of town if I tried that. So, what do you know about solid state electronics?"

"Not much yet. When Dean Calder said the project would involve solid state electronics, I picked up the textbook for your EE351 course and I'm about a third of the way through it."

"A third, in how many days?"

"Four, Sir."

"How do you expect to understand and retain material from a cursory scan?"

"I'm reading it carefully, Sir. I can remember things as long as I understand what's being said."

"That's absurd Mr.–uh–Pillage. Don't see how you can be of any use to me but I can't renege on Calder now."

He reached over to a book case and pulled out a reference book, then picked a small collection of technical papers off a foot high pile.

"When you're finished with the textbook, read chapters four through seven in this one and these papers. Don't come back until you think you know what's in them. I'll give you a test to assess how well you have mastered the material and we'll decide then whether or not to continue."

"Thank you, Professor Medan."

"It's Medane, not Medan. If I was a caveman, I would say 'Me Dane'. Got it?"

"I'm sorry Sir, I must not have heard Dean Calder correctly."

"Hearing's important for this project. Our goal is to be able to pass a scanner over a printed Braille page and get this."

He flipped a switch on the box and played a series of notes, singing out a letter for each: "N O W B E G O N E".

"Yes Sir." He picked up his load of material and left. Medane shook his head and buried it in the test paper again.

~~~

Delbert had to balance class work with the books and papers. It took three weeks to feel comfortable with the material, not that he felt truly comfortable with Professor Medane's threat hanging over his head. Another two days passed before he could get an appointment.

He was greeted with, "Are you claiming to have mastered that material already? Before you say anything, if I decide you only have a superficial knowledge we're through. I have no use for coddled Prima Donnas. So what's your answer?"

"I think I understand the textbook and material you gave me."

"Then answer these questions," and he thrust a paper across to Delbert, then went back to his technical journal, as if Delbert didn't exist.

It took almost thirty minutes to answer the questions since the last three were design problems, the final one quite involved. He placed the paper back on the professor's desk and waited. It was ignored for at least five minutes. Finally, the professor put down his journal, sighed and picked up the paper. He skimmed down through the initial questions and found them all. correct. More time was spent on the final three, particularly the last one.

. Slowly he raised his head and stared at Delbert. "You never saw this material before a month ago?"

"No Sir."

"Come with me." He led them to his lab, which was as messy as his office. He picked up a sheet of paper. "This is what the Braille alphabet looks like."

"Yes Sir. I decided it would be wise to learn that so I got a Braille primer from the library."

"Good. The characters are all the same size from book to book. Now I've done an analysis of how many optical sensors are needed to detect each character. I want you to perform an independent assessment and see how it compares with mine. The first obstacle we run into is that optical sensors today are not small enough to fit into the space available. Even when I staggered their height to overlap them it was still too tight. I think it will take future miniaturization to be successful. Anyway, get back to me when you've had a shot at the analysis."

"Yes Sir."

"And Delbert, call me Mike as long as we work together. If you end up in one of my classes, it will be Professor Medane again, but not here. For what it's worth, I'm impressed with what you learned in a month. Some of my third year students never get that far."

"Thank you, Mike."

Delbert realized the analysis wasn't trivial. As the scanner passes over the page, there is nothing to center it over the character. If it is handheld rather than run on tracks, it might be rotated to at least a small angle to the line. It would have to ensure that it isn't looking at pieces of two adjacent characters. Since he knew the thickness of available sensors from the material read, he could see Mike's overlapping design wouldn't work. They would have to wait for smaller sensors.

But why not use optics rather than cram the sensors into a space which may remain too small for years to come? Why not start with a lens that bends the light so it can be read by an array of sensors mounted as though they were stuck into half a tennis ball? Mike probably thought of this and found a problem with it. Maybe not.

To satisfy his curiosity, he decided to find a lens which might accomplish what he envisioned. He researched lenses in the library without success. In the end, he found a book on lens design and adapted the dimensions of a lens with the desired characteristics to fit the Braille characters.

He arranged an appointment with Mike to present his analysis. Mike studied it for some time.

"You're even more conservative than I am and it makes sense. I want to see this project work so bad I probably kid myself with too crude a sensor array. Damn it, that pushes it even farther out into the future."

Delbert was afraid to show his optical approach. Still, he wondered if Mike had considered any possibility along that line.

"Is there perhaps an optical way to spread the light to the sensors?"

"Do you mean a magnifying lens? I've looked at that and the gadget gets so unwieldy we can't expect a person to use it as a handheld scanner."

"I was thinking of a refraction lens."

"Explain what you mean."

"I did some work on a possible lens design if you would like to see it. It looks like it would work to the dimensions required by the Braille but I may be all wet."

"Let me see that. What's the scale?"

"Twice full size."

After careful study, "Will this lens really spread the light out like that?"

"The data says it will."

"I'll get a guy over in the Physics department to look this over and unless he finds a problem, to grind us a lens to these dimensions. And we'll give it a try. If it works, you'll go from being a pain in the ass to my hero in less than a month."

~~~

A week later, Mike showed him a lens. It was even smaller than Delbert anticipated, about the size of a penny. That made sense, however, since the area to be scanned was smaller still.

"Delbert, let's get something straight. Don't ever hesitate to make suggestions or show me your ideas. That's what research is all about. What you came up with may well be the breakthrough we need. Promise me you won't hold back in future."

"Yes Mike."

"OK. Your next challenge will be to come up with a way to mount this lens with the sensors positioned correctly. Don't try to be elegant with your design. We just want to kluge up something to see if the optics work. We've a long way to go before a real design."

"Seems like we'll have to control the height above the paper and maybe shine some light on the paper to get good contrast between dots and space, won't we?"

"Yes. We'll probably need some sort of roller balls under it. Unless you can think of a simple way to include lights, you may want to put that off until later. We can shine some light into it for the optical tests."

"OK."

The design problem intrigued Delbert. He sketched possibilities during the best part of two lectures, fortunately undetected by professors. Students near him thought they were doodles which they had come to expect. I don't like Mike's idea of roller balls, he thought, the device will scoot off at all angles. We want to encourage it to go in a straight line once the user gets oriented with the book. It should have little wheels which would naturally move it in a straight line.

He decided the simplest design would probably prove best. That would be half an aluminum sphere a little smaller than a tennis ball. Holes would be drilled in it to hold sensors in the desired positions. The bottom would be a flat plate with a large hole drilled in the center to hold the lens. He could see how light emitting diodes could be mounted in the base plate along the outside edge. He made scaled drawings of his design.

About this time he realized his preoccupation caused him to overlook a scheduled chemistry test until he showed up for the class. The test didn't bother him too much. What scared him was that he might not have attended the class at all. He determined to pay better attention in future.

He took his sketches to Mike with a mixture of excitement and nervousness. Mike liked them and said he would get the mechanical engineers to fabricate the case.

"Are you confident that the sensor positions are where you want them?"

"I'm concerned that the lens won't behave exactly as expected. And converting the signals to recognized Braille characters will be scary complicated."

"Scary complicated," Mike laughed, "yes, scary. But first things first. If the sensor array can give us an electrical picture of what's scanned, that will be a giant step forward."

"Well the sensor positions are my best estimate of what will work with the number of sensors we have."

"That's good enough for me. I'll get it made up. Incidentally, I like your idea of light emitting diodes around the circumference. And I agree on wheels rather than roller balls—very clever and easier to mount as well. Good work. I'll let you know when the case is ready so we can hook it up and see if it works. I'm excited, Delbert."

"Me too."

CHAPTER TWENTY-ONE

Mike called him the following Wednesday to assemble the scanner. The housing had its little wheels attached to the base which snapped into the hemisphere.

"Professor Jones gave me static on this, said we should have given the damn thing to a dentist to make, not a mechanical engineer."

With sensors and lights installed, they connected wires from the sensors to a bank of transistor amplifiers which fed a panel of little lights that Mike had built. Anxious to see if it worked, Mike positioned a test pattern under the scanner and turned it on.

"My God, look at that!"

The pattern on the light panel reflected the printed test pattern. Mike moved the scanner across the page and they watched the pattern move off the light panel. He slapped Delbert on the back, "We've done it! We've done it!"

They ran it over a variety of Braille characters and watched them repeated on the light panel.

"OK, we need to get more scientific. I want you to set up experiments, take measurements and calibrate its accuracy and resolution. Make sure dots will always be detected. No blind spots—perhaps a poor choice of words."

The scanner success boosted Delbert's self-confidence. At dinner that night, he described what happened in the lab. The scanner felt like half a tennis ball on little wheels so the size problem had been licked.

Dan smiled, "Great!" From a conversation with Mike he knew how much Delbert had contributed to their success. He decided not to mention that in front of Charlie. He was proud of his son's academic and athletic accomplishments. Still, Charlie might become jealous of what Delbert achieved in so short a time. Better not make a big deal of this.

He needn't have worried. Charlie had long since decided he couldn't compete with Delbert on an intellectual level. They developed a strong friendship to which Charlie contributed much needed social leadership. He took pride in getting Delbert into shape, onto his soccer team and into a social life with other students.

They developed a symbiotic relationship; Delbert helped Charlie work through concepts and problems he found difficult, Charlie kept Delbert advised of upcoming assignments and tests. They often hung out together in the commons area, called the Hub, or in the bookstore cafe. Charlie had a way with girls and conspired to combat Delbert's bashfulness through introductions. He succeeded to the extent that Delbert learned to talk at ease with the more extroverted girls.

However, their presence always brought Sylvia to mind. He wouldn't ask even the most desirable girl for a date. When they took the initiative and asked him to go some-where, he always had something else to do. He apologized to Charlie for his reluctance to date.

"I don't want to betray Sylvia by dating another girl. Sounds ungrateful but that's how I feel."

"She must be some sort of goddess. I hope she appreciates you as much."

"She is and I think she does."

Two of the girls most intrigued with Delbert confided to Charlie that they wanted to date him. He told each that although Delbert liked them, he was committed to his girlfriend back on Saltspring. This just fueled their ambition. They often bumped into Delbert, whether he was with Charlie or not.

~~~

Spring mid-term exam results were a replay of the Fall but without the concern he felt earlier. The Braille scanner project captured most of his attention. While he calibrated its optical characteristics and resolution, his mind leaped ahead to the design requirements for the circuits needed to recognize characters and generate sounds for each.

He dreamed of a machine able to speak the words or letters represented by the Braille characters. That would be the ultimate. No, the ultimate would be to scan ordinary typed pages, recognize words not letters, and speak the words. Now that's a dream, he thought. It will be years before electronics are miniaturized enough for Braille words, let alone printed ones.

~~~

One afternoon in early April Dan invited Delbert into his study.

"I talked to Ross MacKenzie about the Air Force Reserve program. He investigated your qualifications and potential for acceptance. Today he told me they are interested, in spite of your age. The man who commands the school at Malton wants to come out in a couple of weeks and talk to you in person. Shall I say yes or no?"

The moment Delbert both longed for and dreaded arrived. I can't say no now, he thought, and I want more than anything to try it—well, not more than anything. But there'll only be one opportunity. Will Sylvia understand what it means to me?

"Yes—I think. Thanks for getting this opportunity. I know you helped make it happen."

"You're not in yet, though you have a reasonable shot at it. I'll tell Ross to go ahead. By the way, he wants to meet you first and there are some medical tests required. He wondered if you could drop by his office tomorrow at four?"

"Sure."

"Fine. I'll confirm that with him too."

Ross MacKenzie turned out to be a tall, thin man with a ruddy complexion that bordered on Rosacea. Perhaps the result of too much whiskey.

"Delbert Pillage, pleased to meet you. Have a seat, my boy."

This, after a bone-crushing handshake that revealed his thinness concealed the wiriness and muscle tone of a man obsessed with fitness.

"Dan Martin painted an impressive picture of your talents. I've investigated on my own and it bears out what he said. You may have what we look for in our pilot ranks. Of course, there's tests we want to subject you to before we make any offer."

"Yes Sir, Dan told me there would be tests."

"I need to describe the commitment and responsibilities expected of entrants into the program. Sometimes people let the word 'Reserve' cause them to forget they join the Air Force. True, the Air Force will not interfere with your university education and any choices you make related to that. Naturally, we're interested in students in programs which can prove valuable to us. However, we make no demands on what you study.

"We take advantage of your summers away from university to give you flight training to get a leg up on what's ultimately required to enter our experimental flight test world. If you wonder why we bother with university students, the answer is that test pilots don't simply have to fly jets. They need to understand airplane design, the theory which allows planes to do what they do and the ability to communicate to engineers what should be done next to fix or improve the aircraft.

"There are strings attached. You don't learn to fly and say 'thanks, see you later'. When you sign on, you commit to a minimum of three years full time after university. Obviously, we hope you want to stay longer. If we make you an offer, I would encourage you to think about the life of a test pilot and assess whether or not it will appeal to you on an ongoing basis. Don't let yourself be swept away by the euphoria of jet flight.

"Here endeth my lecture. If we and you decide the Air Force is a good fit, you will spend your next few summers back in Ontario. Basic training is a bit rigorous but not like the army or special forces. You look fit enough to handle it. In the winter, we ask you to spend one weekend a month over at Comox. We fly you over Friday night and back Sunday afternoon. You would have to plan any school assignments around that absence."

"I understand. I'm a little concerned that I don't know what the life of a test pilot is like and that maybe I glorify it too much."

"That's a very healthy concern, my boy, very healthy. If you pass the medical tests, the commander back at Malton, 'Bentwing' Carson, will fly out and meet with you. He's a great one to describe what experimental test flight is all about. Just don't ask why they call him Bentwing, he may decide to show you."

"OK. How do I take the tests?"

"Call this doctor," MacKenzie passed a card across. "His receptionist will expect your call and you can pick a time and date which fits your schedule. Thanks for coming in. I hope this works out."

The tests surprised Delbert with their thoroughness. Along with physical examinations, there was a long session with what must have been a psychiatrist. It included a battery of questions, some quite strange, and a series of mental tests clearly designed to determine his reaction to stress. He resisted the temptation to guess what they wanted to hear since he suspected the tests exposed contrived responses.

Ross MacKenzie called less than a week later. "You came through in fine shape, my boy. You might like to know you have unusually strong eyesight, equal to that of Ted Williams. He can see the seams on a baseball sixty feet away and you could too, not that I recommend you take up baseball. Point is, that eyesight helped to make him an ace in W W Two. It's a great asset for a pilot. Have you had second thoughts about the program?"

"No Sir, I'm interested in it."

"Good! I'll pass everything on to Bentwing. He'll want to fly out and meet you."

Actually, Delbert overflowed with second thoughts. How do I compete with older full-time pilots? Can I learn to control a jet? Flying has increased my self-confidence but will this push my luck too far? Inevitably his thoughts returned to Sylvia. She encouraged me to take on university life. Will she encourage me to do this too? Or will she be hurt that I'll be gone all summer? I don't want this opportunity to jeopardize our life together.

Chapter Twenty-Two

Although not revealed to Delbert, the Training Command was excited with his test results. His combination of mental and physical abilities, together with emotional stability under stress, was exactly what they wanted. The report did say he was humble and lacked self-confidence, though it was felt that could be remedied with maturity. Bentwing decided to push a few things off his plate and fly out to Vancouver that week.

"Delbert," MacKenzie began on the telephone the next day, "Bentwing wants to come out this week. Can you spend Saturday with him?"

"I have an eight thirty lecture but I'm free from ten on. The lecture's important because there's a test scheduled."

"That's fine. That'll work. He wants to take you up in a jet trainer. He'll fly it from Comox and pick you up at Vancouver International later in the morning. I'll firm up the time this week and plan to drive you out there myself."

The rest of the week was spent in anticipation. When Dan heard what happened, he cautioned Delbert not to be in awe of the jet.

"It's like any other airplane, just a lot faster. You have to think ahead so you control it instead of the other way around. What's his name, Bentwing, will be more impressed if you remain calm than if you act like an over-excited puppy."

So Delbert reined in his enthusiasm and tried to assume a blasé demeanor, without much success. Concentration on class work, though difficult, helped pass the hours at something above a snail's pace. Saturday arrived at last and Ross MacKenzie rang the doorbell. Delbert answered before the last chime died out.

"Before we leave, you need to put on this flight suit. It should fit you based on the doctor's measurements. Don't wear anything under it other than your skivvies. And put on these flight boots."

When he re-emerged Dan chuckled, "If I didn't know better, I'd say you're in the air force already."

Delbert admired the RCAF insignia on his chest. Both men got a kick out of his obvious excitement.

"Don't get shot down," Charlie chimed in, "we've got an important soccer game on Tuesday."

On the way to the airport, Ross MacKenzie explained that he needed the flying suit because he would wear a g suit on the airplane. It was important to know there wasn't anything between him and the suit which could cause problems.

"You probably could get by without the g suit for this flight, however, it's standard protocol and you never know what old Bentwing might do. If he does pull a few g's, the suit will automatically inflate. If that happens, you want to flex your abdominal muscles as much as you can while it's inflated. Do you know what the suit does?"

"No."

"It puts pressure on your legs and body to restrict blood flow away from your brain to your lower extremities. If your brain is deprived of blood very long, your vision will grey out, then vanish and finally you lose consciousness. But don't let me scare you. He won't put you in that position."

Delbert spent the rest of the ride flexing his abdominal muscles. When they arrived at a guard gate via a side road, MacKenzie showed his credentials and they were waved through. Straight ahead was a small building with a number of military aircraft parked nearby. They were confronted by a short stocky man in a flight suit like Delbert's except with additional patches on the sleeves.

"Damn, Pillage, you almost look like a fly boy already. I'm Tom Carson but most people insult me with the nickname Bentwing." The gruff voice reminded Delbert of his examiner. He wondered if vocal cords suffered abuse from too many flight hours.

"It's an honour to meet you, Mr. Carson."

"Bull shit. Call me Bentwing. We'll be flying buddies in a few minutes. Did MacKenzie here tell you we'll wear g suits?"

"Yes Sir."

"Bentwing!"

"Yes, Bentwing."

"OK, let's go get them on. Ross, we should be back by two. Can you drop back then?"

"Sure, Bentwing."

Decked out in a g suit and shiny new flight helmet, Delbert walked on air as they approached the jet trainer.

"This is our basic trainer, the CT-133 Silver Star. You sit up front. Step here, then there with your right foot and swing your leg into the cockpit, then slide down into the seat."

Once seated, Bentwing leaned in and connected his g suit and interphone, showed him how to fasten the harness, then climbed into the back seat and hooked himself up.

"You hear me, Pillage?" came over the interphone.

"Yes, S–Bentwing."

"Instruments look familiar?"

"The basic ones do. Engine instruments are all new to me."

"Adjust your seat so the rudder pedals feel right. Grab the joystick and move it around. Side to side is roll, front to back is pitch, just like you would expect. Gotta warn you though, this bird is frisky compared to what you've flown and the stick forces will be higher. The thrust lever is on your left, forward for more thrust, idle is back. There are limits on how hot you can run the engine but I'll look after that—OK, Chuck, we're ready to crank. Fire that bottle." This last bit was over the ground interphone to the crew that manned a cart with a hose connected to the engine.

What started as a low hum increased to a high whine as the turbine spun up to a self-sustaining speed. The canopy closed and muffled it a few minutes later. As the cart pulled away, Bentwing requested taxi clearance and within moments ran the engine up briefly to get them rolling.

Well at least taxiing is a lot like Dan's plane, although it takes a lot longer for the engine to accelerate. When lined up on the runway and Bentwing had received clearance for takeoff, he said, "Hang on Pillage, here we go."

They began the takeoff roll but not much happened as the engine spun up. Then the thrust kicked in and flattened Delbert against the seat back as the jet hurtled down the runway. In almost no time Bentwing pulled back on the joystick and the aircraft leaped into the sky. The rate of climb amazed Delbert but it gibed with the rate the ground fell away. They were already well above the restricted airspace around the airport. Bentwing had the jet in a graceful turn out towards the open ocean. The rate at which they crossed Vancouver Island gave Delbert a true perspective of the jet's speed.

"OK Delbert, grab the joystick but be gentle. This bird jumps when you yank it around. Try a gentle turn to the right." Delbert gingerly moved the joystick a little to the right to feel out the controls. Gaining confidence, he put the airplane into a perfectly coordinated thirty degree banked turn.

"Good. Now show me a forty-five to the left." Delbert rolled the jet smoothly over to the left bank angle. Bentwing was impressed but said only, "I'll take it now. I want to show you what a roll is like. This is a barrel roll which means we maintain one g throughout. You could have done it in Dan's rig."

Without thinking Delbert said, "I did."

"Well in that case, you show me."

He wished he had kept his mouth shut as he started a slow roll to the right, pushed the joystick forward while they were inverted and pulled it back as they came out of the roll. Damn, Bentwing thought, that was near perfect on the first try.

"Not bad, now I'll show you a snap roll."

And he did. Wow, thought Delbert, that was great and it looked like he didn't do anything more than use roll control.

"Want to try it. Just hold the joystick over until you come upright again."

Delbert swung the joystick hard over, the airplane rolled violently. He barely leveled off in time.

"You're quite a mustang, kid. Now I'll show you a loop. Hang on."

For the first time, Delbert felt some significant g forces. He began to flex his abdominal muscles even though the g suit hadn't triggered.

"You want to try that, kid?

"Sure."

"Push the nose down to build up a little speed, then keep the joystick back all the way through the loop, back off the thrust as we go over the top. If you have any trouble pulling out of the descent segment, I'll take control so don't fight me. I'm not much of a swimmer."

Delbert had no trouble with the first half but as they went over the top he had an urge to roll out of the loop. He forced himself to hold the joystick back. The sea came into view from above. Exhilarated, he felt an urge to pull back even further to get out of the loop as soon as possible, which he did. The g suit triggered and he immediately felt intense pressure on his legs and torso. Bentwing decided to let him continue to see how he handled the g forces.

"Can I do another one?"

"Sure."

Delbert climbed straight into the second loop. Over the top, still with considerable g's, he pulled the loop even tighter and madly flexed his abdominal muscles under the extreme pressure. He pulled high g's as he exited the second loop. As Bentwing felt his vision fade, he tried to tell him to back off, tried to push his joystick forward as he passed out. Delbert leveled off above the original altitude, elated as never before.

After a minute of silence, he looked back and saw Bentwing slumped in his seat.

"Bentwing, what's wrong?"

No answer. My god, he thought, I've got to get him down in a hurry. I've got no idea what the approach speeds are for this thing. Better head for Comox and get on the radio for a quick tutorial. He banked to a heading in the general direction of Comox. Damn it, I don't even have charts, he's got them all back there. Better contact commercial air traffic control and tell them what's happened. They can pass me over to the military.

"Shit," came weakly over the intercom.

"Bentwing, are you OK?"

"Wha' happened?"

"Don't know. After I pulled out of the second loop, you had passed out. Thought I had better get us down in a hurry so I'm headed for Comox."

"You talk to anybody on the radio?"

"Not yet. I was about to call ATC to get instructions."

"Stay off the radio and make a one eighty turn...gently."

Once they were headed back over water, Bentwing came on again, "Look Pillage, you ever tell anyone I blacked out and ole Bentwing will get you renamed Bentass and it will be well deserved! And you'll never fly in a military plane again. Understand?"

"It never happened, Bentwing."

"Obviously you didn't black out too. Did your vision fade?"

"No."

"You like acrobatics, don't you?"

"I love them."

"I was going to show you a hammerhead stall but my heart's not in it now. Or have you already tried that in the Cessna too."

"Actually I have...but if you tell anyone and it gets back to Dan, Bentwing will become Bentass too."

"OK kid. It's a deal. We've both got a secret to keep," he said with a laugh. "Turn to zero two zero, let's go home."

Back on the radio, Bentwing requested clearances for descent and approach. As the clearances were received, Delbert executed them with a precision Bentwing enjoyed. Now fairly comfortable with the jet, Delbert felt a camaraderie with the machine as it responded to his direction. Bet this is how a jockey feels with a racehorse, he thought. Bentwing took over to land the jet. They touched down at a speed even higher than Delbert expected. Then taxied to the previous parking spot with canopy open, braked to a stop and shut down the engine.

"Remember to unhook seat harness, g suit and interphone. Getting out is just the reverse of getting in."

As the two pilots walked towards the building, Bentwing put his hand on Delbert's shoulder. "You've got a real future in experimental flight test, son, if you want it. Any questions?"

Being called son sure beats kid, he thought. What was I going to ask him? Oh, yes.

"Mr. MacKenzie said you would be a good person to describe what experimental flight test is all about."

"Lot of people think of test pilots as a bunch of daredevil cowboys and to be honest those in the fraternity like to keep it that way. They pride themselves on staying calm in even the most dire situations. But the truth is far different. A good test pilot uses most of his time to learn about the test airplane, work with the design team to influence the design and look for potential problems before the airplane ever leaves the ground. Unforeseen things happen but they can be minimized through careful groundwork.

"Don't get me wrong, superb flying skills, quick reactions and rapid, clear thinking are a must. So is a keen analytic mind and an ability to judge people and assess the validity of what they say.

"As for typical workload, a test pilot spends a lot of time in simulators, classrooms, meetings with engineers, especially before the test plane flies. Once flight test is underway, each flight is carefully planned and the pilot's job is to execute the test steps with precision. He also watches for anomalies and provides feedback to complement the data recorded. With fighter aircraft in particular, he gradually expands the speed/altitude envelope and investigates handling characteristics.

"I've avoided the flyboy glamour aspect. Tight situations do develop that can be survived only with split second analysis and action. Maybe you don't realize it but you saw a sample of that today when you pulled out of that loop and realized you were on your own in a jet with only a few minutes experience. You handled it like a seasoned test pilot. In fact, I see in you the attributes we look for and seldom find. I hope you take a serious look at our program. Does this make sense to you? Anything else I can tell you?"

"No. That gives me a good idea of what it's all about. I like the combination of flying and engineering design. I really appreciate the exciting introduction to it today."

"Just between us, it got a little exciting for me today too. Here comes MacKenzie now. Look son, if you come up with any questions or topics you want more info on, call Ross and he'll put you in touch with me."

"Thank you Sir, uh Bentwing."

"You nearly screwed up there, son," he chuckled as he waved to MacKenzie and swaggered back to the jet.

CHAPTER TWENTY-THREE

At dinner, all three Martins wanted to know how it went.

"Did you get to control the airplane?"

"Yes."

"What did he let you do?"

"He taught me to fly a barrel roll, a snap roll and a loop."

"Did you actually control the jet through a loop?"

"Yes, twice."

Charlie thought that cool, Dan envied him and Samantha could see flying captivated him. She wondered what his parents would think of this possible career choice and worried that it might somehow limit what he might achieve in life. She had a nagging concern about the danger involved. Still she joined in the spontaneous celebration that blossomed.

Still on cloud nine that evening, he wrote letters to both Sylvia and his parents, in which he raved about the day's experience. Fortunately, he couldn't mail them until the next morning. By then he decided on a more discreet approach and tore up the letters.

Instead, he wrote to Sylvia to ask if he could take her to the prom and if so, when was it? Almost as an afterthought, he mentioned that an air force man that Dan knew arranged for him to get a ride in a jet trainer.

He was a little more candid with his parents. Still, he started with assurance that studies were going well. Then brought them up to date on the Braille reader project. Finally, he mentioned the jet trainer ride and confessed that the pilot had let him control the airplane part of the time.

He confided his dilemma to Charlie. "It looks like they might accept me into their program and I really want to do it. But it will rob Sylvia and me of a summer together. How can I expect her to wait?"

"A cold hearted person would say if she really wants you she'll encourage you to do it. You're not cold hearted, so what other options are there? Can you spend some time on the island before and after training?"

"Probably a few days although it's a jam-packed schedule by the sound of things."

"Why don't you ask them for a specific schedule so you know for sure?"

"That's a good point. I'll ask."

"Then, Del, I think you have to come clean with Sylvia and tell her this is a chance of a lifetime and ask her if she can support you taking advantage of it."

"Guess you're right, as usual."

~~~

As so often happens at crucial times, the fickle finger of fate intervenes to throw the best laid plans into a shamble. The prom date fell right in the middle of final exams. No way could Delbert get away. Heartsick, he had to tell Sylvia. Dashed hopes left her desolate, although she tried to put up a good front. She understood the exams had to come first.

"Perhaps, if you don't mind, I'll see if Sal Lightfoot wants to take your place. He's the easiest boy in our class to deal with."

"Yes, of course. I'm really sorry, Sylvia."

"I understand Delbert."

He was afraid to bring up the air force program.

"I'll get away the weekend after this next one and come home. Can we spend some time together then?"

She brightened, "Sure, that would be great!"

"Good! I'll let you know my schedule as soon as I can figure it out. I love you, Sylvia."

"I love you too."

~~~

To take his mind off the dilemma, Delbert threw himself into the Braille reader project. With what he learned about solid state electronics, he designed four circuits. The first detected the space between lines and generated a buzz to represent the gap. From a blind person's viewpoint, he decided there should be no sound with the sensor centered over the line. A low pitched buzz would tell the user to raise the sensor and a high pitched buzz to lower it.

The second circuit would look for gaps between characters. The position and size of this gap would determine when a character could be read. It triggered the third circuit which identified the Braille character. The fourth circuit generated the appropriate sound for each character.

Finally, he cleaned up all four designs and wrote a short report to describe his approach. He was afraid Mike would be annoyed with him for taking the design too far too fast. Still, Mike had encouraged him to bring forward his ideas.

After three days of worry, he decided to arrange a time to meet.

"Now that the optical characteristics are defined and documented, I got carried away and worked up a circuit design which might convert sensed signals to sounds. Hope I didn't jump too far ahead."

"Well...let me look at what you've done. Frankly, I can't imagine how you could design the circuitry this fast. Promise me you won't get mad if I have to tell you it's naïve."

"Sure. That won't surprise me."

However, the more Mike dug into the design the better he liked it. Damn it, he thought, the kid's a genius. He laughed to himself. Well, that's what Calder told me, wasn't it? Still it's awesome to witness. He could see where some tweeks would make the circuit more stable. Other than that, he saw no reason not to go with Delbert's design.

"We may have to name this gadget after you. Wouldn't be fair to call it the Medane Reader now. Perhaps the Delbert Burper."

"I like Medane Burper." They both laughed.

"Well, let's make the lab unit work first, before we worry about its name. I'll have my lab technicians build the circuits and a compatible power supply. They should be ready next week or the one after."

CHAPTER TWENTY-FOUR

The fateful weekend arrived sooner than Delbert liked. He still didn't know how to broach the subject with his parents, much less Sylvia. As he walked through the door, Paul badgered him about the jet flight. He tried to play it down but both parents sensed it meant more to him than claimed.

When Paul left for a softball practice, Phil said, "Well son, what's it all about—this flyin' thing?" Teresa let him kick off the discussion while she studied Delbert's reaction.

"After a few months at UBC, I realized that while it's harder than high school, the classes are very straight-forward and don't really challenge me. Dean Calder sensed this and worked to introduce extra things. Professor Medane and I have made tremendous progress with the Braille reader and will soon have a working model. The project has been great for me, we've created something that's never been done before and something that will benefit a lot of people—"

"That's good Delbert, but we're talkin' flyin."

"Flying is in the same category. Dan Martin saw I could handle more than class work. The first time he took me up, it was just for company and to let me experience something new. He could see on that first flight that I'm a natural pilot and I love to fly. So he offered to teach me but only on the condition that it didn't interfere with studies. He was strict about that."

"Are you tellin' us you have a pilot's license?"

"Yes, Dad."

"An' how're yer grades?"

"I've aced every test. I'm at the top of the class. Dean Calder is delighted with my progress. He says the Braille reader is a fine example of the kind of contribution I can make to the university and people in general."

"Well, I trust Wally but where's this flyin' business goin'?"

"Well," Delbert cringed, "with Dean Calder's approval, Dan talked to the Air Force Reserve representative at the university. He met with me and described their experimental flight test pilot program. They pick a few promising university students who want to try out for their summer program. They train the accepted students each summer in exchange for a commitment to spend three years with them after graduation."

"C'mon Delbert, you're too young to git in the Air Force, let alone be a test pilot."

"That's what I thought but I did so well on their tests and the flight with the head of their training school, they want to enroll me this summer." He didn't mention Bentwing's nickname.

"They want you to sign up fer their jet flyin' program this summer?"

"Yes, Dad."

"Where's this trainin' goin' to happen, Comox?"

"No, they send me back to Malton, Ontario."

"An' they're goin' to pay fer everthin'?"

"Yes, Dad."

"Damn, things are happenin' awful fast, son. First yer off to UBC, now it's Ontario. I dunno. Whata you think, Teresa?"

"I don't know what to think. It does seem like a lot in a short period of time. Do you really want to do it? Have you considered what it will be like through the additional three years? And does it have to be this summer?"

"I've thought about it a lot and I do want to do it. They described what it would involve through those three years and it sounds both exciting and rewarding. If I turn down this summer, they may take me next year but it means one less summer before I graduate and I might lose the chance altogether."

Teresa could see he had his heart set on it, yet she couldn't shake her uneasiness. "Isn't it dangerous?"

"Not as long as one's careful and methodical, which I am."

"Have you told Sylvia?"

Delbert blushed, "No, not yet. I wanted to know you would let me do it first."

"Well son, can't say I'm happy about it but there comes a time when a boy becomes a man an' makes his own decisions. Reckon you're 'bout there, assumin' you agree, Teresa?" She nodded, reluctantly.

He had a date with Sylvia that evening to take her to the movie. If ever a situation compromised his desire to meet her, this was it. Still, the prospect of seeing her again swamped his qualms and he set off eagerly in Phil's pickup.

He was overwhelmed when she came to the door. So beautiful, her smile and the light in her eyes so intoxicating, he could barely stammer a "Hi".

"I'm glad you're back," she said in her soft quiet voice, a tinge shyly. They headed for the pickup. As soon as they rounded the first corner and were out of sight, she leaned over and kissed him on the cheek. "I've missed you so much."

He pulled over to a wide spot in the road and they embraced. Kissed. A tear rolled down her cheek. He wiped it away.

"That's a tear of happiness. Do you really want to go to the movie, Delbert?"

"What do you mean?"

"We could go down to Rainbow Beach and talk."

"OK." He made a U-turn and headed back to the beach.

"Tell me what you've been doing at university."

"Well, the school work is a little like high school. Perhaps it would be more accurate to say it's a cross between school and church sermons. The professors give lectures. Some are good, most are boring."

"That sounds about the same as church sermons." They both laughed. "What about outside of school?"

"Well, I train with Charlie and he's got me on a soccer team which plays once a week and practices in between games. And I work with a professor on a research project to develop an electronic scanner which will let blind people read printed Braille books."

Delbert parked with a view of the ocean. The sun still shone above the low hills on the island to the north. A golden river shimmered across the water.

"You haven't mentioned flying."

"Yes, I've been doing a lot of flying on weekends. I've now got a private pilot's license and I told you about the flight I got to take in the jet trainer."

"Did the pilot let you actually fly the jet?"

"Yes, for quite a while but not for takeoff or landing."

Almost afraid to ask, "Why did they pick you to take for a ride?"

"Dan Martin knows the Air Force Reserve representative in Vancouver and he thought, because of how fast I learned to fly, they might want to consider me for their experimental test pilot training program. So the rep set up some tests and arranged for the flight. It was awesome and I did well with the jet."

"Do they want you in their program?"

"Yes."

"What does that mean?"

"They want me to enroll in the program. They train me during the summer while I'm in university and then I agree to stay with them for three years after graduation. They pay for everything. And from what I can see about experimental flying, I may well want to make a career of it. That is if you're there with me."

Her hand caressed his arm. "Where do you go for the training?"

"Malton, Ontario." He felt her hand tremble as she caught her breath.

"You'll be gone both winter and summer."

"I'll get some time off in the spring and fall. And after this year, I should be able to get home more often on weekends. Sylvia, I've been worried sick about being away from you. I don't want to lose you. I want to get married and spend our lives together. This is a chance of a lifetime and I desperately want to do it too. Can you let me do it and hold on until we can be together full time?"

"I can see you really want to...the flying scares me. It must be dangerous...the thought of being apart for years is almost unbearable. But I'll wait for you as long as it takes and live for the times we do have together." She couldn't hold back another tear, not one of happiness this time.

"I love you so much it hurts. Perhaps you could get a job in Vancouver and we could be together a lot more. And perhaps we wouldn't have to wait until I graduate to get married."

"You haven't asked me to marry you."

"Will you marry me when we can afford it?"

"Yes."

They held each other as the sun slid over the hills and turned the sky from yellow to orange to rose to a darker red and finally from mauve to darkness. She wondered if their love might fade from sunlight to darkness the same way. Would she lose him, out of sight out of mind. He wondered if she would wait for him. So many things can happen in a few years which might pry us apart.

As if to measure the risk she asked, "Do you date other girls in university?"

"No. Never. Charlie tried to get me to ask out a girl he said was interested in me but I refused. I told him you're the only girl I'll date. He said you must be some sort of a goddess. I said yes." She squeezed him gently.

"To be honest, what scares me about separation is that you'll succumb to some girl's charms and we will drift apart."

"Trust me. It won't happen. You're my soul mate. When I think back to our early school years, it was true even then. And my love for you gets stronger each year."

"I feel the same way."

"So I won't come home some day and find you ran off with another man?"

"Don't be silly. You know better than that."

They kissed and held each other tight for a long time, too overwhelmed with their thoughts to experience the arousal they usually felt together. Finally, they broke the embrace and Delbert started the pick-up to drive home.

Back at her place he said, "Would you like to walk up Mount Maxwell tomorrow and take a picnic lunch?"

"Sure. I'll make the lunch. You bring something to drink—coke for me."

"Great. I'll pick you up at ten."

They kissed again, exchanged whispers of love and he walked her to the door. It was hard to let go of her hand as she entered.

CHAPTER TWENTY-FIVE

Next morning Sylvia looked fantastic in a light weight top and shorts. The road up the north side of Mount Maxwell started paved, turned to gravel and finally became a pot-holed narrow road not much better than a trail. It ended about a mile from the peak.

Picnic lunch, a blanket and cokes in hand, they hiked up the trail to the peak. Halfway up they came across the remnants of a little six by eight shack. Like hundreds of hikers ahead of them, they looked through it. The roof obviously leaked and newspapers had been stuffed between the studs as insulation.

"Can you imagine living up here?" she asked.

"No, he must have been a hermit."

"What makes you say it was a he?"

"Would you live here?"

"No."

"I rest my case."

As they neared the peak, the trees and underbrush gave way to bare rock covered in places with moss. The approach from the north is a gentle grade, the south face a different story. A sharp vertical drop-off of about three hundred feet ends in a steep, rocky slope which falls away to the forest below. The peak provides a spectacular view of Burgoyne Bay and Sansom Narrows with Vancouver Island beyond.

"What a view! I can't go near the edge, it makes me queasy. Be careful, Delbert, the moss can be slippery."

"OK, I'll stay back. Unless you want to eat here, I seem to remember a neat place down that way where there's a little pool."

They followed a narrow path back in a north east direction and found the spot about two thousand yards along. A clear, spring-fed pool surrounded by a mossy slope with a fringe of small trees made it an idyllic hide-away.

"It's like a little Eden," she said as she spread the blanket and unpacked their lunch.

They ate more or less in silence. Afterward, she kicked off her shoes, then pulled off Delbert's shoes and socks. The cool moss tickled their toes. Delbert noticed a tear form in her eye and trickle down her cheek. Putting his arm around her, he asked, "What's the matter?"

"I'm afraid of losing you while you're away. I can't help it in spite of what you say." The tears flowed more freely. He held her tight.

"I could never look at anyone else."

They kissed. She unbuttoned his shirt, pulled it out of his pants and slid her hands down his arms, pushing the shirt off. They kissed again. While he held her loosely in his arms, she unbuttoned her blouse. This time he pushed her blouse off and unhooked her bra. She unfastened his belt, opened his fly and slid her hand inside.

After a moment, she said softly, "Darling, I want to go all the way."

Before Delbert could object, she slid off her shorts and underpants. Stark naked, she was truly a goddess. In awe, he wanted her so much it hurt yet worried about later regrets.

"Are you sure, Sylvia?"

She pulled him over on top of her, pushed down his pants and underwear.

"Please be gentle," she whispered in his ear, as she wrapped her legs around his.

Still confused, he slowly entered her, then stopped, uneasy. Her hands on his back pulled upward and she gave a little gasp as he penetrated fully. Passion took over and swept them to levels they never thought possible.

Exhausted, they remained locked in an embrace, both with tears of happiness. After a time, Sylvia felt they were not alone, opened her eyes and turned toward the pool. A doe and fawn stood by the water staring at them.

"Look at the pool," she whispered in his ear.

While the doe continued to stare, the fawn stepped forward to the water and drank. Then, while the fawn stared at them, she stepped forward and drank in turn. For a little longer, they both stared at the couple. Delbert blinked and the doe blinked back, the universal sign of friendship. Then she led the fawn away, looking back one last time before they disappeared into the trees.

"I could swear she smiled, maybe in approval," he said.

"She's probably never seen animals mate face to face before."

"I can't imagine anything so fantastic as that but I'm worried you'll regret it tomorrow and what will we do if you get pregnant?"

"It's the safest time of the month and I will never regret what we did. I may have to say a thousand Hail Mary's for it and if I do I'll smile the whole time. Our first time will live with me forever."

"Me too. God how I love you!" They kissed again.

"We better get dressed before something more human than a deer comes along."

"Sometimes I wonder if anything is more human than a deer. Certainly nothing with our curiosity."

They dressed, packed up, enjoyed one last kiss and started back up the path. A family sat on the peak as they sheepishly passed, telling themselves they had not been spied upon.

"When do you have to go back?" she asked on the way down.

"I've got a ticket to fly on the new seaplane service which leaves Ganges at seven tonight. After I take you home, I have to get back to our place. Promised Mum I would be there for an early dinner and then Dad will drive me up to catch the plane."

They parted reluctantly at her place and Delbert rushed home. A little after seven he was on the seaplane as it taxied over the choppy water to find a clear takeoff path. It seemed to take forever to gain enough speed to break free of the water. With engine roaring and spray flying, he could see how much harder it was than a land takeoff.

It was tougher to leave Sylvia too. The thought of her started to arouse him again. He had to concentrate on different things to keep from embarrassing himself with the other two passengers.

Now introspective, he wondered how he could leave her. Is an education and flying worth the absence from her? A tear formed. I'm committed to this course. I want to fly. I've got to have faith in her. Still, a foreboding persisted.

Chapter Twenty-Six

Sylvia spent the next week in turmoil. They had reached a new plateau with a declared commitment to each other. She felt a mixture of elation and anxiety which left her confused. She wanted to dedicate herself to him but he wasn't there to receive the dedication. And to go to the Senior Prom, she had to turn to another date.

It took only the merest hint to Sal Lightfoot to trigger a prom date request. She accepted with a hidden reluctance. When his family learned he would take Sylvia to the prom, Robin collared him.

"Sal, I want to hire her to work in the office after she graduates this spring. Let her know there's a good job available. It won't take long to learn the ropes. Don't let me down, Sal." It almost sounded like a threat.

~~~

Prom night arrived and a nervous Sal drove over to pick up Sylvia. The vision of her in a prom dress left him gawking, unable to make any coherent comment. He almost dropped her corsage. While flattered, she couldn't help think, I wish you were Delbert, I wish you were Delbert. She immediately felt guilty and took the corsage, thanked him and pinned it to her dress.

He followed her to the car like a puppy, a happy puppy, trying not to slobber like a puppy.

"You're stunning," he stammered.

"Thank you, Sal."

The jealous looks they received at Christmas were eclipsed this night. Sal had to fend off classmates who left their fuming dates in hopes of a dance with Sylvia. Again, they both had a good time. Some furtively spiked punch relaxed her so that she let him kiss her when they arrived back at her place.

"Thanks, Sylvia, it's been fantastic! Can we date again?"

"You're a great guy, Sal, but I'm promised to Delbert. I'm sorry if that disappoints you but I won't date anyone else. It has nothing to do with you. Most of the girls in our class want to date you."

"Except the one I want."

"I'm sorry."

"Guess I understand. Delbert's a lucky guy. Thanks for going with me tonight, at least."

"Goodnight Sal. It was fun."

A dejected fellow drove home.

Robin called first thing in the morning.

"Well, did you convince her to apply for my job?"

"I didn't have an opportunity to bring it up."

"Damn it Sal, get on the ball or I'll kick your ass 'til your nose bleeds." He hung up.

Convinced Robin might carry out his threat, Sal caught Sylvia after class a couple of days later. "Got a minute, Sylvia?"

"Sure, Sal, what is it?" She hoped it wasn't a date request.

"Don't know what you plan to do after graduation but Robin asked me to tell you he has a job opening in his office. He thinks you would be an ideal candidate and could quickly learn what's required."

"I'll keep that in mind. I plan to look for a job in Vancouver in the Fall. He probably wouldn't want to hire someone just for the summer."

"He might. I'll tell him."

Robin of course thought the summer months would give him enough time to achieve his real goal. So he waited a couple of days and called Sylvia.

"Hi Sylvia. Robin Lightfoot. Sal tells me you might be interested in a job in my office through the summer."

"Actually, I said you probably wouldn't want to hire someone just for the summer months."

"I desperately need someone to handle sales and orders when I'm busy in the field. I'm not able to get away enough to give good service to my customers and they get mad if I'm not around when they come in. You would be a great help, even if it's only for the summer."

"Well—"

"Why don't you come in on Saturday and I'll show you what the job involves. We can talk about hours and salary and see if it interests you. How about ten o'clock?"

"Well, OK, ten o'clock." If he needs help so bad, why hasn't he hired someone else already. Still I need to do something this summer. Maybe it could work out.

She showed up Saturday morning just before ten. Robin was dressed in a tee shirt and jeans designed to show off his muscles and he reeked of aftershave lotion. Sylvia almost bolted from the interview.

"How's Barry, haven't seen him for a while."

"Fine. He's logging with the Cummings brothers."

"Good. Sylvia, this job involves running the office while I'm out in the field. Actually it's as much a store as an office. We have a lot of equipment for sale. I also own a bulldozer. I take on jobs which means I'm out on it quite a bit. Besides the stock in the store, I take orders for stuff shipped out from Vancouver or Victoria. So the job involves sales, orders and billing."

"Did Sal tell you I plan to look for a job in Vancouver in the Fall?"

"Sure. I hope you like what you're doing here so much you want to stay. But if you decide to go, that's fine. Summer's the hard time for me. By the way, I'll pay you $3.50 an hour to start. Does that sound OK?"

It was more than she expected. Despite a premonition that she should pass up the opportunity, she couldn't ignore the fact that it would give her a summer job. She had no other prospects on the island so she accepted.

~~~

Back at university, Delbert was confronted with enough to draw him out of the melancholy mood fallen into on the return flight. Final exams approached. The Braille reader circuitry was ready and Mike anxious to try it out.

"Can you join me at two tomorrow afternoon, I want you here when we fire it up?"

"I'll be there."

Shortly after two they connected everything together. Mike explained how he had added an amplifier and speaker so they could hear the "music of the letters". With mounting suspense, they powered it. Other than a very low hum, there was no sound. "Good so far," Mike commented as he checked voltages at a few different points.

"Well, here goes," he moved the scanner onto a page of printed Braille characters.

As he slid the scanner down to the line, a buzz came down in volume and then was replaced with a single tone as the scanner passed over the first character. Then silence, followed by a different tone when the second character passed. Excited, he rolled the scanner over the rest of the line and was greeted by a series of tones that sounded like some kind of weird melody.

"Delbert, it works! It works!" he shouted.

He moved the scanner back and down. As he left the first line the low pitch buzz started and increased in volume. Then suddenly, it was replaced with the high pitch buzz which then decreased in volume. Centered on the second line, he rolled the scanner across and heard again the weird melody of letters scanned.

"We've done it!" He slapped Delbert on the back. "You've contributed so much, Delbert, you should be proud of what you added to the project."

"I may have done some of the leg work, but the concept, inspiration and direction is all yours. I've learned more with you than I would have in two or three years of lectures— other professors' lectures, of course."

Mike laughed, "I will never have to show you the quality of my lectures or lack thereof. I must confess, I've never enjoyed anything in my career as much as this. We need to measure and document how it works. The equivalent of a carriage return generates a lot of buzzing. Maybe we should silence it when the scanner moves backwards over the page. Also, we need to be sure the notes are distinctive enough to prevent errors. If you find time with finals a couple of weeks away, you might start work on that. Well Delbert, we have a working model of the Pillage-Medane Reader."

"Medaner. You created it. Just to see it work is enough for me."

Still excited when he returned home, he couldn't wait to tell the Martin's about their success.

"To be honest, I had my doubts that blind people would be able to teach themselves to interpret the tones as the letters they represent. But after I heard the 'music of the letters' as Mike calls it, I really think they can. I thought Mike would have a conniption when we first heard it. It was great!"

"Fantastic, Delbert," Dan said, "I think we should toast the project's success after dinner." He retrieved a bottle of champagne from the bar and put it on ice.

Charlie added, "It's amazing what you've done in three quarters of a year, Del. When you're famous, I'll tell anyone who'll listen how I lived with you when you first burst onto the university scene."

"You've helped me grow more than you'll ever know, Charlie. Without you I'd still be the nervous, bumbling island hick that showed up last September. I'll always be indebted to you—to you all."

They went to bed that night with a happy intoxication, more than could be attributed to the champagne.

CHAPTER TWENTY-SEVEN

Final exams proved no harder than Christmas ones. Delbert couldn't concentrate on prom night. Desperate to be there, he wandered into fits of depression, felt sorry for himself and worried that Sylvia might have too good a time with Sal. That triggered remorse. He wanted her to have a good time. How could he wish her anything else? He was in a vicious cycle.

Charlie tried to distract him with questions and requests for help with problems that might be on the exam. He already knew the answers for most of them. When Delbert appeared to come out of his funk, Charlie challenged him to a game of ping pong.

"We need to clear our minds of all this crap so we can think straight tomorrow."

A series of hard fought games raised their spirits. Delbert went to bed refreshed and grateful for the distraction he knew Charlie deliberately supplied.

Late the next afternoon, Ross MacKenzie called. "Training school begins boot camp on the seventeenth and Bentwing hopes you can join it. Any chance you can?"

"I don't see how, my last exam is on that day." He would have no time on the island.

"Well if we flew you back the next day, you would be two days behind. I'll let him know and see if he wants to go ahead with it anyway."

"OK," spoken at a barely audible level.

"I'll get back to you tomorrow." He hung up.

Things seem to conspire against us, he thought. Is this some kind of divine intervention to test our resolve? How can I tell Sylvia we can't be together until the Fall? Please, Bentwing, don't let me join the class late. But Bentwing let him down.

"He wants you there as soon as possible," Ross said. "Thinks you can catch up to the others. It's like boot camp the first two weeks and you're already quite fit. You'll have some aches and pains after the first few days but the others will too. I'll make the reservations to fly you out first thing in the afternoon on the seventeenth."

"OK."

"You don't sound very excited, my boy."

"Well, I hoped for a gap between school and training."

"Normally there would be one. The camp schedule screws it up this year. Sorry."

"OK, I'll be ready." He began to grope for a way to tell Sylvia. How many times can I disappoint her? It took two days to summon courage to call.

"Hi Sylvia, how was the prom?"

"It went well. Sal was a perfect gentleman but I wished all night he was you." The sword of guilt twisted deeper into his butter-flied stomach.

"Sylvia, a terrible thing happened. Because of their schedule, the Air Force insists I go back to camp right after my final exam. Normally there's a gap but not this year. I'm sorry Sylvia. I'm mad but there's nothing I can do about it."

After a pregnant pause, "That's a big disappointment but we'll just have to live with it."

"My heart aches, darling, I don't want to be apart until Fall."

"Me neither, Delbert, but what can we do? On the bright side, I intend to look for a job in Vancouver in the Fall so you won't be able to avoid me for such long periods."

"Fantastic!"

The conversation turned to recent events and Delbert told her about their success with the scanner. She knew he contributed a lot and was proud of what he accomplished. He's already a great man even though he's still a boy, she thought. Will he be my great man? They hung up resigned to separation until Fall.

~~~

Three hours after the final exam, Ross MacKenzie drove Delbert to the airport. Bentwing met him in Toronto and drove him to the barracks. Late that night he entered his home for the next four months.

"Breakfast is at eight if you can make it. Your camp-mates will have finished a five mile run by then but we don't expect you there. Join in whenever you can, hopefully by noon. There's a set of fatigues on your bed. Your other gear is in a locker next to it."

"When do they start the run?"

"Oh, they're up and ready to go by seven. Get a good night's rest."

As Bentwing might have guessed, Delbert showed up at seven in his fatigues more or less ready. He soon found out how much harder the run would be in boots. It was a good thing they didn't have to carry packs too. Exhausted after four miles, he began to wonder if he could even make five. He lagged behind the group.

I let myself get out of shape this Spring with so little physical activity, he thought. What if I can't keep up with the rest of them? I'm just a teenager up against men in good condition. Did I make a mistake taking this on instead of a summer with Sylvia? What if they send me home after a month? Dan will be embarrassed and disappointed. So will Dean Calder. Dad will say he knew I shouldn't have jumped into flying. I've got to push harder. He finished the run over a thousand yards behind the rest.

When Bentwing arrived in his office, he asked his adjutant for any new developments.

"Nothing important. The new kid you brought in ran this morning, far behind the pack."

"That was on less than four hours sleep and a fifteen hour day. Told him he didn't have to join in before noon but I'm not surprised he was out there first thing. Watch that kid, Sam, he'll be one of the best test pilots of all time."

"If he makes it through boot camp."

Delbert dragged through the day's drills, unable to keep pace with the rest of the class. When they had an hour's free time at five o'clock, he collapsed on his bunk and slept right through to the next morning. The men laughed at the kid and thought he would never last. But he was up for the morning run and this time managed to keep up with the pack.

With each new day, his stamina increased and the earlier pains slowly disappeared. He thrived on the firing range once he got over the anxiety of pulling the trigger. They didn't need to run his targets back for inspection. He could see exactly where each bullet struck no matter how far away the target. That allowed him to make corrections after each shot. His fear of failure gradually subsided.

Ground school classes began in the third week. Minor points where the military differed from his civilian experience made it a good refresher. Finally, they met their first airplane, the CT-133 Silver Star he flew before. The whole class had pilot's licenses and flight experience so they started right off in the jet trainer.

As if to blunt their eagerness, they spent the first four hours in ground familiarization of the airplane. Then, instead of flight, they were ushered back into the classroom for four days of Silver Star ground school.

When they formed up on the parade ground at eight the morning after that, Bentwing addressed them.

"OK, larvae, today you turn into butterflies. An instructor will take each of you up for a familiarization flight. Twelve instructors, twelve planes. When I read off your name, report to the quartermaster for your flight gear. Then, report to the instructor next to the plane number I read off, in full flight gear by 0830."

He read off the first twelve names. Delbert was assigned to plane seven. He reported to his instructor, ready to fly, before eight thirty.

"Pillage, my name's Schroeder. Let me check your gear and then we'll go pillaging," he laughed at his own joke. "You wearing a belt?"

"No Sir."

"Necklace?"

"No Sir."

"Anything hard at all under that flight suit?"

"Nothing Sir."

"OK. Better not be or you'll be damn sore after that g-suit gets through with you. Here's how you get into this animal."

"I'm familiar with that Sir, the commander took me up in one out in Vancouver."

"Just my luck to get one of Bentwing's pets. Well Pillage, you need to unlearn anything he showed you. Mount up if you think you know how."

Delbert did and had everything connected before Schroeder could say or do anything other than check his work. With a sigh he climbed into his own seat and strapped in, "Can you hear me Pillage?" came over the interphone.

"Yes Sir."

"I'll read the checklist, you perform the actions and confirm."

It was done without error and Schroeder noticed Delbert started the action before he read each item. Impressive, he thought. Guess I should expect it from one of these university nerds. His true colors will surface when we get airborne. Ready for engine start, he called for the ground crew to fire the bottle. He wouldn't let Delbert touch the controls until they reached 20,000 feet over northern Ontario.

"Bentwing let you fly the airplane at all?"

"Yes Sir, he had me fly it for about half an hour."

"OK, the controls are yours. Show me a thirty degree bank 360 to the right."

Delbert executed it flawlessly. As the flight progressed, the maneuvers became more difficult but not for Delbert. Snap rolls, barrel rolls, stalls, Immelmanns.

"Think you can handle a loop?" Schroeder was caught up in seeing how far they could go, which already far exceeded the first flight syllabus.

"Yes Sir."

Delbert dropped the nose to pick up speed and advanced the thrust as he pulled up into the loop, then throttled back as they passed over the top. He was careful not to pull too many g's. He didn't want to repeat the Bentwing experience.

"Give it the gun and let's go straight up. You know what a hammerhead stall is?"

"Yes Sir."

"Yes sir, yes sir, is there anything you don't yes sir?"

"I'm not sure how to answer that Sir."

"Good, here we go now. If I tell you I want control, you let go immediately. Understood?"

"Yes Sir."

But he didn't have to take over. Delbert flew the airplane through the stall and brought it out of the spin which followed.

"Take us home, Pillage. Got to tell you this has been one hell of a first flight. Bet the ground crew thinks we're scattered over the tundra. Since you've done everything else, take a shot at landing this crate."

Delbert was in seventh heaven as he lined up with the runway and captured the glide slope. He felt his way down to the runway and landed a little long as a result. Schroeder took over to make sure they got it stopped in time. Then he had Delbert taxi in.

"Well Pillage, your air-work is impressive for this early in the program. Next time we'll concentrate more on takeoff and landing."

The ground crew started to refuel the jet. They noticed Schroeder had used a lot more than the other instructors and assumed he had a hard time with his student. Probably a washout, they thought.

~~~

Late in the afternoon, Schroeder burst into Bentwing's office.

"Well you sure got a hot one there, Bentwing!"

"What you talking about?"

"You know what I'm talking about. Pillage is what I'm talking about. Kid was married to that jet the minute he took over the controls. It was like the plane was in love with him and vice versa. I never seen anything like it. We'd still be up there pulling g's if we weren't low on juice. Damn, it was a joy to watch!"

"Skip, that's why I assigned him to you. The kid's special. I don't want you to just make a great combat pilot out of him, although he could be one of the best. I want you to make him into the best damn experimental test pilot in the RCAF. That means he's got to know combat flying better than anyone and along with that know how to push the envelope in a reasonably safe way. Get him to think about what we need in the future."

"Yes Sir."

"Don't give me that yessir shit, Skip. You're our best instructor. Take him under your wing. Don't worry about what the others are up to. Go at your own pace—or his. Just give me the best damn test pilot we ever had."

"OK Bentwing. I get the picture and truth to tell, it'll be a pleasure."

That marked the start of an arduous four months. Delbert's classmates wondered why he was in the air before them and still there when they debriefed. They also didn't understand how he could make them look like fools in mock dog fights. One minute they would have control of the situation, the next he would be on their tail. How the hell did he do that became a frequent refrain. They knew nothing of his ability to often anticipate their thoughts and actions, the benefit of hours spent studying classmates in school.

CHAPTER TWENTY-EIGHT

After the first Saturday, Sylvia showed up for work each weekend. Robin continued to find every excuse possible to lean over her shoulder and rub up against her body. She drew away as much as possible and frequently asked him about his wife and kids in an effort to fend him off. Fortunately he realized the need to teach her the job. The sessions soon made her able to manage the store in his absence.

When school ended, she worked full-time. Robin was too busy to harass her more than three or four times a week. On the other hand, word spread amongst loggers and farmers that a visit to Lightfoot's Welding paid dividends. Before a month of summer passed, business almost doubled.

Even devout husbands couldn't resist an urge to drop in. They asked technical questions just to prolong each visit. Sylvia struggled with them. She often had to promise to get back with an answer. To avoid a call to their home, they usually told her not to hurry—they'd drop back in a few days after she had a chance to touch base with Robin. She accumulated answers to most of these questions within a few weeks.

For his part, Robin realized he should stay away from the store. Business boomed. That didn't stop him from pursuit of his sexual goal but it did lead him to confine it to late afternoons. On one of his more explicit attempts to get her to join him for a drink after work, she first used her age as an excuse and then told him he should go home to his pretty wife instead.

"After the two kids were born she became frigid. Frankly, it's like screwing a penguin on a snowfield."

Shocked, she replied, "That's no way to talk. You're married. You owe it to her and your children to be a good father."

"OK," he said, smart enough to back off. "Go on home, I'll lock up."

~~~

Freed from store work, Robin found time to pursue an idea toyed with for months. Switchback turns and even downhill curves forced logging trucks to slow to a crawl at times. He thought he could do something about that. If he built a cab under the trailer and put in a steering system, they could negotiate those turns a lot faster. And they could haul longer logs. And they wouldn't have to put the trailer up on the truck to drive back for the next load. The more he thought about it, the more excited he became. It took his mind off Sylvia for hours at a time.

When one of the island loggers bought a new rig, Robin persuaded him to sell his old trailer for next to nothing. From a junkyard in Victoria, he found the front wheels and steering mechanism from a demolished truck, along with other junk which might prove useful.

He became engrossed in the project. He cut and welded heavy beams to suspend wheels about six feet in front of the trailer. A small cab just wide enough for a driver's seat was attached to a cross beam behind the front wheels. It was positioned just inside the left beam so that the steering mechanism could be attached with minimum modification.

In spite of his moral paucity, one had to admire his ability to improvise a complicated design. Caught up in the project, he left Sylvia alone for over two weeks.

He finished the cab, complete with a small windshield, seat and steering wheel. To test it, he had a local logger bring his truck over to tow it around. It worked! He could steer the trailer back and forth across the road. Backing the rig up was a snap since he could steer the trailer and all the driver had to do was follow.

He had to extend the trailer tongue for the longer logs which gave the trailer an added advantage over current designs. He realized a rigid tongue would stick up too far with the empty trailer loaded on the truck so he designed it to telescope. All in all, an ingenious creation. He had visions of fame and wealth. It would be perfect to spring on the big outfits at their annual convention in Nanaimo in the third week of July.

He cleaned and smoothed the trailer, painted the cab fire engine red and had a local sign painter stencil "Lightfoot Steerable Trailers" on the side. He photographed it from various angles, one loaded on a truck with the tongue retracted. Sylvia took pictures with him in the cab. The best of the photos he had enlarged to hang on the booth at the convention. Some of them went into a small brochure he put together and printed in quantity.

"Sylvia, you need to come to the convention. I need you to man the booth while I'm out demonstrating the trailer. I'll take care of everything, get you a room at the hotel and cover all expenses." It obviously meant so much to him, she couldn't refuse.

Just before the convention, Robin went over the brochure material with her, explained the benefits of his trailer until she was conversant enough to handle the booth.

"I'll need to drive the truck and trailer up to Nanaimo, so you'll have to drive my car, OK?"

"I can do that."

"I've booked two rooms for us at the Malaspina Hotel. Your room is reserved in your name so you won't have any trouble with check-in. I'll call you when I arrive. I'll pack all the booth material in the trunk. Just leave it there, I'll unload and set it up. Damn, Sylvia, I'm excited. This might be the big break I've been after."

It was not hard to share his happiness until he suggested they have a drink to toast the new venture. As usual, she begged off and headed home.

~~~

Seldom off the island, the drive to Nanaimo made her nervous, especially with the new small ferry at Vesuvius. Wednesday morning, Robin picked her up at home, drove back to where he parked the truck with his trailer on top, gave her a quick lesson on his car and left her to head out on her own.

She was amazed at the Monarch's power and luxurious ride. Although the car had a powered convertible roof, Robin told her not to lower it because there wasn't room to stow it with all the material he had in the trunk. She inched her way onto the little ferry, afraid of scraping a side. The ferry crew laughed at her and gestured emphatically to speed things up.

"Must have a sugar daddy with a car like that," one said to the other.

"I'd like to be that sugar daddy," he retorted.

Robin had to take the ferry from Fulford Harbour to Swartz Bay because of the size of his rig. That meant a six hour drive to Nanaimo. He arrived at the hotel just after four in the afternoon, plenty of time to get the booth set up once he got in touch with Sylvia and located his car. She had checked in about two and taken a walk through the downtown area, fascinated by all the stores and the old fort that overlooked the bay. The hustle and bustle unnerved her after a lifetime on the laid back island.

Whistles and "Hi Babe's" left her flustered and eventually drove her back to her hotel room haven. It was almost a relief when Robin called.

"Hi Sylvia, I'm checked in. They gave me the room next to you. Where's the car?"

"It's in the lot right behind the hotel. Do you need the keys?"

"I'll come and get them as soon as I get unpacked."

The room next door sounded a lot closer than she would have liked. She checked that the interconnecting door was locked. Just in time as she heard him open the door on his side and try to open hers. When he found it locked, he knocked on her hall door. She met him there with the keys.

"Do you need help to set up the booth?"

"Sure, why don't you help me. It'll give you a chance to get familiar with the convention layout."

Together they packed in the materials. Robin found their booth location and they set things up.

"Let's grab dinner in the hotel dining room. It'll be a long day tomorrow so we don't need a late night tonight." That was fine with Sylvia.

Although he had wine with dinner and suggested she try some, she declined. He didn't press it so after a relaxed dinner they parted ways to their separate rooms. Or so it seemed to her. He waited a reasonable time, then quietly left in hunt of accessible women and staggered back in about three in the morning. She didn't see him at breakfast which surprised her in light of the early night. He appeared bleary-eyed at the convention room about noon.

"Will you be OK alone in the booth, Sylvia? I want to collar some company honchos and set up a demonstration."

"I think I can handle it."

Even though she dressed with a skirt that reached over half way from knee to ankle, she stood out in the convention hall crowd. Before long a group of loggers jostled to get close and ask questions about the trailer. Most had no intention or wherewithal to buy one. However, a few owners gradually worked their way to the booth.

Amongst them was the owner of the Gold River Logging Company. Some of the lecherous loggers backed off when they recognized him. He was not immune to Sylvia's charms yet he could see the potential of the trailer concept. He asked intelligent questions and Sylvia did a credible job with her answers.

Eventually he allowed, "Young lady, you are very persuasive. I would like to see a trial with a load of logs and if it's all it's cracked up to be, I'll order a fleet of them. Can you arrange a demonstration?"

"I'll have to talk to my boss but I'm sure we can. I know he's anxious to show what it can do."

"My name's James McAfee. Here's my card. Talk it over with him and get back to me. I'm in Room 412 here in the hotel if you or he want to reach me before the convention ends. Now I'll let these lecherous devils back to harass you. Don't allow them to get you down."

CHAPTER TWENTY-NINE

An irritated Robin showed up back at the booth late in the afternoon.

"Spent all day trying to find people with clout to make a contact and sell them on a demonstration. Couldn't find anyone who matters."

"Is this someone important?" She handed him the card.

"Is it ever! How did you get this?"

"He came by the booth, asked a bunch of questions and wants a demonstration. Said if it works as advertised, he'll order a fleet of them."

"Sylvia, this guy owns the biggest company on Vancouver Island. This is fantastic! You're fantastic!" He hugged her before she could back away.

"He says you can reach him here at the hotel. He's in Room 412 until the convention ends." With reluctance, he released her.

"I better give him a call—strike while the iron's hot. I'll be back to help you close up the booth."

He charged off in search of a hotel phone. Ten minutes later he was back.

"No answer. I'll catch him first thing in the morning."

With the booth closed, he persuaded her to go to dinner with him at an upscale restaurant that faced the bay. Although she would only drink ginger ale before dinner, she succumbed to a glass of wine with the meal. She had to admit that it was good and was tempted to have a second one when he urged it. His insistence triggered her silent alarms and led her to ask for coffee instead.

He was too excited about the sales prospect to argue when she said she was tired and wanted to get back to the hotel. With uncharacteristic politeness, he thanked her again for the contact and said good-night. She was relieved to not have to fend him off again. Perhaps he's finally got the picture, she thought. He was out on the prowl an hour later.

The next morning he did manage to make contact and reached agreement that he would drive the truck and trailer up to Campbell River on Saturday. The owner would arrange to have one of his regular drivers make a run to the nearest camp where they would load the rig. They would haul the load down with Robin in the trailer so they could assess just how well it performed on the switch-backs.

During the course of the day, Robin made contact with two other owners. They promised to talk with the Gold River folks to find out how well it worked. They were definitely interested. Robin was in high spirits.

As the convention wound down, he and Sylvia dismantled the booth and stored what was left in the trunk of his car.

"Sylvia, this has been successful beyond anything I could hope for and it was all started by you. I owe you. Dinner at the best place in town is on me."

After a two wine dinner for her, more for him. they returned to the hotel.

"Sylvia, we need to have a nightcap to celebrate our good fortune," he said, heading towards the bar. "I'll order you a nontoxic drink," he laughed. Reluctantly, she went with him.

"Bring the lady a grasshopper and me a scotch on the rocks."

A grasshopper sounded tame enough to her unaccustomed ears. When she excused herself to go to the restroom, he caught the waiter and slipped him a twenty dollar bill to make her drinks with double vodka. Then he proceeded to talk her into a second and third drink to keep him company. She felt more relaxed, thanks to the vodka she had no knowledge of, and began to enjoy the euphoria of their success. It was short lived.

"I don't feel too well, Robin. I better call it a night."

"OK, let me pay the bill and we'll be gone."

On the way out of the bar she felt wobbly and it dawned on her that grasshoppers weren't really harmless little insects. By the time they got into the elevator, she was dizzy and fought to stay awake. On their floor, he half carried her down the hall. When she collapsed entirely, he lifted and carried her the rest of the way.

He glanced up and down the hall to be sure they were alone, then held her with one hand and rummaged through her purse to find her room key. He opened the door. Carried her in after a quick glance again. Nobody was in the hall. She had totally passed out. He carried her to the bed, pulled the covers back and laid her down.

He took off her shoes, then her blouse and skirt, her bra and nylons. The more of her body he exposed, the more aroused he became. Somewhere in the recesses of his mind he knew this was wrong. He pulled down her panties. It was more than he could resist. He undressed quickly and laid down with her. Tomorrow, when she knows there's nothing to hold back for she'll want it. He rolled on top of her. True to his basest nature he raped her unresponsive body.

CHAPTER THIRTY

As morning light filtered through the shades, Sylvia struggled towards consciousness. An alien snore swept away the cobwebs of her first hangover. She felt the naked body next to her and leaped out of bed, only to grasp her head in agony. The enormity of her situation sent her into a state of shock. She first shivered then began to shake uncontrollably.

No! No! It couldn't be, raced through her mind. Please, God, don't let him have touched me. But the truth was hard to put aside. She couldn't.

In shock, she retrieved her panties, bra, nylons, blouse and skirt. She shook violently now, tears rolled down her cheeks. No! No! ran through her mind as she moved to the closet and stuffed things into her suitcase.

Frightened that she might wake the monster, she quietly found his wallet and keys in his pants pocket. She took some bills which looked to be enough to get her home, along with his car keys. Then, with her shoes, purse and suitcase, she stole out of the room and down the hall. She stopped to put on her shoes at the elevator. She looked back, afraid that he would wake up and come after her.

In the lobby, the valet asked her if she wanted help with her suitcase. "Are you checking out, Ma'am?"

"I have to leave. The room cost is being taken care of by my boss."

"Yes, Ma'am. Would you like me to turn in the key."

Flustered, "I left it with him." She realized how bad this looked but could only think about escape. The valet smirked as she walked away. Lucky boss, he thought.

She didn't feel safe until on the highway south of Nanaimo. She tried to remember what happened. Had she let him into the room? Into her bed? No. Impossible. I remember feeling groggy in the elevator, then nothing. He got me so drunk I must have passed out. Surely he didn't do anything more than lie down with me. But she didn't believe that.

Robin woke up about the time she passed through Ladysmith. He reached over for her and found the bed empty. "Sylvia?" he asked the silent room. No answer. He got up and checked the bathroom door. Damn it, she's gone, he thought. She woke before me and got scared off. Oh well, she'll calm down by the time I get back to the island and we can get it on in earnest then. He had something more important to do, get the rig up to Campbell River for the demonstration.

Sylvia drove nonstop to the ferry dock at Crofton and parked in line for the next ferry. A glance in the mirror revealed how disheveled she looked. She fixed her hair and makeup. Fortunately, she used little makeup since the constant tears would have washed anything more substantial away.

When she drove onto the ferry this time, she could care less about the car and perhaps as a result managed to scrape the side on a barrier. She sat in the car for the thirty minute trip to avoid recognition. At Vesuvius, she drove off and headed home, dropped her suitcase beside the road, drove back into town and left the car behind the shop with the keys in it. Then walked home.

On the way, she thought of the times Delbert walked this road with her. The pain in her chest almost strangled her. How can I ever face him again? I've failed him. I've failed him. Can I tell him? Would he forgive me? Do I have to tell him? She was still in this spiral hell when she reached home at one thirty in the afternoon. Her mother met her at the door and immediately realized something was wrong.

"Are you alright Sylvia?"

"Yes."

"How did the convention work out."

"OK. I quit the job. I can't work with...him again."

"Here, let me take that suitcase."

"No. I'll take care of it myself." She went straight to her room.

Her mother called after her, "Have you had lunch? Can I fix you something? Make tea?"

"No thanks."

She closed the door, threw herself on the bed and cried again. After a while, she got up, went into the bathroom and ran a bath. Half an hour later, her mother tapped on the door.

"Are you alright, dear, you've been in there a long time?"

"I'm OK."

Even after she dried off, she still felt dirty. Her father would be home soon. She went back to her bedroom and dressed in clean clothes. Nothing helped. She was still crying when her mother called her for dinner.

"I'm not hungry."

"I'll tell Dad you're worn out."

For the first time, she confronted the impact of her predicament. She couldn't tell her father or Barry what happened. They might go after—him—she couldn't say his name. They might think I'm a slut to let him take advantage of me. What if it gets out in the island gossip? How do I explain quitting so soon? What can I do? The tears returned.

Next morning she waited until the men left for work, then ran into the bathroom to take another long bath. She just couldn't feel clean, even though she had no proof that Robin had violated her.

"I've fixed you breakfast," her mother said through the door. By now, the problem was clear to her.

"You need to eat, dear, come to the kitchen and try to eat something."

A while later, a red-eyed Sylvia appeared and tried to force down some food.

"When you want to talk about it, I'm here and anything you tell me will be our secret, even from your father."

Sylvia nodded, felt her mother's love and concern. But the fragile bubble burst when she added, "By the way, there's a letter from Delbert on the counter." Sylvia fled to her room, devastated again.

Late in the morning, she walked to the Catholic church and asked the priest if she could take confession.

"I have sinned, Father."

"How have you sinned, my child."

"I—I don't know how, father"

Confused, "Don't know how?" The tears started again. "There now child. Tell me what you don't know."

"A man got me drunk without my knowledge and when I passed out he must have carried me to my hotel room bed and undressed me. When I woke up he was in bed with me and I think he might have violated me. I don't know. Help me Father."

"If what you say is true, my child, you may be the victim of a sinner, a grievous sinner. If in your heart you did nothing to encourage him but rather while you were able tried to discourage him, it's hard to find you sinned."

"He made advances many times before and I always rejected them. I detest him but since I worked for him, I couldn't avoid him. Oh Father, what if he violated me?"

"Without evidence to the contrary, my advice is to assume that didn't happen and to pray to Our Father in heaven to make it remain so. What has happened has happened, my child. Turn to God to ask his help to strengthen your resistance to this man and to alcohol."

"He called the drink a grass-hopper and said it was nontoxic."

"If memory serves me right a grass-hopper is made with vodka, which is very difficult to detect. What you can detect is the onset of drunkenness and now you know what that feels like."

"Yes Father."

He could feel her pain as she left. He could also see why the culprit was tempted into his evil deed. He knew it was Robin and knew he would never see him in a church, much less a confessional. He was well aware of some of his other exploits on the island and heard confessions from more than one of his victims.

"Forgive me, Father, but I wish you would mete out retribution for his evil ways," he muttered aloud.

CHAPTER THIRTY-ONE

Saturday morning Robin met with James McAfee and his driver, Arne Axelsson, for breakfast.

"Arne'll run you up to Camp Five and I've told them to have a crew there to load you up and there'll be a crew to dump the load down here. Arne, I want you to get a feel for how much faster you can take the corners with Rob in the trailer. Also, get a feel for how it helps backing up. Told them to load you up with logs twenty feet longer than usual but if the trailer works, that shouldn't cause any trouble on the switch-backs. Take this walkie-talkie with you so you can talk back and forth."

"OK, Boss. Let's get going Rob. I got some salmon fishing to do this afternoon."

They left for Camp Five both in the truck cab. At Camp Five, they dropped the trailer off the truck and Robin adjusted the tongue for the longer logs. With them loaded, Robin climbed into the trailer cab and they checked the walkie-talkie units to ensure communication between truck and trailer. And they were off.

They hadn't gone a quarter of a mile when Robin realized the dust kicked up by the truck caused a problem. It made the gravel road hard to see and he began to cough from the dust that seeped in. He should have radioed Arne to stop the rig and let him out. But the lure of a lucrative trailer business blinded him like the dust so he pressed on.

On the first few turns, Arne noticed that steering the trailer really helped so he increased speed. That increased the dust and Robin soon steered more by feel of the trailer dragged into the turn than by sight of the road. Fortunately, Arne's conservative nature made him slow down at the first switchback because Robin was now choked with dust and essentially blind. The trailer started over the bank on the inside of the turn before Robin recognized it and wrenched the wheel to the outside. They made it around.

Barely conscious, he managed to get them around the two other switchbacks. A few minutes later, when Arne called back on the walkie-talkie there was no answer. Damn walkie-talkie's on the blink, he thought and brought the truck up to speed for the run into town. Robin lost consciousness, suffocated by the dust. After a hair-raising turn in which Arne almost lost control of the rig, he slowed down to less than his normal speed.

"That contraption aint working, I could of been killed back there," he swore out loud.

McAfee waited at the dump area until they pulled up. Arne shook his head.

"Don't ever do that to me again, Boss. We damn near lost it."

As the dust cleared, they could see Robin slumped over the steering wheel in his little cab.

"Pull him out boys."

They laid him on the ground and one of the crew started artificial resuscitation. Each time he pushed down on Robin's chest a little puff of dust came out of his mouth. One of the onlookers started to laugh. Soon they all roared.

"Keep pushing Bill, now I know what they mean when they say puffer belly...always thought they were talking about a train."

Robin finally started to breathe on his own and coughed out more dust. He regained consciousness to the sound of laughter and looked around just in time to see McAfee drive away.

"If you seal that thing tight enough to keep the dust out you wouldn't have no air to breathe," Arne offered. "Anyway, the Boss aint interested in pursuing it."

The crew dumped the logs, loaded the trailer back on the truck and left Robin with his rig. After a half hour, he felt he could drive the truck so he headed off to the nearest beer parlor to drown his sorrow and the last of the dust. Unfortunately, the crew arrived ahead of him.

"Hey, here comes the puffer belly now."

He soon realized he was the talk of the town. All it took was for someone to mention "puffer belly" and the whole crowd broke into gales of laughter. He left after one beer, too weak to start a fight to regain his honour. Humiliated, he drove to Courtenay, proceeded to get drunk and spent the night in a cheap motel.

Sunday morning he set off for Victoria, spent that night in Duncan and reached Saltspring Island late Monday afternoon. He found his car out behind the shop, with the keys in it. The shop had not been open since he left the previous week. Damn it, why didn't she open up today? God, I need some sex to make up for that fiasco. It never dawned on him that his wife had no idea where he was or when he would be home.

He opened the shop, called the Cairns house and asked for Sylvia. Her mother's frosty voice told him she would not talk to him.

"Just let me talk to her, I need to find out if she can open the shop tomorrow."

"She won't ever set foot in that shop again." Click. Disgusted, he went home.

CHAPTER THIRTY-TWO

Days became painful routine for Sylvia. Stay in bed until the men left, take a long bath, stay in the house as much as possible and avoid conversations with Barry. Often, in the afternoon she would walk down to Rainbow Beach and sit on the log she had shared with Delbert. Staring out over the water, she anguished over him. Again and again the question arose. If I tell him what happened, will he believe me or will he think I was just seduced? Or worse, wanted it to happen? Can he find a way to forgive me?

A malignant fear wedged its way into her mind from time to time. She felt changes in her body and tried to dismiss them as caused by misery and missed meals. Yet she knew that wasn't a good explanation. After three weeks, the fear turned to panic because the period that should have started hadn't. She prayed fervently that she wasn't pregnant but with each day the evidence mounted. Too ashamed to go to a doctor, she had no one to turn to for help or advice, not even her mother.

Convinced of pregnancy by mid August, the thought of his monster growing inside nauseated her. She knew about abortion but had no idea how to get one and knew it was a terrible sin in the eyes of her church. The conflict of sin versus bringing the evil thing into the world raged in her mind. The shame of pregnancy and what that news would do to her family as much as her was too much to bear. She stole a table spoon from the kitchen and tried to give herself an abortion.

When she didn't come to dinner after a couple of calls, her mother went into her bedroom and found her in a pool of blood. She screamed. The men ran in. Sylvia was unconscious, barely alive. Barry picked her up and carried her to his car, then raced to the hospital in Ganges. The doctor on call stopped the bleeding and put her on an intravenous drip.

"We need to get her to the hospital in Victoria tomorrow morning," he told the family, "she needs a specialist to repair the damage she did to herself."

"What do you mean?" Barry asked.

"She tried to give herself an abortion and made a terrible mess of it. Such a shame."

"That's why she's been different since that convention. That Lightfoot bastard did this to her. The son of a bitch!" He stormed out as his mother called after him, "Barry, no!"

The next morning an ambulance boarded the ferry with Sylvia inside. The event was soon common knowledge throughout the close-knit island community.

~~~

At the Jubilee Hospital, Sylvia underwent two hours of surgery. Blood transfusions brought her off the critical list. She regained consciousness the next morning, confused about her whereabouts and what had happened. Gradually memories returned, terrifying memories. The nurse came in.

"Good morning. You've been through a lot but things are under control now."

A lot more than you think, went through her mind, and it's not under control.

"The doctor will be in to see you later this morning. Can you eat this consommé now, it will give some strength back."

Sylvia made a half-hearted attempt to swallow some.

A kindly looking doctor showed up just after ten. "How are you, Sylvia?" he asked as he checked her pulse.

"Sore."

"I'm not surprised. You've been through an ordeal but it will get better. You're on the mend now. I must tell you Sylvia that you did considerable damage to yourself. There was no way to save your ability to have children. I know that's the farthest thing from your mind at present, however, it's something you need to know as you go forward in life."

What life, she thought, I have no life. "Yes Sir."

"Thing's probably look bleak right now, dear, but rest and gather your strength. There'll be brighter days ahead." He patted her hand gently. "I'll check in on you again this evening."

"Thank you."

She slept for a few hours. Later, the nurse came in with lunch and coaxed her to eat a little.

"Does a priest come to the hospital?" she asked.

"Yes, Shall I tell him you want to talk with him?"

"Please."

She slept again. When she awoke, the priest was by her bed.

"Father, forgive me if I've kept you waiting."

"Sylvia, may I call you Sylvia?"

"Yes."

"I've only been here a little spell, Sylvia, admiring your angelic beauty while you slept."

"Angelic? Father, will you hear confession?"

"Of course, my child."

"Father, I have sinned. An evil man got me pregnant without my knowledge. I grew to hate the thing he created and...and I killed it before it could grow."

"You know our Lord tells us that the taking of life, even unborn, is forbidden. It is a sin that can only be atoned through persistent penance."

"Yes, Father," the tears came unbidden.

"Now, now, child, now is not the time to address this issue. First you must get well and regain your strength. Then it can be addressed. Let us pray for a speedy recovery."

He took her hand and prayed for help with her recovery, physical and spiritual. He promised to return tomorrow.

When the doctor checked her that evening he appeared pleased with her progress. The blood transfusions helped significantly. Examination of his handiwork from two days earlier embarrassed her. He told her the operation appeared to be successful under the circumstances. She would recover to a normal life, other than inability to carry a baby.

~~~

"How are you today?" the priest asked next morning. "Your color looks much better."

"The physical pain is going away, Father, but the other pain isn't. In a sudden outburst, "I don't know what to do. I've ruined everyone in my family's life. I've lost the man I love. I've taken a life. I don't deserve to live."

"No, Sylvia. You mustn't talk like that. Time heals the mental wounds as well as the physical ones. It just takes longer."

"But I can't face them again. Where can I turn?"

"You can turn to our Lord, my child. He helps all who seek help. Sometimes I think he sends these tragic events to test our strength. I have seen other women who have been dealt more than they seem able to bear, yet overcome their hardship through dedication to God's work."

"How Father?"

"In a convent."

"What convent would accept someone who has lost control of her life as I have?"

"A decision of that type is yours to make, not theirs. But now is not the time for life decisions of this magnitude. You should heal your body and let a passage of time clear your perspective first."

"Thank you Father, you give me comfort. I'm very grateful for your time."

"It pleases me, Sylvia, to be of some small service to you. I can't get away tomorrow but I'll drop by the next day. Rest and eat."

"Yes, Father."

When he returned, he found her in an agitated state again. She would soon leave the hospital and she didn't know where to go. She didn't want to return to the island even though her mother tried to talk her into that. Her father wasn't at all enthusiastic which hurt her although it wasn't a surprise. They changed the subject when she asked about Barry. She assumed he was ashamed of her by his absence which increased the hurt.

"Father, how do I find out more about the convent?"

"I can ask the Mother Superior here in Victoria to have someone come and talk to you if you wish?"

"Yes Father. Thank you."

The next day a nun appeared. It was the Mother Superior herself. For two hours they talked, Sylvia described her plight and Mother Agnes described life in a convent, what they offered and what they expected. She described how there was a trial period of one to two years which allowed the novice time to see if dedication of her life to God was what she really wanted.

"Mother Agnes, could I come to the convent straight from the hospital?"

"Yes, child, if that is what you want. You are welcome to come and stay with us before you decide if you want to join us as a novice."

"Thank you, Mother, I appreciate that."

"Let me write down the convent address and phone number. We will expect you."

For the first time since Nanaimo, Sylvia slept soundly. A weight lifted from her shoulders and she could see a path ahead. A poor substitute without Delbert but all she deserved now.

The nuns were kind to Sylvia. They welcomed her to the convent and showed her their routine. No one questioned her reason for coming. Obviously, her past was past to them. Within a week, she wanted to become a novice and work as a nurse.

"Are you sure, Sylvia? Have you given it enough thought? Although you can leave the sisterhood at any time, you will lose contact with your family, friends and acquaintances."

"That is exactly what I want, Sister Emily."

"Then, with Mother Agnes' approval, I will take you to your home on Saltspring Island so you can tell your parents of your plans and collect whatever personal possessions you wish to keep."

"Must we do that?"

"It's best that we do so your parents can see first-hand that it is your free choice to follow God's path. If other friends deserve to know what will become of you, you should tell them also. I'll talk to Mother Agnes about taking you over."

Other friends deserve to know what will become of you, she thought. How can I tell Delbert? He needs to know. Suddenly, the stress returned. I have to write and tell him.

She struggled with words to explain why she felt unworthy of him and how she hoped to find peace in the convent. The next morning she read the words again and made some changes before writing a final letter.

Two days later, Sister Emily drove her to the island. Arriving mid-day saved her the anxiety of facing her father and Barry. Her mother asked if she was sure this is what she wanted.

"What about Delbert?"

"I'm not worthy of Delbert. If he looks for me, will you give him this letter? And please explain to Dad and Barry that this is what I want to do."

Sadly, "Yes, dear."

Sylvia put the things she wanted to take in a small suitcase, hugged her mother and left the island for what she expected to be the last time. Tears came to her eyes when she looked back from the ferry to Mount Maxwell's cliff face. The following week she became a novice and was assigned to a nursing convent.

CHAPTER THIRTY-THREE

As the summer wore on, Delbert's flying skills became finely honed. He was now smoother than Skip. As his instructor, Skip took pride in that, tinged with a little jealousy to be honest. Delbert mastered all the maneuvers he could teach and sometimes invented new ones when the situation warranted.

Skip introduced him to the technique used to stretch an airplane's operational envelope. They pretended it was a brand new model and started with simple low speed flight. Then, gradually explored low speed characteristics through all types of stalls.

After that they addressed the high speed end, taking it beyond the published maximum speeds in power dives. Again they explored handling characteristics and a couple of times took the aircraft into maneuvers that made Skip sweat. Delbert remained cool and Skip told himself Delbert had it under control. It always amazed him how an insecure boy was transformed into a powerful man in the cockpit.

Concentration required in flight took his mind off a growing concern. Sylvia had not written in over a month. He found it hard to believe the strength of their love could wane. Unable to stand not knowing, he phoned Sylvia. When her mother answered, he asked for Sylvia.

"She's not here," followed by a click as she hung up.

Her curtness startled him. Was she told to do that? Have I really lost her, he wondered in panic. Perhaps her mother was just busy when he called. His faith was sorely tested.

Skip reported back to Bentwing that afternoon, "I've taught him everything I know. He flies better than me, he takes the airplane into maneuvers I'm afraid to try and he's wrung everything from that airplane it's got to give."

"Do you think he could handle the Canuck?"

"He could get it up and down safely with a couple of hours of preflight."

"Don't get carried away, Skip. Will you give a one on one ground school? We don't have enough time left to run him through the regular ground school."

"Sure."

"See if you can get him scheduled in the simulator to follow that. He's here for another two and a half weeks so if we can't get him into the Canuck by that time, save it for next summer."

"Let me see what I can do."

"Thanks."

Skip told Delbert he would be grounded for a while. "You're going to take a crash course, no pun intended, on the CF-100 Canuck fighter. I'll teach you. You're scheduled into the simulator a week from now and when you're ready you'll go up in our front line interceptor."

For the next week, he soaked up everything Skip could teach him and added to his knowledge by reading manuals. Every spare moment was spent out on the flight line while mechanics worked on the CF-100's. He sat in the cockpit when they let him. By the end of the week, he knew more about the airplane than any ground school graduate and was thoroughly familiar with all controls and their locations.

He felt at home in the simulator and started the engine before the instructor could go over the procedure. A little irritated, the instructor decided to just be quiet and let the kid get himself into a jam. It didn't happen. Delbert went through the preflight perfectly, taxied to the simulated runway and took off.

The simulated airplane controls felt sluggish although the airplane acceleration was way above that of the trainer. The lack of maneuverability disappointed him. No wonder they call it the "Clunk", he thought. Still, he put the simulated airplane through its paces with a smoothness that further irritated the instructor.

Determined to put the kid in his place, he introduced equipment failures. Delbert adapted to them with a calmness that infuriated the instructor. I'll bring the brat down, he thought and failed both engines. Delbert realized he couldn't eject from a simulator. He fought to control the airplane and rode it down to a dead stick landing on simulated tundra. The simulator went into a hold mode when it reached the boundary of its design. Delbert remained unperturbed.

The instructor had to admire Delbert's calmness and to admit he hadn't seen a student perform like that before. Delbert merely kept in mind that it was only a simulation. No need to panic no matter how realistic the flight sensations appeared.

The instructor reset the simulator on final approach and had Delbert fly half a dozen touch and go's, followed by a full stop landing. The first touch and go was a bit clumsy but each successive one became smoother. Near the end of the session, Skip walked in.

"Well, Buzz, what do you think? Another session be enough to clear him for the real thing?"

"Hi Skip. We've never cleared anyone for flight with only two simulator sessions."

"This kid isn't anyone. What else do you need to teach him?"

"He's good. I'll grant you that. Let's see how the next one goes. I put him through the paces today and he held up well. I'll give him more touch and go's, along with spin recovery and failures he didn't see today. If he comes through that as well as he did today, I'll clear him for flight, if you'll co-sign it."

"That's a deal. He's scheduled for the same shift tomorrow."

As Skip expected, the second session went as well as the first.

"OK Skip," Buzz said grudgingly, "I agreed to sign him off. It's unprecedented, even in wartime, but a promise is a promise."

"Thanks, Buzz, here let me countersign the flight clearance."

A little later, he told Delbert he would take the real thing up in the morning. I've come a long way from Dan's Cessna, Delbert thought. Hard to imagine this four months ago. I wish Sylvia could share my happiness. It's now been over two months since her last letter. Her father answered a second phone call as curtly as the first. Why? Has she found someone else so soon? Tired of waiting for me already? That's hard to believe.

When we were together I could feel the flow of her love to me. Given like a gift—the gift of love. Even apart, I can feel it. Surely she can feel my love for her the same way. I'll be back home in two weeks. Have to trust in her until then.

The day dawned chilly but clear, not a cloud in sight, air almost still. A great day to solo in a new airplane. Skip repeated last minute instructions, far more nervous than Delbert. He cautioned Delbert about the airplane's many shortcomings and warned him to stay ahead of the airplane to remain in control.

"Now just take it up and get the feel of it. Don't do anything fancy. Treat it tenderly like a new airplane. Then bring it in carefully."

"OK, Skip. Relax, I won't embarrass you."

But he almost did. The takeoff uneventful, he was surprised how well the simulator mimicked the airplane. It was equally sluggish in response to control inputs. Acceleration anything but sluggish, he could see why the Canuck was a good interceptor but decided he wouldn't want to take one into a dogfight.

Once he had a feel for the airplane, he put it through some maneuvers and began to explore its speed and altitude envelope. In the middle of a tight turn, the airplane suddenly rolled violently. He pushed the joystick hard over to arrest the roll and ended upside down with the nose up pitch sending the airplane into a dive. It took most of the joystick travel to hold the wings level. The altimeter was spinning down at a rate he didn't like. Panic swept over him. His mind pushed it aside. He brought the engines to idle and decided to finish the inadvertent loop as the only way to avoid crashing. Did he have enough altitude left?

He pulled more g's than ever before. Vision faded as he leveled off and began a slow climb. Fixated on the attitude indicator he could barely see to keep the wings level, he almost stalled the airplane. Felt it coming just in time to push the nose down and gain speed. Cursed himself for forgetting to add thrust. He was flying half blind, mainly by feel. Why on earth was he thinking of Sylvia at a time like this? But he was.

Gradually his vision cleared enough to take better stock of his situation. He had the airplane stabilized in a climb to a safe altitude. The base was behind him. He had to make a one eighty turn. The only way was to ease off on the roll input to bank the airplane and hope there was enough roll control to pull out of the turn again. It took forever to reach the heading to Malton. Time to let them know what happened on the radio.

"Malton, Canuck 532 inbound five miles west of Orillia at fifteen thousand feet declaring an emergency."

"532, state your emergency."

"532, I have an equipment failure leaving almost no roll control. Request a straight in approach to runway two three."

"Rodger 532, cleared for straight in approach to two three."

Skip had a bad feeling when the siren sounded and fire trucks pulled out toward the runway. Where the hell is he? Should be down by now. Is this for him?

Delbert maintained a high approach speed with the jet in a long gradual descent. A wind gust could flip the airplane out of control if he didn't catch it immediately. A strong gust would be deadly. As his subconscious mind struggled with the airplane, he thought again of Sylvia. I can't die without seeing her again. Sight of the runway, still far in front of him, brought his full attention back to the airplane. He carefully lined up with the runway, slowly extended flaps and finally landing gear.

Skip watched the jet touch down almost on the runway threshold, obviously carrying far more speed than normal. As it entered the ground effect height one wing lifted up. It seemed to take the pilot forever to get it back down. He knew now it was Delbert and found himself yelling "Brakes!" as he watched it careen down the runway. Smoke from the tires answered him. Fire trucks roared after the jet which ground to a stop with less than five hundred feet of runway left. One wheel was on fire, the other poured out smoke.

Skip flagged down an air force vehicle starting toward the runway. By the time they reached the jet, its wheels were smothered in foam. The canopy was up and Delbert was standing at the side of the runway peering up at a drooping aileron on the wing.

"What the hell happened?"

"The aileron jammed in that down position. Took almost full roll to counter it. I think it must be a mechanical failure. Happened when I rolled the airplane into a tight turn."

"Is that how you treat a new airplane tenderly?"

"It was behaving fine before that."

"Well, guess that will bring your flying to an end for this year."

"No Skip, don't end it on a sour note. I want to go back up tomorrow."

Skip shook his head. You can't hold this kid down, he thought, maybe that's a good quality for a test pilot and I sure as hell don't want to discourage him.

"OK, Pillage, let's draw up a flight syllabus for tomorrow's flight. I want to treat you like an experimental test pilot."

Every day of the last week in Ontario, Delbert put a second CF-100 through its paces as if it was the first one off the production line. In fact, it was one of the early Mark IV versions, the same model that test pilot Jan Rakowski took supersonic in a dive. Aware of that, Delbert duplicated the feat on his second to last flight. It exhilarated him but he could see why it was forbidden territory. The controls were unpredictable and he returned to a more manageable speed with relief.

On Delbert's last day in Malton, Bentwing called Skip and him into his office.

"Well, kid, it's been quite a summer. Thanks to Skip here and your skill, you've covered more than we expect in two summers."

"Skip's a phenomenal instructor Sir."

"Sir! That's one thing you never seem to learn."

"Sorry, Bentwing."

"Did they tell you that Canuck had a broken aileron linkage? Pure chance that it jammed in the down position."

"Yes, they told me."

"You proved your mettle on that one. I'm proud of what you've accomplished and I take full credit for recognizing your abilities from the outset. Since we dragged you here right out of school, we'll send you home a little early so you'll have a week or so off before classes start.

"I'll send a report on what you've accomplished to the Comox base along with an outline of what I want you to do this winter. My aide has a package for you with your tickets to Vancouver. Any questions?"

"No, well...could I add on a flight over to Victoria from the Vancouver connection?"

"Sure, I'll have Sam add it."

"Thanks, Bentwing, for a summer to remember always."

He couldn't wait to see Sylvia again. She would never hear of the Canuck incident.

CHAPTER THIRTY-FOUR

Delbert called his parents with his arrival time in Victoria. They agreed to meet him at the airport. He wanted to get to the Island quickly. He trembled each time he thought of Sylvia, fearful that she was lost.

Phil and Teresa both did a double take when he walked off the airplane in his air force uniform. He looked taller and with an air of confidence new to them. My God, he's a man, Phil thought. Teresa flushed with pride.

"Hi Mum, Dad. Where's Paul?"

"Stayed home. You're both so big now we can't all fit in the pickup."

"Guess that's right," chuckling, "you both look good. How's the neck, Dad?"

"It's OK most a the time. If I do a lotta liftin', it gits to actin' up. The doc says don't do a lotta liftin' then. Easy fer him to say, he makes a livin' just proddin'."

On the drive to the ferry, Phil said, "Sorry to hear about Sylvia Cairns, Delbert, know you had a bit of a thing for her."

Delbert blanched, barely able to gasp, "What happened?" Phil and Teresa exchanged looks.

"Thought you would've heard. That Lightfoot bastard raped her and got her pregnant as a result. 'Parently she tried to give herself an abortion and nearly died from it."

A ghastly pause. "Is she OK now? Where is she?"

"Don't know. They took her to the hospital in Victoria. Word is she recovered and decided to become a nun."

Delbert was in shock. Silent. Unable to speak even if there was something to say. Teresa laid a comforting hand on his arm.

"We didn't know she still meant so much to you, dear. We're sorry to tell you this way. It's such a tragedy. She's such a nice girl."

"She's my life."

"If she feels the same way, maybe you can bring her back. Rape leaves a wicked scar on a person's psyche and often causes them to repulse others of the same gender, no matter how they are loved. Sometimes it takes a long time to overcome."

"At least the bastard got his!" Phil interjected.

"Oh Phil, there's tragedy in that too. Barry went after Robin, dear. He beat him so badly he's in a coma on life support. They say he's a vegetable and expected to die anytime."

"Robin? That's no tragedy."

"Barry's in prison with an aggravated assault charge and facing a murder charge if he dies. Two families have had their lives torn apart."

"Three."

They were silent the rest of the way. As the ferry pulled into Fulford Harbour, Delbert on deck stared blindly. He came out of his stupor when Mount Maxwell's cliff came into view. The thought of their afternoon there brought tears to his eyes and a constriction in his chest so painful he couldn't breathe. His mind struggled in panic to find a strategy to get her back. The first step was to find her and talk to her, let her know how much he wanted and needed her, no matter what happened. He would talk to her parents first.

At home, Paul gave a more detailed account of what happened, including the trailer invention and need for her to go to the convention. Robin apparently got her so drunk she passed out before he raped her. She tried to give herself an abortion and nearly bled to death. They took her in an ambulance to Victoria. He said a nun had brought her back to the island for a day and that's the last anyone saw or heard of her.

Right after dinner, Delbert borrowed the pickup and drove to the Cairns house. Sylvia's mother answered the door. For a moment he thought it must be her grandmother. Her hair was devoid of color, her face drawn and her body a frail shadow of its former self.

"Sylvia's not here if that's what you're after."

"I'm sorry. I know how painful it must be for you, because of what's happened to Sylvia and Barry."

"I doubt that."

"I love her too. And I want to talk to her, to find out why she's become a nun and...to talk her into coming back. Can you tell me where she is?"

A little more sympathetically, "No. I have no idea where. She entered the convent in Victoria but they won't tell where they sent her."

"I'll talk to them and beg them to let me talk to her. I'm sorry to bother you and so sorry about what you're being put through." He turned to leave.

"Oh, I forgot. She left a letter for you. I'll get it."

Back in the pickup, he opened it and read...

Dear Delbert,

By now you must know what has happened to me — to us. I'm sorry I couldn't answer your letters or write to you sooner. I just couldn't. Please know that I love you more than I can describe. Believe me when I say I did nothing to encourage him, in fact, rejected him always. I was unconscious when he attacked me. My love for you has never wavered.

At first, I wanted to throw myself at your mercy and beg you to forgive me for letting it happen. But when I found out I was pregnant, I made matters so much worse by taking a life, even though I loathed it, and by injuring myself so that I could never give you children.

Not being able to have children makes me feel useless and unworthy of you. Because of being violated, I never feel clean and - this is so hard to say - I'm not sure I could ever have a sexual relationship again. Forgive me Delbert, it's not you. I have wonderful memories of our time together. Can you understand that?

The only path I can see out of this darkness is to dedicate what's left of my life to God's work. It calms the turmoil in my mind. And by forcing a separation from you, you can move on and find someone more worthy of you and better able to match your brilliance. The world needs little Delberts just like you.

I miss you so much, my only hope is to bury myself in work and prayer. Even so, I will watch for news of the great things I know you will attain. And I will pray for you daily that God will look after you and reward you with a fine family and an exciting life.

With my love always, Sylvia

The tears blinded him. His chest in a vise again. All he could manage was gasping sobs when forced to breathe. He sat in the pickup for half an hour and reread the letter over and over. Why did I go off and leave you? If I hadn't deserted you, I could have protected you from him.

Why couldn't you call me for help after it happened? Was I too far away? How can I tell you I want you always, no matter what? There can be no other woman. I have to find you and bring you back. Finally, he started the pickup and drove home.

~~~

The next morning he dropped his dad off at the current job and drove to the Catholic church in Ganges. He asked the priest if they could talk in private.

"Do you wish to take confession?"

"No, Father, I'm afraid I don't belong to your church."

"You needn't be afraid to belong to our church. You're the Pillage boy, aren't you?"

"Yes, Father. Delbert."

"Then again, you might be afraid to belong to our church. Come with me."

He led Delbert to a small room in back. "Now, what do you wish to discuss?"

"Sylvia Cairns and I were—are very much in love with each other. I need to tell her the tragic events in no way diminish my love. How can I find her?"

A sad look crossed the priest's face.

"Sylvia is a wonderful young woman. Such a shame. Such a shame. God has wreaked his vengeance on that evil man."

He came out of his momentary reverie, focused again on Delbert, "Son, I can see how sincere you are but I know only that she entered a convent in Victoria. She was full of remorse about what happened, which I told her was not a sin. But when she took the life of her unborn baby that was a serious sin in our Lord's eyes."

"How can I get a message to her, Father?"

"You might go to the convent in Victoria and talk to the Mother Superior. Please understand they make no attempt to persuade her to become a nun. It's strictly her choice but once made, it's difficult for outsiders to influence her since she has chosen a higher leader."

"Thank you, Father."

The priest sighed as he watched Delbert leave. "So many lives damaged. So many lives damaged," he muttered.

Delbert would have caught the next ferry to Victoria if he didn't have to pick his father up after work. By that time, it was too late. Early next morning, he walked the mile down to the ferry dock and took the bus from Swartz Bay into Victoria. He hailed a taxi and asked the driver to take him to the Catholic convent. With a snicker, the driver told him he only had one thing that prevented him from becoming a nun. Delbert was in no mood to laugh. Sullen the rest of the way, the driver couldn't resist a parting shot after he was paid.

"Make a habit of keeping it in your habit."

Delbert rang the bell next to the high gate once he determined it couldn't be opened from the outside. Eventually a nun appeared.

"My name is Delbert Pillage and I would like to speak to the Mother Superior."

"I will ask our Mother when Delbert Pillage may speak to her."

She turned and walked into the building. He stood outside the gate for over ten minutes before she returned and opened it for him.

"Follow me, Delbert Pillage."

She led him into the building and down a corridor to the right. No one in sight, an eerie quiet pervaded the building. She opened a door at the end of the corridor.

"Mother Agnes, this is Delbert Pillage who would like to talk to you."

"Come in Mr. Pillage. What would you like to talk about?"

"Sylvia Cairns, Mother. I want desperately to speak to her."

"Are you familiar with the events of the past two months?"

"Yes Mother. I was in Air Force training in Ontario all summer and only found out what happened two days ago. I love her and I believe she loves me. I need to tell her what happened does nothing to change that."

"Unfortunately, what happened did everything to change that. Although you may find it hard to believe, it changed her life completely. She finds peace now in the dedication of her life to God and wants to become a nurse."

"If she knew I still want her she might reconsider."

"Maybe in time she will change and be drawn back from God's love to yours. She will remain a novice for two years before taking her vows and is free to leave anytime during that period. In fact, we discourage novices from taking their final vows if any doubt remains in their minds."

"Can I see her and speak to her?"

"No, she's not here and I am not at liberty to say where she was sent."

"Can I write a message to her."

"You can write a letter to her in care of our convent. I will hold it for her. If I learn she has doubts, I will attempt to get it to her."

"Thank you."

"However, Mr. Pillage, in spite of your love for her, which I believe, my advice is that you make every attempt to get on with your life. I have seen other young women go through equally traumatic experiences and only find the strength to go on through their faith in God."

"She can find strength in our love too, Mother."

"Perhaps, Mr. Pillage. Good day."

She gave him a card with the convent's address, then rang a chime to signal the nun to show him out.

Dejected, he found a hotel for the night and composed a letter to Sylvia, though he doubted it would ever reach her. He enclosed the letter inside a second one addressed to the Mother Superior. He thanked her for seeing him and implored her to send it on to Sylvia. In the morning he mailed it and caught the boat to Vancouver.

CHAPTER THIRTY-FIVE

Embarrassed to just show up at the Martins out of the blue, he apologized unnecessarily. They welcomed him back with enthusiasm. A couple of letters to Charlie and one to Dan during the summer left them anxious to hear more about his experiences back east.

They soon realized something was terribly wrong. He appeared depressed instead of bubbling over with stories. Samantha tactfully brought things to a head.

"Delbert, you're obviously distraught. It's none of our business, however, if you care to talk about it at any time, we stand ready to help you in any way we can."

"Thank you. You have a right to know. It's Sylvia."

After a long pause to gather himself together, "She was raped by her boss. When she realized she was pregnant, she tried to abort the fetus and nearly bled to death. When her injuries healed enough to leave the hospital, she entered a convent. I can't reach her to talk to her or even get a letter to her."

Teary eyed, he took out the letter and passed it to Dan as Samantha held him. Dan choked back tears of his own as he finished the letter and passed it to Charlie.

"Oh shit," was Charlie's comment as he passed it on to Samantha.

"I'm sorry, I shouldn't dump my troubles on you. There's nothing that can be done other than hope Sylvia reverses her decision."

"I know it sounds callous," Dan said, "but if you're right that nothing can be done, it will help to throw yourself into your work in the meantime." That brought a scowl to Samantha's tear-stained face and a nod from Delbert.

"I'll register for classes tomorrow, then I have to go back to the island and get my things."

"Thought you were traveling a little light," Charlie offered in an effort to break the tension. Delbert showed a trace of a smile for the first time.

~~~

Within a week he was settled back into university life. He had an interview with Dean Calder, who had been forewarned by Dan. The Dean was gentle, but straightforward. He told Delbert he was aware of his tragedy and echoed Dan's suggestion. He said Mike Medane eagerly awaited his return.

"You've made a friend for life there, son. Also, now that you have the necessary clearances, you can work with Dan. Let me know if it's not your cup of tea after he describes it to you. As I've told you before, my door is always open to you to discuss your situation or problems, educational or personal. Come to me any time."

"Thank you."

~~~

When they met once more, Mike told him he played with the reader over the summer. He suggested some improvements like a quieter way to align the scanner on each line and perhaps some way to make it less sensitive to vertical alignment. He no longer felt it should be silenced during right to left movement. That would be when the user hunted for the next line. And this year he wanted Delbert to develop a compact packaging design for the electronics.

How could I consider the project ninety percent done, Delbert thought. Well, it keeps me involved in something physical. He spent a long session with Dan on the secret project, which was purely theoretical. The Orenda jet engine manufacturer asked Dan to develop a thermodynamic model of their new Iroquois engine. The model entailed complex analyses. While Dan felt he had some of the general steady state equations worked out, boundary conditions and engine acceleration and deceleration proved difficult.

The model intended to prevent hot spots in the turbine, burner and exhaust sections which could damage metal parts. Designed to produce more thrust than any engine in existence, they blazed new territory in metallurgy and flow control. In addition to overheat, tests on smaller engines caused a concern that surge problems could arise as the engine decelerated. The model was crucial to their success and Dan was now pressed for time.

At first overwhelmed as he poured over Dan's work, Delbert gradually learned what the equations represented and how they related to the engine design. Dan had passed back data that allowed Orenda to refine the burner can design to keep within limits. But soon they would need a precise estimate of temperatures along the length of the turbine blades and a pressure profile for high thrust conditions. A formidable challenge, exactly what Delbert thrived on.

Within a week he was immersed in a three way battle for his time. Classes and tests in particular could not be avoided. Between classes he worked on the Braille scanner. Late afternoon and evenings found him buried in the engine project. There was little time left to mope over his loss.

~~~

With Mike Medane one afternoon, "Mike, we push the limits with this circuitry. It's really a job for one of those new digital computers."

"That one over in the Math department fills a room."

"They'll get dramatically smaller when someone designs a transistor version. And when that happens, it will give us flexibility to interpret what's scanned. Instead of a tone for each character, we could put out an oral rendition of what's scanned, maybe even speak words or at least spell them."

"Sounds wonderful. You're going to obsolete our scanner before it gets into widespread use."

"No, no. The scanner will still be needed. Just the downstream process will change. What would really be neat is if we can refine the scanner to where typed letters can be read. Wouldn't need to translate books into Braille in the first place. Braille would be obsolete."

"Sometimes I think you live a hundred years in the future and can't wait for the rest of us to catch up."

Delbert laughed, "forty years at most."

On a more immediate basis, Delbert worked on a circuit design which would use a vertical scan to locate each line of characters. Vertical position would no longer be so critical. Mike thought it a noble effort but said he wouldn't hold his breath. With all the mental activity, it fell to Charlie to instigate some physical balance.

"Soccer season is almost here, Del, you need to get in shape. We better hit the circuit."

"Don't know if I'll have time for soccer this year."

"C'mon man, you need physical exercise to balance all this brain work or your spindly little body won't hold up that massive head you cart around."

"Argument is useless when you get on a mission."

So a daily workout was wedged into an impossible schedule. Within days Delbert was thankful, amazed at how exercise improved his mental agility.

Charlie pushed too hard, however, when he tried to get Delbert to date a girl interested in him after Charlie casually mentioned Delbert was a test pilot. But Delbert stood firm. He had not come to grips with losing Sylvia. He wrote the Mother Superior every two weeks to ask about Sylvia and his letter. She faithfully responded that nothing had changed. Each time his bitterness towards the church increased.

CHAPTER THIRTY-SIX

The constant pressure on his time prevented Delbert from dwelling on Sylvia. Certainly he often thought of her but as the weeks went by gut-wrenching emotion slowly transitioned into grim determination. Although he couldn't argue with the concept that she needed the convent's emotional support, he remained convinced he could perform that role equally well.

He spent time in the library digging up the address of as many convents in western Canada as he could find. Then wrote a letter to Sylvia in care of each begging her to contact him. It was a long shot. She now would go by a different name and might not be at any on the list. Even if it reached her she might not respond. Many of the letters were returned. He did not hear from her.

Still he remained convinced their paths would cross again. Even if he could not determine her situation, she might discover things about him. She would be disappointed and ashamed to find a dismal failure. A lost soul. He would not let that happen and determined to live up to her expectations with one exception. In spite of urging him to find a new mate, she would retain sole custody of his heart.

By December he refined the scanner circuitry to the point that Mike could offer no more suggestions. They decided to build the new circuits and begin tests in January. Once again,

Mike felt obliged to propose Delbert be included in the scanner's eventual trade name. Delbert refused.

Also by December, Delbert made a significant breakthrough with the engine model. He found a way to predict temperatures along the turbine blades and in doing so developed equations that defined pressure gradients as well. Dan's elation paled in comparison to the excitement at Orenda. They now had the data needed to move ahead with turbine design. More important, it looked like the metals available were up to the job. While a lot remained to handle accelerations and decelerations, it was a significant milestone.

The weekends spent at Comox cemented his skill with the Canuck fighter and introduced him to the Sabre as well. Word spread around that he was Training Command's newest fair haired boy. Local pilots set out to show him up, without success. It didn't take long to impress them with his ability and his humble demeanor left them nothing to dislike. So they accepted him and perhaps because he was a local B.C. boy, became proud of him.

Over the Christmas break, he called on Mother Agnes at the convent to plead his case again. She was aware of his letter barrage.

"Mr. Pillage, please believe Sylvia finds support from the sisterhood beneficial to her emotional and spiritual health. She may still harbour fond feelings for you just as you do for her. If so, and if she feels strong enough to deal with a secular life, you may hear from her sometime in the future. That's not the case to date. I must tell you again my experience leads me to believe it will not change in future. Please try to make peace with that."

"I know you mean well, Mother, but I cannot accept your opinion." After he left, she prayed that he be led in a different direction.

~~~

By mid January, the scanner prototype was available to test. It performed flawlessly. The next step was to determine if blind students could use it. Experienced Braille readers were selected so winning them over might prove difficult. However, incentive to learn the musical language increased when they realized it would make significantly more books accessible. Before long, they were as proficient with their ears as their fingers.

Mike deemed it a success and they published their results in a technical paper. An electronics firm in Ontario was licensed to produce the "UBC Braille Reader", as it was finally named. Mike and Delbert received a humanitarian award from the Prime Minister. The award and their accomplishment was reported in newspapers throughout Canada and the United States.

Dean Calder wrote a letter to Phil and Teresa to tell them how proud he was of Delbert's contribution and how thankful the university was that they had let him attend UBC. This one project repaid Delbert's scholarship many times over. And another project had already contributed significantly to an important military program. He said they should be very proud of their son. They were, even Phil.

~~~

With soccer season over, Delbert looked for something else to keep him in shape. For want of anything better, he began to run around the campus at dawn. He laid out a route exactly ten kilometres long. Within days, Charlie joined him.

Not long after, two girls happened to jog in the same area at the same time. They were hard pressed to match Delbert's pace. The boys' attraction motivated them to far exceed what they otherwise might attempt. Three soccer team-mates next joined the fray, followed by four more girls. Within a month, the "Pied Piper of Point Gray", as Charlie called him, had over fifty students outside the house each morning.

They became known around campus as Pillage's Dawn Patrol. And the numbers continued to grow. Afraid they were now a neighbourhood nuisance, Delbert laid out a new course, still exactly ten kilometres. It started at the Fort Camp bus stop and ended at the Hub. This proved even more popular since they could sprawl exhausted in the Hub and be revived by a cup of hot coffee. The Hub brought in extra help to handle this early morning surge.

Camaraderie made the exercise popular and physical benefit made it worthwhile. The dawn patrol was here to stay as long as Delbert showed up to lead. Only the first two girls were a little miffed to have to share their access to him with everyone else.

~~~

Dan and Delbert finished the engine model by Easter. Delbert had developed equations which appeared to handle acceleration and deceleration. They were so complicated no one else truly understood them. The Orenda engineers found it hard to take them on faith but had little choice.

Delbert advised them that the engine would surge during deceleration unless they could bleed off excess pressure from the compressor section. He showed them how they could use spring loaded check valves which would open when the pressure difference between compressor and turbine sections exceeded the allowable range.

The surge valve requirement led him to think about the engine design as a whole. He told them they could get much better fuel efficiency if they used longer blades at the front to blow air along the outside of the engine. It was a natural outgrowth of their twin spool design. The inner turbine should be designed to handle the bulk of the compression needed to pump high pressure air into the burner cans. The outer compressor should contain long blades to perform the dual function of providing initial compression and extra thrust with bypass air. By ducting this bypass air along the outside of the engine, it would cool the casing and probably reduce engine noise as well.

This smacked of science fiction to the Orenda engineers.

"Yeah, well I think we'll go with what we got." Now they had some doubts about the equations.

Dan chimed in, "one thing I've learned about Delbert, guys, don't sell him short. Maybe you can't redesign the Iroquois at this point. But you might want to get some of your research types to think about this for the future."

"You're right, Dan. And your track record has been very good. We'll take your equations on faith 'cause to be truthful we don't understand them. We'll all be heroes or goats when the first engine runs."

Off the phone, Delbert couldn't resist a comment on what he perceived to be a "not invented here" attitude. They seemed to pooh-pooh his suggestion when it looked like an obvious improvement. Dan pointed out that things he found obvious were not always so to others, at least not without additional contemplation.

"Don't despair, Delbert, the future will catch up to you eventually."

"You sound like Mike." They both laughed.

Late spring at university was as always a time of drooping spirits with exams and summer separations almost upon them. Delbert, however, looked forward to additional flight time in the country's hottest jets. Exams were no longer scary and he breezed through them.

CHAPTER THIRTY-SEVEN

He now had little incentive to return home before heading east. Still there was an obligation to his parents so he spent a long weekend with them. He also met with Hal Lundquist to relate what transpired this past year. As Delbert left, Hal reminisced, what a long way he's come from the gangly kid in high school. You can never tell where the gems are hidden.

~~~

Bentwing welcomed him back.

"Got the reports from Comox on your progress. Looks like you're now checked out on all our top fighters. Well, all but one."

Curious, "What am I missing?"

"The Arrow."

"The Arrow? What's that—some kind of secret? I've never heard of it."

"It is secret so treat it that way. No discussions in public at all, understood?"

"Yes Sir—Bentwing." The jaundiced eye was on him.

"The Arrow is a new interceptor to be designed and built by Avro right here in Toronto. It'll outperform everything in the world, Mach 2 plus."

"Mach 2?"

"Plus. When it gets the engine being developed by Orenda."

"The Iroquois?"

"How do you know about that?"

"I worked on the thermodynamic model used to design burner cans and turbine sections. But that engine is a long way from running."

"Yeah, they're going to use lower thrust engines from the States until the Iroquois is ready. They won't get to Mach 2 with them but they will get supersonic experience. Anyway, I brought it up because I want to get you onto that program."

"Wow, sounds great."

"Don't get excited yet, we have to convince them it's worthwhile. I've set up a meeting with Rakowski for Tuesday at two. He's chief test pilot on the program. You'll go with me. He'll think you're too young so I'll challenge him to take you up in a Clunk and let you show him your stuff."

~~~

Sharp at two o'clock on Tuesday they were parked in front of Jan Rakowski office. After introductions, in which Jan assumed Delbert must be an aide dragged along by Bentwing, they got down to business.

"Jan, we would like to have an Air Force test pilot join your team. Although you know more than anyone about fighters, we think there's a benefit to the program and to us to have some early involvement."

"We have a good team of pilots already. They can look after your interests."

"I'm sure you've got a good team, still I think some Air Force representation would be useful. If for no other reason than to counter any political concerns in that regard."

Jan sighed, "well, who do you have in mind?"

"Pillage."

"The boy?"

"He's young I'll grant you. But he's the most talented pilot I've ever seen. I'd even go so far as to say he's in your class. And he has technical abilities second to none. The Orenda engineers used information he developed to design the Iroquois hot section. What I would propose is that you take him up and see what he can do."

"Christ, Bentwing, if it was anyone but you, I'd toss you out of here. OK Pillage, we'll go flying. I need to get out of this office anyhow. But no promises, Bentwing."

"Sure, we can talk about it when you get back. I'll make one of our new Mark four Clunks available."

"Make two available. Nine tomorrow morning?"

"Fine. Thanks."

"Thanks for nothing yet."

Nine in the morning the two tramped out to their airplanes in flight gear.

"How many hours you got in this crate?"

"A little over a hundred."

"That's almost nothing. Well, try to keep up."

They took off in tandem with Jan in the lead. With afterburners blasting, he climbed near vertically to thirty thousand feet, then kicked the airplane hard over into a twisting dive. Delbert was right on his tail the whole time. Carrying a lot of speed Jan pulled up into a tight loop. Delbert pulled into a tighter loop inside the leader, more g's than he had with Bentwing. Jan pulled as many g's as he cared to, less than Delbert.

"You still conscious, Pillage?"

"Doing fine Sir."

Next he tried some time proven maneuvers to shake off a pursuer. Even though the airplane was not maneuverable, neither had an advantage over the other. Delbert stuck on his tail so tightly, an observer would think they were in formation. His 'Ted Williams' vision allowed him to respond to control surface movement on the lead airplane. That gave him a split second advantage over tracking the airplane itself.

Jan climbed to forty-five thousand feet and put the airplane into a power dive which pushed the airplane supersonic. Delbert followed him. He remembered how touchy control would become and moved laterally to put more space between them. When they pulled out of the dive, Jan told him to head for the barn.

Bentwing met them when they walked in. Neither talked. A bad sign he thought.

"Well Bentwing, you're a sly old bugger. You knew a flight would make it hard. We wrung those planes out like they never been wrung out before. The boy is the best jet jockey I've ever seen. But when we went supersonic, he put a little extra space between us. That's when I knew he'd been supersonic before. That's when I knew he isn't just a jet jockey, he's a test pilot. He's on the team."

"Supersonic? One day you guys are going to clunk one of them Clunks for real," Bentwing said with a laugh.

Jan wanted Delbert on the program full time, at least to start. Bentwing had no choice but to agree. So Delbert moved into the Avro flight test building and shared an office with Peter Copel, an Avro test pilot. At first a little aghast at the prospect of a teenage test pilot, Peter soon gained an appreciation for Delbert's abilities.

The fact that he would return to UBC in the fall presented a problem. A large gap in his involvement appeared inevitable. Still, the summer months allowed him to become familiar with engineers on the design team. Flight control stability in particular gave him an opportunity to contribute. There was concern that the airplane would not be naturally stable.

Delbert pointed out that a fighter designed to be stable would compromise maneuverability. However, after hours with the design team, he had to agree there might be more maneuverability than they were prepared to cope with. The answer was to introduce a stability augmentation system, basically an electronic system which superimposed a signal on top of the pilot input to the hydraulic flight controls. There was a fine line between a fighter too wild to fly and one too docile to get the job done. Delbert guided the designers down that fine line.

By the end of the summer he had a good knowledge of aerodynamics as well as flight controls and hydraulic systems. Because of the confined area available for flight control actuators, the Arrow introduced a radically new high pressure hydraulic system and flight control cables were replaced by electrical signals directly to the valves. He helped ensure sufficient redundancy was designed in and introduced a valve approach which would allow automatic over-ride of a single valve failure by the two remaining ones.

In many respects the Arrow design was ambitious, with features significantly ahead of anything on the design boards at the time. This made test pilot input doubly important. While all of the test pilots actively worked with the design team, Delbert was better able to dig into the more complex design areas. By the time he left for UBC in September, he took with him a number of issues. One particular concern was that internally stored missiles could de-stabilize the airplane in supersonic flight when they were extended and fired. For security reasons, he could not take written material with him. He didn't need it. He remembered everything needed to continue work on the issues in which he became immersed.

CHAPTER THIRTY-EIGHT

Return to UBC produced mixed feelings. He knew it was important to get a degree and wouldn't dream of reneging on his scholarship obligations. On the other hand, he would miss a key phase of the Arrow design process. Now in his second year of engineering, it was hard to reconcile the importance of what he could contribute to the Arrow with many of the introductory courses in this year's curriculum.

At what had become a traditional start of the year meeting, Dean Calder quickly sensed a concern that Delbert would not divulge on his own.

"Alright Delbert, tell me what's bothering you."

"Nothing Sir."

"Something is. 'Fess up son."

"Well, I worked on a classified project this summer. Now, when I look at some of the introductory courses I take this year, they seem very unimportant in comparison. I know they're intended to help us decide which branch of engineering to pursue and to give us a well rounded education. I think I can achieve both of those ends without a year's classes. There's an important reason to get my degree a year early, although I realize that's not possible."

"I wonder how many times I've counseled students to not dwell on what is impossible but instead think of a way to make it possible."

"I'm sorry Dean."

"No, no, I don't mean that as a rebuke. We have to figure out how to get you that degree a year early. Remember, you skipped a year once before. Maybe the same strategy will work again. The first step is for you to list all of the courses that remain between you and the degree. For each, jot down your thoughts on why the course is or isn't important to you and what you would have to do to be able to pass the exams. Then, bring that back to me, preferably in the next week so we can take action at the outset of this term."

"I can have it back by Friday."

"Fine, make an appointment with Sheila on your way out to be sure you're on my calendar. This is a busy time of year."

"Thank you Sir."

The courses fell into three categories; those that appeared valueless, those with value but easily mastered by reading the textbook and those which truly warranted class attendance. He didn't want to demean any course so he lumped the first two categories together and suggested they might be handled by reading the textbooks only.

When he reviewed the list, Dean Calder asked why he need study things like Economics, Geology and Surveying.

"I don't," he agreed, as Dean Calder ticked off most of the courses originally on his "valueless" list.

"OK, let's cross these off. Now, which courses from next year can we add to this year? We need a combination of some which are exam only and some which are attend class.

And we need more than a full load because schedule conflicts will rule some out."

Together, they worked up a heavy load for the year. Then Delbert was sent off to build a class schedule. A day later he was back with a proposed class load. Dean Calder made the rounds of the impacted professors to apprise them of the situation and gain their support.

In the end, about three quarters of this year's courses were moved forward from the third year curriculum. If combined with a heavy load next year, it looked possible to graduate a year early. Excited, Delbert threw himself into the new textbooks. The time previously dedicated to the Braille reader allowed him to devour additional course material.

He still found time to work on the Arrow issues and within two months had put together a technical paper on how to compensate for the weapons delivery system during supersonic flight. MacKenzie had it sent by courier to Bentwing who passed it on to the Avro team. They were amazed by the technical detail he included without reference to any printed data. His analysis looked sound and the recommendations were adopted.

In spite of the heavy workload, Charlie successfully persuaded him to turn out for soccer. And due to popular demand, Pillage's Dawn Patrol started again. Within a week close to a thousand runners turned out each morning. Even a couple of young professors showed up. Tradition now dictated that Delbert lead the run. Early in October, a Vancouver Sun reporter heard about it. A week later an article appeared with a picture of Delbert in front of the procession. Almost overnight participation doubled.

Many of the newcomers found ten kilometres too hard and had to drop out along the way. Most persevered until they could handle the distance in stride. The general level of fitness on campus rose. The gender split remained fairly constant. The Dawn Patrol provided a good opportunity to meet people. Since the paper article pointed out that Delbert was an Air Force jet pilot in the summer, the mystique that surrounded him continued to grow. He certainly didn't fit the Hollywood image of a fighter pilot and he seemed very quiet, even shy.

A number of girls pushed hard to be near him on the run and jockeyed for a position to talk to him at the Hub afterward. One extremely attractive girl with long, jet black hair and a beautifully developed body repeatedly matched him stride for stride. One morning she ended up next to Charlie with Delbert on his other side.

"Hi, I'm Charlie."

"Virginia."

"Oh, Virgin for short but not for long." Wham! She slapped Charlie so hard he fell over backward, partly from surprise.

"It was just a joke."

"My virginity is not a laughing matter," she said flashing a dazzling smile.

"Take that, Charlie," Delbert laughed. "Hi Virginia, my name's Delbert Pillage. With a name like mine you'll never hear me make fun of anyone else's. So you can safely reveal your surname."

"Karakan."

"Virginia Karakan. That sounds Hawaiian."

"Actually, my ancestors were Russian."

Her smile and dark, twinkling eyes stirred an emotion long buried. Disturbed by a sense of betrayal to Sylvia, he excused himself and left.

"Did I scare him away?" she asked Charlie.

"Guess he didn't want to expose himself to getting decked for saying something wrong."

"OK, I'm sorry. I didn't mean to slap you that hard. I've heard that line too often."

"I'm sorry too. Should have realized that."

"Well, we're a sorry pair," she said with a laugh. "You a friend of Delbert's?"

"He lives with us during the school year."

"Does he date?"

"No. That's a long, sad story."

"Tell me."

"Well, to make it short, he loves an angel he grew up with. While he was back east the summer before last, she was raped by her boss. When she found she was pregnant, she tried to give herself an abortion and almost died. She recovered physically, although she could no longer have children. She had a harder time emotionally and ended up in a convent. Delbert can't contact her so he has no idea how she is. It's been damned hard on him."

"Oh, that's sad." A tear trickled down her cheek. "He's a very lovable man. I was going to ask you to tell him I'd like to go out with him but now that would be disrespectful."

"He's as strong a character as I've ever seen. He distracts himself with a tremendous load of extra courses and outside work for the Air Force."

"That's not a surprise. Look Charlie, I'm really sorry I slapped you. Can we be friends?"

"Certainly, Virgin, I mean Virginia." They both laughed as she left.

~~~

Delbert's appeal overwhelmed Virginia. Attractive in spite of his ears, intelligent, famous because of the Braille reader, jet pilot and victim of a tragic romance. What could allure her more than the challenge of replacing sadness with happiness?

More than ever, Virginia was determined to run near him and sit near him in the Hub. Now introduced, conversation was easier. She offered friendship instead of flirtation and Delbert found her easy to talk to, even interesting. When he learned she was a biology major, he steered the conversation in that direction and surprised her with his knowledge of her field.

"How do you know so much about this stuff?"

"It's interesting to read about."

As the year drew on, their friendship grew. She never asked about his past love life. He never mentioned it. She was bright, cheerful and extroverted, a perfect counter to his natural shyness. She made time spent together comfortable and though there was a sexual attraction, they kept their friendship platonic. She sensed he would draw away if she infringed on the love he refused to abandon.

Charlie could see Virginia was good for Delbert. He became more relaxed, more cheerful. Charlie contrived to get them to campus events, along with whichever girl he dated at the time. They were never called dates or made to appear like dates.

At the dinner table one evening, Dan asked what they had planned for the weekend.

"Del and Virginia and Katie and I are going to the Ella Fitzgerald concert Saturday night."

"Delbert, you haven't mentioned any Virginia, who's she?"

"She's a girl who runs with us in the morning." Dan, Samantha and Charlie exchanged glances while Delbert continued to eat.

"Does her family live here in Vancouver?" Samantha asked.

"No, they live up in Nelson."

"I bet it gets lonely on weekends, so far from home."

"I don't think Virginia ever gets lonely."

"Still, I bet she misses home-cooked meals. Why don't you invite her over for dinner on Sunday?"

"We're not dating."

"I would hardly call Sunday dinner at the Martins a date," Dan interjected.

"Well, I'll ask her tomorrow morning." The three conspirators suppressed a smile.

~~~

Virginia, Charlie and Delbert talked after the next morning's run.

"Oh, by the way, Charlie's folks wonder if you'd like to come over for a home-cooked meal on Sunday?"

She glanced at Charlie. "That's right. Thanks for reminding me Del."

"I'd love to. Cafeteria food gets old real quick. What time do you want me there?"

"We eat about five on Sundays. But why not come over around two and we can play ping pong or something before dinner."

"I don't know where you live."

"How about I call for you at two?" Delbert asked.

"That would be great! I look forward to it."

The concert Saturday night and dinner Sunday certainly felt like dates to Virginia. She was excited even though she knew they couldn't be treated as such. Ella en-chanted them. They thoroughly enjoyed the whole concert and spent the ride home singing their favorites. Charlie swerved back and forth up Tenth Avenue in time with the music. That is, until a burly officer on a motorcycle pulled them over.

"Do you want to know what I pulled you over for?"

Instantly Charlie responded, "You wanted to practice dangling your participle?"

While they snickered, the officer stared at him, dumb-founded. Still confused, he stuck his head in through the window and sniffed.

"You been drinking?"

"No Sir."

"I pulled you over because you were weaving back and forth in your lane."

"I'm sorry Sir. We were singing an Ella Fitzgerald song and I was waggling to the music."

"Well, knock off the waggle before you cause another car to swerve into trouble."

"Yes Sir."

On their way again, Delbert remarked, "Very witty Charlie but I feel obliged to point out that he actually dangled his preposition."

"OK smart ass, give me an example of a dangling parti-ciple."

"Well...thinking it over, the participle dangled if he said, 'Weaving down the road, I decided to pull you over.'"

In an attempt to get the last word in, Virginia added, "You should know better than to argue grammar with 'He Who Knows All' Charlie."

To make it the last word, Delbert began to sing the next verse of the interrupted song. The others joined in on the chorus. Charlie drove straight ahead. Back at Virginia's dorm, Delbert walked her to the door. She squeezed his hand and said, "Thanks, Delbert, I had a wonderful time. See you in the morning."

"Sure, Virginia, it was a great concert."

~~~

At two the next afternoon, she appeared in a skirt and top that somehow looked casual and formal at the same time.

"That's a stunning outfit," he said.

"You're the most gorgeous girl in the world," she heard and felt a warm glow.

"My God, you're a beautiful young woman!" Dan said when they were introduced.

"Don't embarrass Virginia, dear. Save those comments for me." They laughed.

"You boys didn't tell me you live in a palace. You're really spoiled. You even have a grand piano!"

"Do you play," Samantha asked.

"I do but there's not much opportunity here at university."

"We'd love to hear you play something."

"OK, but I'm rusty so please don't feel you have to stick around and listen. And if you threaten to leave the house, I'll stop."

She sat down at the piano and played a piece by Chopin, with finesse and feeling. Then followed with Mendelsohn and Mozart concertos. Each brought an enthusiastic response from the family. When she launched into Beethoven's Eloise, Delbert was entranced. It always haunted him. It also reminded him of Sylvia. He wondered where she was and what she was doing. He became misty eyed. Virginia noticed and immediately guessed the cause. That was the wrong thing to play, she thought. Don't ever do it again. Why can't he divert a little of that love to me?

"That's enough of that," she said. "I don't want to wear out my welcome in the first hour."

They contradicted her simultaneously and praised her talent.

"Can I help you with anything in the kitchen?"

"Let's go find out," Samantha responded.

"She has a wonderful touch with that thing," Dan said.

The others agreed. For want of something to do and a way to break the mood Delbert was suddenly in, Charlie challenged him to a game of ping pong. Dan turned on his new TV to watch a football game.

Dinner was accompanied with nonstop banter that tickled everyone's sense of humor. With her gregarious nature, Virginia fit into the family instantly. After dinner, they coaxed her back to the piano. This time she played Ella Fitzgerald standards and they all sang along. The evening inevitably came to an end and Delbert drove her back to the dorm. At the door she gave him a kiss on the cheek, pausing slightly in hopes that he would return the kiss in a more ardent location.

He just said, "We had a wonderful time, thanks to you."

"I'm the one who's thankful. The Martins are great people! It's rare to come away from a first meeting feeling like one of the family. Thanks Delbert."

Alone with Charlie later, Delbert bared his soul.

"Why can't I open up to her, Charlie? She's a great person, beautiful, sexy, intelligent, great sense of humor, everything a guy could want. And the more I want to be with her, the guiltier I feel. I immediately think of Sylvia. As long as she's alive and out there somewhere, I can't move on."

Charlie placed a hand on Delbert's arm. "You're in a hell nobody deserves."

"You know even though I don't go to church I am quietly religious. Science can explain how one thing evolves into another but it has yet to explain how the seed was created in the first place. It seems like a divine power tests me, tests Sylvia. I tell myself if that divine power is benevolent, we will eventually be rewarded. It drives me to keep doing my best to challenge it to give evidence of that."

"What if you are on your deathbed when the reward arrives? How many happy years with Virginia will you have squandered?"

"You apply logic where it doesn't apply."

"It's hard to imagine how anyone could shun Virginia. She's perfect but I understand your position. How I wish there was some way to talk to Sylvia so you could get closure one way or another."

A quiet, "Yes."

CHAPTER THIRTY-NINE

To distract himself from this emotional turmoil, Delbert turned back to the Braille Reader project. Although successful, he felt that use of Braille characters was not a long term solution. Braille books printed with ink on paper were far better than embossed paper. Yet, books still had to be translated into Braille. They represented a drop in the bucket of world literature. The real solution would be to scan typed words and vocalize them.

When he shared this with Mike, the reaction was, "noble thoughts, Delbert, but face it, technology for that kind of thing hasn't been invented yet. We barely got the resolution needed for Braille characters with your optical wizardry...and signal processing would be formidable. Or as you once said, scary complicated."

"You're right. A number of inventions are needed. But why can't we start work on one of them anyway?"

Sighing, "Okay, where do you want to start?"

"Well, I wonder if we should try a different approach to scanning."

"What do you mean?"

"Instead of dragging light sensing diodes over the page, what if we bounce a thin beam of light off the paper and sense the reflected light. The thin beam could sweep across the page and search for lines and characters to identify. We would need a digital computer to process the data generated by the sweeps but it would allow us to increase the resolution by using a very thin beam."

"Isn't that sort of how those television cameras work?"

"Not really. They use a tube that scans across the image collected by the lens and outputs an analog television signal. They don't get anything like the resolution we need for typed characters. There are things called drum scanners used to make copies of printed material. They have better resolution and may be a workable approach. But you have to mount each page on the drum which would be too cumbersome for a blind reader.

"I picture something where you place the open book on a base plate and lower the device onto the page. It would flatten the page as much as necessary and scan it. For each new page the operator would raise the lever, flip the page and lower the lever again."

Mike thought for a moment. "Well, It could be a first step to the scanner of your dreams. Make that your next project if you want."

So Delbert thought seriously about how such a scanner could be designed. By the end of the school year he concluded the tray should align pages vertically when the operator slides the book onto it. The lid should block outside light as well as flatten the page. The light beam would have to be extremely thin yet able to reflect enough light to drive the sensor. The beam would have to be aimed electronically although it could be moved mechanically across and down the page.

Control of the light beam would be the toughest nut to crack. Not sure it could be done, he decided to put off further research until after exams, perhaps even until Fall if Arrow work consumed his time during the summer.

~~~

The Dawn Patrol continued right through the exam period. Attendance fell off since many of the students crammed for exams. Students who still ran included those who knew the material well and those in no hurry to graduate. Charlie and Virginia had qualms about missing things that some last minute study might pick up. On the other hand, they agreed with Delbert that exercise would keep their minds sharper during exams. In any case, Virginia was not about to abandon Delbert's morning runs. So they pressed on and probably enjoyed higher marks as a result.

After exams, Delbert went home by way of Victoria. Mother Agnes, now accustomed to his twice yearly visits admired his persistence. The answer to his question never varied. As far as she knew, Sylvia had no inclination to leave the sisterhood. She did say she had sent his letter on but didn't know if Sylvia had received it. Delbert thanked her for doing that and gave her his summer address in case anything changed. Again, she urged him to move on even though she resigned herself to the fact that he wouldn't.

Life on the island changed little. Paul was now in high school and taller than Delbert. Phil prospered by island standards with his carpentry skills. Teresa no longer worked for Roy Bracewell much to Phil's relief.

Robin had come out of the coma but his brain remained useless. He couldn't talk, recognize anyone or care for himself in any way. He was a vegetable. His long suffering wife looked after him. She sold the business and with some help from his father managed to get by. Barry was out of jail on parole for good behavior, a murder charge now out of the question.

Delbert spent a teary evening with the Cairns family. No one had heard from Sylvia. By now she might be nearly through the novice period. He related what Mother Agnes told him. There was no relief in sight for the sadness they all felt. When he left, he drove down to Rainbow Beach and walked to the log they sat on. He watched the sun sink down in the west like they did together. His heart ached, tears flowed. Drained, he drove home.

It was too hard to stay on the island so he returned to Vancouver the next day. Virginia was invited over for dinner since she would leave for Nelson in the morning. Now adept at reading Delbert's moods, she could tell the island visit had been traumatic. It's not going to change, she thought. I've got to move on without him. What a shame for both of us.

Before the evening ended they managed to cheer Delbert up and it broke up on a happy note. Charlie drove Virginia back to the dorm.

"It's become pretty clear to me that Delbert isn't going to look beyond Sylvia for companionship. I can't wait for him to change."

"He's a fool," Charlie replied.

"You're a good friend, Charlie, to him and to me." She placed her hand on his arm. He felt a warm glow.

At the door, he said, "Have a good summer, Virginia."

"You too Charlie. See you in the Fall." Cupping his head in her hands, she kissed him quickly and turned to go inside. Damn, he thought on the way back to his car, I feel guilty but I hope he doesn't change any time soon.

CHAPTER FORTY

Within three days, Delbert was back at Malton and immersed in Air Force life. Bentwing insisted he spend two weeks in refresher training and drills before he joined the Avro team.

"You'll have to go through survival training later this summer so stay in shape."

The Avro engineers were glad to see him. They discussed the material he sent and he became familiar with current design releases. Most of the mechanical design was complete and fabrication of various subassemblies already underway. It fascinated him to see drawings transformed into hardware.

He was surprised to find the hole for the Iroquois was wider than before. They told him the engine team had come up with a way to increase thrust by blowing extra air along the outside of the engine. They didn't know why he grinned.

Delbert settled into a routine of running in the morning and exercise at the base gym each evening. In between, he spent the bulk of his time with engineers. Other flight test pilots preferred to work on cockpit and flight control design issues, which left the more complex systems to him. He was gratified to see his influence reflected in the final design.

He was particularly intrigued with the new military digital computers in the airplane. More powerful than a room full of computer back at UBC, they fit into a two cubic foot box. They were programmed with a very primitive language and the code had to be extremely efficient because their memory was so limited.

Computer code was to Delbert what catnip is to a cat. He couldn't stay away from it and soon proved as competent as the vendor's programmers. They were irritated when he suggested ways to streamline code but the suggestions were too valuable to ignore.

It was impossible to determine if the computer could complete a pass through the code fast enough for real-time control since the lab computers were all far slower. Delbert came up with a technique where computer performance could be evaluated on the slow computers by putting a time tag on each instruction. Then the airplane program could be run on the slow computer at its pace and the times added up to determine how long the airplane computer would take to do the same job.

~~~

Survival training interrupted his work for two weeks in August. He came back sunburned and thinner than when he left.

"What do maggots and beetles taste like?" became a frequent question.

"Don't knock them until you try them," said with an involuntary gag at the thought.

By September, his contribution to the computer design wrapped up and the first airplane neared completion. He gazed at it lovingly. It's even bigger and more beautiful than I pictured, he thought. He hated to go back to school when the airplane would roll out, go through ground tests and fly before he returned.

CHAPTER FORTY-ONE

With Dean Calder's help he put together a course schedule which allowed him to complete his degree requirements in the upcoming year. It was a heavy load.

Pillage's Dawn Patrol swung into action once more and quickly proved as popular as last year. Although still friendly, Delbert detected a change in Virginia's demeanor towards him. She had moved on to other romantic possibilities. He could only blame himself and knew that the situation wouldn't change until closure with Sylvia could be reached.

Surprisingly, she moved towards Charlie to Charlie's obvious delight. The situation came to a head a week later when Charlie hesitatingly asked if he could date her.

"Wondered when you would come out of the closet. Of course. You're my two best friends and I hope something wonderful comes of it."

"You're a great friend, Del."

"Keep in mind Charlie, you better treat her right or she'll slap you silly." The conversation ended on that light note.

He has a great heart, thought Charlie, big and broken.

~~~

Mike called in October, "Hey hotshot, where's your new scanner design?"

"Sorry, Mike, I've been buried in class-work. I put together some concept sketches if you want to see them?"

"Beats marking student papers. Bring them by. I'm free after three tomorrow."

Damn, thought Delbert, they're crude. He'll be disappointed. He worked most of the night to clean them up.

Mike commented, "reminds me of one of those presses used by dry cleaners."

"Well, it does have to press the page flat and block out the light."

"Don't get sensitive on me, kid. Actually, I like it. Looks like the big challenges will be to get a thin enough light beam and direct it precisely."

"Right. If it was an electron beam we could bend it with magnets but light doesn't bend. For the speeds we want, the moving part has to weigh almost nothing. I think we need to slide the light assembly from side to side and up and down the page. To actually scan each character, it might be possible to rotate a lens instead of the whole light assembly. That's as far as I've gone with it."

"Fair enough. It's a start. Not sure what you'll do with the scanned signal. Seems like it will be a small version of a television signal."

"Guess you could say that. It'll take a high speed digital computer to analyze the signal and figure out what character it represents."

"Can't help but think that kind of computer is a long way in the future."

"Perhaps not as far as you think. I've seen some amazing military computers. Civil applications usually follow close behind."

"OK, so let's sum up. You'll work on the scanner and if you can provide an analog signal of each typed character, that will be success. Conversion to a character or word by a digital computer of the future will be a follow-on project."

"Sure, that bounds it."

~~~

The school year settled into a routine. Run in the morning, classes and soccer during the day, project in the evening or at least some evenings. Charlie and Virginia saw a lot of each other, however, they still dragged Delbert out whenever possible. They never gave up on introduction to new girls, in hopes one of them would seduce him into a replacement for what had now become his imaginary romance.

When Dan invited him to go flying, usually on weekends, he couldn't resist. For each of them, the cares of the daily grind melted away as they climbed out of Vancouver. While different than a father/son relationship, the camaraderie between pilots caused a bond of similar strength. They explored the mountains and inlets along the coast, never tired of the unsurpassed beauty.

Delbert introduced Dan to some acrobatics that at first left him concerned for his airplane. Delbert assured him he wouldn't do anything which might damage it. Dan tried to believe him and in time actually did. Both returned to Vancouver exhilarated and refreshed with a clear mind to start the next week.

Once a month Delbert flew to Comox for a weekend with jets. He was now proficient in all of their fighters and continued to show up the full time pilots. Those that had flown with him before knew better than to challenge his skills and they now enjoyed watching newcomers put in their place.

He went home for Christmas but couldn't stand to stay on the island for more than two days. He worked on the scanner design most of the Christmas holidays. The movable lens assembly had to hold the light sensor as well to keep it positioned to collect reflected light. Even then, it looked like a curved mirror would be needed to capture the reflected light.

From tests he had done on a lens mockup, it looked as if light could be focused into a thin enough beam. He designed the lens and sensor assembly to rotate with a rocker action, driven by electromagnets to give it the necessary speed with a minimum of parts subject to wear. This assembly, together with the light source, was mounted on a track running across the page. An electric motor on one end moved it. The whole assembly was mounted on tracks running up and down the page, driven by an electric motor at the back. The bottom plate consisted of two pieces, mounted on springs to accommodate different page heights on each side. The front and sides of the housing slid over the back plate to hold the book surface flat.

In January he showed the design to Mike. After a few minor modifications, they gave it to the fourth year mechanical engineering class to build. Delbert then moved on to the circuitry needed to control the electric motors and electromagnets.

His search strategy was to move the sensor assembly to the middle of the page and zigzag back and forth as it moved down the page until a line was detected. Then, with vertical motion stopped, move to the left edge and begin a scan to the right until the first character was detected. But as he thought about it, the amount of motor activity bothered him.

It would be a reliability problem. Better to use a rocker design for the zigzag movement. Wait a minute. What if we rotated the rocker assembly ninety degrees during the line search phase? That would speed up the search and minimize motor activity.

He worked most of the night to redesign the rocker assembly to allow the ninety degree rotation. It proved more complicated than he first thought so next morning he called Mike and asked to put a hold on construction of the rocker assembly. It had to be as light as possible to allow quick rotation and yet be sturdy enough to handle the shock of stopping at each end.

A week later he had an all new design for Mike. "They better call in the dentists for this one."

Mike laughed. "Let them eat filings."

Increased mechanical complexity at least simplified search circuitry. He incorporated an adjustable speed control in the rocker control circuit since they didn't know how fast it could be rocked. In fact, all circuits contained adjustment flexibility. He passed the designs to Mike for his scrutiny. Mike suggested some modifications, then had the circuits built in the electronics lab.

"Damn it Delbert, I don't know how you come up with these complicated designs so fast?"

"Superior education by my professors."

Mike reflected on how Delbert's self-confidence had grown in the last two years.

"Hell, you haven't attended enough classes for any professor to take credit. If anyone asks me, I'll tell them you got your degree through correspondence courses."

~~~

It took a month and a half to build the first unit. They put it all together on a lab bench. Then gingerly applied power.

"Well, we didn't fry it."

They ran the assembly from side to side and up and down the imaginary page. It looked OK. Next they set the rocker assembly in motion, slowly at first. When that worked, they increased speed until it became a blur. Still no failure. They rotated it back and forth between search and scan position.

"The mechanical design seems to work Delbert. That's a success in itself."

"Let's see if the light beam and sensor work."

They put a small mirror where the paper would be and turned the beam on. The reflection missed the sensor but the curved mirror behind it redirected enough light to activate it. Then, they tried it with a piece of white paper. It still produced a signal.

"We need to adjust the sensor location but let's run a black line through the beam anyway."

They slowly slid a piece of paper with a single line drawn across it under the beam. There was a dip in the output signal when the line crossed the beam.

"That works but it may be quite different with the rocker assembly in motion. Want to try it with a typed page?"

"Sure. Let's back the speed off and go for it."

They put a page on the plate, lowered the scanner onto it and turned the power on. The scanning unit moved to the top center of the page and began down with the rocker vibrating horizontally. Suddenly it stopped and slid to the left edge. The rocker rotated ninety degrees and began moving right. When it reached the right edge, it slid back to the left margin, rotated ninety degrees and started down again. They watched it repeat this process down the page. The grins on their faces expanded with each new line.

"Even at this speed it works faster than the Braille scanner. Obviously it senses typed characters. The big question is whether or not there's enough resolution."

The next step was to hook the output to the cathode ray tube. The vertical signal was driven from the rocker position. The horizontal signal was set up to scroll at the speed of the scanner's horizontal movement. The sensor circuit put out an off/on signal which would be off normally and switch on when there was a dip in sensor signal.

The moment of truth arrived. They started to rescan the same page. When it reached the first character, a somewhat blurred version of it appeared on the screen as it moved across the line. Mike slapped Delbert on the back. Delbert simply stared at the display in an effort to figure out what caused the fuzziness.

"Lighten up Delbert! It works! Better than I would have thought possible."

"You're right. And I'm excited. There's a lot of refinement needed but it works."

~~~

Anticipation of flying the Arrow made the year drag on. Even a heavy workload didn't take his mind off it. By final exam time, he and Mike had refined the scanner resolution so that it could clearly distinguish characters and punctuation. The scan speed reached a level sufficient to support verbalized words at a pace consistent with reading out loud. A massive leap was still needed to convert the signal to spoken words. Still it met all objectives of the defined project. They co-authored a paper that described the scanner and its performance.

~~~

Finally, exams finished and Delbert graduated with honours. He had one last meeting with Dean Calder.

"Well son, you did us proud in four short years. Hal Lundquist's faith in you was well placed. High grades even while skipping a year, two if you count high school. Pioneer work on the scanners, your contribution to the jet engine design and who knows how much you contributed to that development program back east. A very productive four years."

"Thank you Sir."

"There's one area I had hoped you would delve further into; namely, your thinking about the physics of matter and energy. You said once you thought the mathematics might give physicists a direction to pursue in their search for unknown forces."

"So far it's proved too elusive. If I come up with anything, I'll send it to you."

"Fine. I'll look forward to that. Good luck with your project back east. Please drop in when you're in town and bring me up to speed on your life."

"I will Sir. Thank you again for all you've done. You transformed my life."

Saying goodbye to the Martins proved harder. They held a bon voyage dinner, as Dan called it. Teary eyed by the end of the evening, promises were made all around to stay in touch. Delbert was not to spend a night in Vancouver unless under their roof.

~~~

The next day Delbert took his diploma home to his parents. Phil put his arm around Delbert. "Son, you've made us very proud. Wally's bin keepin' us up to speed on what you bin doin'. All those early years, I spent worryin' fer nothin' about you. Yer a man to be reckoned with."

"Thanks, Dad. That means a lot to me."

Ready to leave for Toronto the next morning, Teresa gave him a hug. "Please be very careful with those airplanes, dear."

"I will Mum."

He agonized over Sylvia. How I wish she were here to share in this success. We could be married or at least engaged by now. What's she doing? Is she happy? Why won't they let me talk to her?

CHAPTER FORTY-TWO

In March, Jan Rakowski flew the Arrow for the first time. Subsequent flights proved the unique new fly-by-wire control system performed as advertised. By the time Delbert arrived back on the scene the speed/altitude envelope was expanding. Peter Copel brought him up to speed on progress.

"It's an absolute joy to fly, Delbert. I've never experienced anything like it. You and the engineers did a magnificent job on those control laws. Looks like it's good for Mach 1.5 with the Pratt engines, can't wait to see what it will do with the Iroquois."

"That's exciting! Hope Jan will give me a shot at taking it up."

"The only real concern is the weapons situation. They call for advanced weapons that haven't been built, let alone tested. When those programs get cancelled, they move on to something else. At least we've got the modular weapons bay design so they don't force changes on the aeroplane."

"Why don't they start with something proven and upgrade when these other systems are ready."

"That would be too logical, Delbert, old boy."

Jan was as enthusiastic about the airplane as Peter.

"You better spend some time in the simulator to get a feel for how it handles. Get up to speed on how we use the second pilot position. When you're ready, I'll take you up for a ride."

That's all it took for Delbert to rack up simulator time as fast as possible. When the simulator was unavailable he poured over flight test procedures and notes. His feedback to Jan brought a smile.

"OK kid, we go up together on Thursday."

Visibility from the back was severely limited with only two small side windows. Still, the airplane thrilled him, bigger than any fighter he'd been in yet far more agile than the Canuck. He longed for a chance to move into the front seat. In the meantime, he performed his back seat duties conscientiously.

His chance came a month later. By that time, he had logged more hours in the simulator than anyone else and was intimately familiar with every system on the airplane.

"Well kid, we'll fly together again on Tuesday. This time I'll take the back seat just to see you don't do anything stupid. Make sure you get the test program memorized."

"Thanks, Jan, I won't let you down."

"If I thought you would, you'd still be in the back seat."

Control of the big jet as it leaped into the sky was a thrill that eclipsed everything before. As usual, Delbert soon mated with the airplane, learned its quirks and nuances, dealt with them automatically. Mission requirements were filled so quickly and smoothly it left the crusty old pilot in back smiling to himself.

From then on, Delbert took his turn in the pilot rotation. Although the temporary Pratt engines wouldn't let them reach the Mach 2.5 region for which the airplane was designed, they had pushed it beyond the Mach 1.5 expected with these engines. In fact, they reached Mach 1.9 with no problems encountered. Rumors swirled about the program's future.

"The farmer we elected Prime Minister and his boys can't begin to understand the importance of this program to Canadian industry. They only see that it costs too much and they've been led to believe the Bomarc missile can better intercept Russian bombers."

"Have they even looked at it," Delbert asked. "It has only a few hundred miles range, if it gets off the ground in the first place. We'd need missile sites every six hundred miles all the way across the north. Besides there's no substitute for a pilot to make sure the threat is real and not some poor airliner off course."

"We know all that but they don't. It won't surprise me if they stupidly cancel the program."

"There will always be a need for a high performance fighter. Soviet bombers aren't the only threat in the world. It'll be years before the U.S. or anyone else builds a plane that matches the Arrow."

~~~~

The flight test pace over the winter months left Delbert with time on his hands, especially in the evening. He dedicated some surplus time to a more strenuous exercise program in the gym. Still, he realized other interests and activities would have to be pursued in this phase of the project. He couldn't wait for the Mark 2 Arrow with the new Iroquois engines to enter flight test. Flight frequency would escalate with their appearance.

CHAPTER FORTY-THREE

Then, on Tuesday, February 18th Bentwing summoned Delbert to his office.

"Come in son. Close the door and sit down."

"What's up Bentwing. You're not taking me off the Arrow, are you?"

Bentwing ignored the question. "You must have heard the rumors about cancelling the program."

"They can't be serious. There's always a need for a top of the line fighter. And surely they know what would happen to our technological capability."

"You and I know that, Delbert. The farmer from Prince Albert has no clue. If we built a titanium tractor, we'd stand a chance. But that's off the point. Can I get your word that what we're about to discuss will never be mentioned with another human being?"

"Sure Bentwing. I understand classified data."

"This goes beyond classified, son. You know what will happen if they cancel the program?"

"Guess they'll shut it down and go look for other funds."

"No. They'll bulldoze the airplanes. Scrap them totally. Destroy the tools and all the data."

"Are you serious?" All of a sudden his stomach knotted. "They couldn't. How could they?"

"They can and they will. There's concern the technology might get lifted by the Soviets. It's not good enough for us or the Yanks but it's too good to let out. Shit, I hate it as much as you do."

Delbert was shocked into silence. Bentwing continued.

"Someone up the line, who I won't name, wants to save one of those birds. I've been told to put together a plan to do that and I have. But to make it work I need you."

"Anything Bentwing."

"Not so fast. First, as I said before, you have to take the secret with you to the grave. No mention of what we're up to even in your old age."

"I will Sir."

"I'll let that go this time, son, only because it's such a grave issue. A little formality is appropriate. Here's the plan. I call it Operation Sleeping Beauty. As you know, everyone is familiar with the Arrows currently in flight status so they will obviously be accounted for in the destruction.

"There's less awareness about those still in the factory although they probably feel they aren't going anywhere. The first Mark 2 bird is ready even though it hasn't been rolled out. No one will expect it to fly without a lot of ground test, what with new unproven engines and all.

"Our only chance is to take that bird right out of the factory into the air. I've got an insider ready to move the airplanes behind it up a slot and change the markings. It will take significant effort to find the gap back in the production line. With the trauma of bulldozer destruction, detection of a missing airplane is unlikely.

"Bottom line, we need someone to take that airplane on its first flight with new untested engines. Someone in the Air Force, no civilian pilot can be involved. We can't protect a civilian like we can a pilot in the service. See where I'm headed?"

"I'll do it Bentwing."

"Hold on. Think it over. There's high risk involved. No way can I order it. You've got to weigh both sides and decide if you want to do it. Certainly wouldn't blame you if you decide it's too risky. I wouldn't take it on."

"I've thought it over and I'll do it."

"You're always a quick thinker, son. If you're sure, here's my plan. Tomorrow morning you show up at 0445 in flight gear. The airplane will be rolled out before daylight, fully fueled. A trusted mechanic will be with it to start engines. You immediately taxi onto the runway and take off to the south no matter what wind direction exists. Wheels up at 0500. Use just enough thrust to get off the runway and fly out over the lake below 500 feet.

"Stay under 500 until you're out of the terminal area radar coverage. About thirty miles out turn to a heading that will take you to this airport," he said, pointing to it on the air navigation map on his desk.

"When you think you're in the best position to avoid radar detection, hit the power and take it as high as you can. Fly to the destination and then spiral down using as little thrust as possible and land to the north at 0600.

"Let it roll out and make the turn onto the first revetment ramp on the right. Control your speed and roll down the ramp nose in. When you're inside the bunker, shut her down and close the doors on your way out. There's a switch on the inside just right of the opening. Walk up the ramp and I'll be there in a Silver Star to pick you up and bring you back for breakfast.

"We've got bulldozers and trucks scheduled to break up and fill in the ramp tomorrow. They'll churn up a big rectangle so the scar in the Spring won't look like a revetment."

"Perhaps you should plant wheat on it. He couldn't bring himself to tear that up." That brought a snort.

"We'll count on two things. They don't realize there's a plane missing and even if they do, don't expect it to be hidden there. It's very risky. You'll take off and land with no radio communication. No one knows how these engines will hold up. Gotta ask you again, you sure you want to do it?"

"It's well worth the risk Bentwing."

"OK...God speed son."

~~~

Delbert arrived on schedule the next morning. The mechanic told him to wave when he was ready to crank the first engine. Delbert climbed in, turned on the panel lights and waved to the mechanic. Within seconds the first engine began to crank. He didn't know exactly what rpm was needed for ignition with the new engines so he let it crank longer than usual. When he introduced fuel and ignition, it caught and kept accelerating. As soon as it stabilized at idle, he opened the cross-feed valves to crank the second engine. At the same time, he released brakes and started a roll towards the runway. The second engine was up to idle as he turned onto the runway so he advanced thrust to accelerate the airplane.

It bothered him to be on the runway without a clearance but all was quiet as dawn was about to break. He could see well enough without lights. Even with modest thrust, the jet accelerated nicely. He balanced speed with runway left to lift off at the far end, climbed to 500 feet, pulled back the thrust and leveled off. Once over the lake, he eased the airplane down to 200 feet and increased speed to 300 knots.

He had the radio tuned to tower frequency to listen for anything that would indicate he had been spotted. There was only silence. He wondered if Bentwing had greased that part of it as well. About twenty miles out, he began a slow turn toward his destination. When it looked like he was in a good place to climb out, he advanced the throttles to maximum thrust, pulled the nose up and hit the afterburners.

The Arrow pushed him back into his seat and shot straight up at a rate he'd never seen before. This is what you were born to do! And you know it too. Like a racehorse's first step on the track. You're magnificent! Way better than they led us to believe!

In less than five minutes he shot through sixty thousand feet and began to level off. At close to sixty-five thousand feet, he was level and accelerating still with afterburners on. The speed went through Mach 2 within a minute, then Mach 2.2, 2.4, 2.5, ... 2.6 and he switched off the afterburners. He made a gentle turn to the right, then back to the left with a steeper turn. Everything was smooth so he cranked it into a sharp turn to the right and slammed it back to the left. Wonderful!

~~~

A traffic controller on the American side of the border stared at his radar display. He turned to a co-worker.

"Ben, you see that?"

"See what?"

"That bogey. It shot straight up out of the lake, leveled off at something over fifty thousand and took off faster than any plane I've ever seen. Think it might have been a rocket?"

"Out of the lake, c'mon Sam, you're seeing things. You've stared at that thing too long. Take a break."

"No Ben, it was real. Maybe it was a UFO."

"Don't go there Sam. They'll make you think you're loonie and bury you in paperwork. Just forget you saw anything."

"Maybe you're right—but between you and me, I did see it."

~~~

Delbert slowed down as he approached the airport and began to circle at sixty thousand feet. At five thirty-five he started to spiral down with engines at idle. To get down in time, he pushed the nose down and let the speed build up. As he dropped through ten thousand feet, he pulled the nose up to slow the rate of descent and speed. At a thousand feet, he leveled off and put the jet into a downwind leg. Judging speed, altitude and distance to the runway, he turned to a short base leg, then inbound to the runway and touchdown, still with the engines at idle. No one in the neighbourhood heard him.

He let the jet roll out toward the far end of the runway, turned off on the rightmost revetment ramp. He rolled through the bunker doors, braked to a stop, cut the engines, opened the canopy, then shut down all power. Once out, he manually closed the canopy, patted it and whispered, "sleep well, you beauty."

At the door, he turned and took one last, glassy-eyed look at the Arrow. Then he turned and pressed the button that cranked the doors shut. Half way up the ramp he looked back to make sure they had closed, then continued up. About the time he reached runway level he spotted Bentwing rolling toward him. Bentwing turned by the ramp with the aft canopy open. Delbert climbed in and Bentwing was already taxiing back to the takeoff end.

"Set?" came over the intercom.

"Set"

Bentwing requested and received takeoff clearance from the tower and within minutes they were airborne on their way back to Malton by a circuitous route.

Over breakfast, Bentwing asked, "How high?"

"Sixty-five."

"How fast?"

"Two point six."

"Control?"

"Flawless."

Bentwing sighed and shook his head.

~~~

Word came down the next day. The program's cancelled. No more flights. Lock up the factory. Mounties were stationed onsite to secure everything. Within days, bulldozers and cutters attacked the airplanes on the ramp and in the factory, reducing them to scrap. Jigs were cut up. Parts and sub-assemblies bulldozed onto the scrap pile. Drawings and documents destroyed.

The first day Delbert watched for a while. It felt like murder. He stood next to a young Mountie with a glum look on his face.

"What a tragedy," Delbert muttered.

"Yes Sir," the Mountie responded, "this is the toughest assignment I've ever had. Rather walk up to a sociopathic killer with a shotgun than watch this."

"You're too young to wish that."

The Mountie glanced at Delbert, "How were you involved with this airplane?"

"I flew it."

"You look too young to be a pilot."

"I'm a lot older now."

"Yeah, I know what you mean. Was it as good as they say?"

"Better."

"Hear about fourteen thousand employees here at Avro will be out of work."

"That's the tip of the iceberg. The whole aviation and electronics industry in Canada will go down the tube. All our top technical people will be gone to Europe or the States within months. Aeronautical and electronic engineers coming out of universities will be gone too or work out of their field. It'll take years to recover, if ever."

"Shit! ...If you'll pardon the expression Sir."

"My feelings exactly."

CHAPTER FORTY-FOUR

There was a round of sad farewells, in no way could they be called parties. NACA hired a lot of the top technical engineers to work on American space programs. Others went to aerospace companies, like Peter Copel who headed to Boeing in Seattle.

Peter asked Delbert what he planned to do.

"I have three more years committed to the Air Force. After that, I don't know."

"Well, I'm fed up with the capricious nature of military aviation. Boeing offered me a desk job on the commercial side and I've accepted it."

"Won't you miss flying?"

"I dare say but I'm no longer a young pup like you. I can put it aside."

"Please let me know how to reach you once you're settled in. If you don't mind, I would like to touch base with you once in a while to see how things are going."

"That would be wonderful. You're the brightest young lad I've ever encountered. I surely hope they find a way to put that brilliance to good use."

"Thanks Peter."

~~~

Naturally, the media had a field day with the Arrow demise. Any number of stories to be told and most were. Pilots were especially sought out since they could attest to the airplane's performance. Rumors had been spread that it really didn't live up to expectations so it shouldn't be missed.

Before long, Delbert was the only test pilot left in the Toronto area. He rejected most interview requests on the basis that he was in the Air Force and therefore not at liberty to be interviewed. With Bentwing's permission, he did issue a statement that the airplane actually performed better than expected during flight test. Suggestions to the contrary were untrue.

The few reporters who did get to meet him were shocked by his youth. This prompted one to dig further into his time at UBC and in the Air Force. Bentwing allowed him to interview Delbert as long as he stayed away from the controversial Arrow topics.

"Are you sure you want me to do this, Bentwing?"

"Sure son, it would be good for the Air Force image. Maybe help us recruit better people."

So the interview occurred, along with some picture taking. A month later, Bentwing called him into his office.

"Got an advance copy of this month's Macleans magazine for you. Take a look."

His picture was on the cover. The caption read "Air Force's Boy Flying Genius". He looked at Bentwing who grinned from ear to ear.

"Go on, read the story. I wanted publicity. I got publicity."

The story reviewed his rapid passage through university and his meteoric rise in the Air Force's flight ranks to the test roll on the Arrow at an unheard of young age. It mentioned his scanner inventions and his role in the Pillage Dawn Patrol. An Orenda engineer disclosed that his contribution to the Iroquois design was significant and so complex no one else understood it fully.

Much of his interview material was included, particularly that related to technology. He made the point that with the world over-populated and starvation rampant, the only alternative to humane population control through education was to bring technology to bear on food production.

In his words, "Technology will become the yardstick to measure a country's position in the world. And the backbones of a dominant technology are education and industrial opportunity." One could easily read into that a condemnation of the Arrow cancellation.

He continued, "Technology grows exponentially because inventions feed on one another. Some people worry that technology might run amok, almost turn into a religion. I agree to the extent that we should be concerned that cultural maturity keep pace with any technology explosion. On the one hand, failure could expose us to the very thing that happened in Germany and on the other, it could lead to crass materialism, greed and loss of moral fiber. We must hold parents, schools and media accountable to achieve a balance."

The article concluded with an accolade on Delbert's brilliance, common sense and maturity far beyond his years.

"You're famous, Delbert. A million girls will write the magazine to find out if you're single and how to get in touch with you. We may have to station you in Port Churchill to protect you from them."

"Very funny. The real question is what do I do next?"

"That is a real question, son."

CHAPTER FORTY-FIVE

If Delbert worried about how to fill his days before, it was nothing compared to now. No airplane to test depressed him, made worse by thoughts of what might be happening with an Arrow program. In an effort to keep him busy, Bentwing told him to put together a training course based on the dogfight maneuvers he had come up with before the Arrow program.

"I want you to create a series of sessions for our students to go through after they've finished normal training. It's not just a matter of a few maneuvers. I want you to build their skills to a level which makes these maneuvers flyable and safe, at least in peacetime."

"The first thing they should do is take a muscle building program so they can horse the Canuck around. It's like flying a concrete block after the Arrow."

"There is no Arrow, son. Move on."

"That's the second time I've been told to move on from something I love. OK, I hear you. Do you want to be my first student through this course?"

"Hell no! It'd kill me for sure."

Delbert found it hard to define what Bentwing expected. Most of his simulated dogfight maneuvers were instinctual rather than planned or thought out. Gradually, he pieced together a curriculum. It turned into a conditioning course designed to get pilots comfortable with flight on or beyond the edge of published airplane design limits. Once they mastered that the maneuvers became easy.

Fewer than half the students could handle his course. Those that could became known as Pillagers, they were at the top rung of the jet jockey ladder. Every new student aspired to join their ranks. It was exactly what Bentwing wanted. To reinforce this status, he created a special insignia for their uniforms. It was a front view of a small fighter with one wing higher than the other. Delbert didn't think that was nearly as funny as he did.

~~~

In his spare time, Delbert decided to develop a computer program to translate scanner signals into letters and maybe even words. He started by assuming each letter scanned would be translated into an array of dots in digital memory. His code would analyze the dot pattern to identify letters and punctuation. For simplicity, he would generate the same tones the first scanner used. For punctuation, he took a page from Victor Borge's repertoire, though he kept the sounds more compact than the exaggerated, spit inducing version Victor loved to employ.

He programmed it to collect letters until a complete word was identified. When he reflected on the difficulty of generating spoken words, a good interim solution dawned on him. He could use the original scanner sounds to generate words if he lumped them together. For example, to generate the word "cat" he would play the "c", "a" and "t" sounds in rapid succession. Since people had learned the "music of the letters", they could expand their ability to handle the "music of the letters and words".

No longer would they have to wait years for someone to invent a voice synthesizer. Now the digital computer need only be used to store and interpret dot patterns. He began to wonder if there was a way around that too.

Perhaps I could design a processor to do just that task, sort of a subset of a digital computer. Over the next two months he researched digital memory devices and processors. It became apparent that a ferrite core memory was his best bet.

It was time to bring Mike into the picture. He described his thoughts in a letter and asked Mike if the university could get their hands on a ferrite core memory. He estimated how much memory would be needed to store the data and interpretation program. He said he would work on the rest of the circuitry if Mike could find the memory.

A week later he received a reply. The Physics department had a ferrite core memory. It was big enough, however, they were not about to give it away. They would share it long enough to try the scanner design provided they controlled the schedule. He promised to mail design data for the memory within a week.

Delbert's Air Force duties stretched out the design process. However, within three weeks he designed circuits to convert the sensor signal into a dot pattern stored in memory. He allotted enough memory to hold three letters. That would give enough time to analyze the first before writing over it, sort of like a wave action.

Next, he wrote a program using the military computer language to perform both the memory scan and character recognition. It required only a small subset of the instructions available. From his research, he thought he could design a partial digital computer using transistors. Even with a limited instruction set it would be a complicated and lengthy project.

~~~

Charlie and Virginia graduated this year. Delbert asked for leave to attend the graduation ceremony and bring Mike up to speed on his progress. Bentwing went him one better.

"We'll fly you out and when your leave is over, report to Comox and introduce them to your Pillager program. I'll let them know when you'll arrive and stress the importance of the course."

"OK, I need about two weeks leave for what I want to do."

"You got it." Bentwing appreciated that there had been no mention of the Arrow in over two months.

CHAPTER FORTY-SIX

It was like home-coming week when Delbert showed up at the Martin's. A lot to catch up on. Delbert told Dan that the Iroquois engine was even better than expected. Charlie took the first opportunity he could to get Delbert aside.

"Del, hope you're not annoyed but I proposed to Virginia last week and she accepted. We plan to get married in October."

"Annoyed? That's great! My two best friends in the same house. What more could anyone ask? You two seemed to hit it off right from the start—literally. I'm real happy for both of you!"

"Happy enough to be my best man?"

"Are you sure? I'd love to be your best man. It would be an honour. You did so much to help me transition from country kid to more or less informed adult, you'll always be my best friend and I'll always be indebted to you."

"Don't get maudlin on me, Del. I've learned more from you about how to live one's life than you'll ever know. And we've had some damn good times together over the years."

"True."

When Virginia showed up the next evening, she and Delbert hugged.

"Congratulations Virginia, I won't say good luck as the custom dictates. You two don't need luck to make a happy marriage."

"Thanks. You'll always be our best friend."

~~~

The next day, Delbert met with Mike.

"Don't fly off the handle and tell me I'm nuts. I have a concept design which might get us a reader without waiting for digital computers."

"Why doesn't that surprise me?"

"We need that ferrite core memory. I've designed circuitry to convert the scans into a dot array in memory. The next step is to design a digital processor that behaves like a digital computer but is much simpler. I've figured out what instructions we need and have a decent feel for what's involved. It's complicated though and it'll take a number of months to design."

"A few months to design a digital computer?"

"What excites me is an alternative to a synthesized voice. We can use the same sounds used in the original scanner but with a key difference."

"What do you mean?"

"Well, you know how we learn to recognize words by their sound when we're infants?"

"Sure. So?"

"Well, I don't think blind people need to have words spelled out letter by letter. We can give them sounds which represent words instead of letters."

"Delbert, you would need a hundred thousand different sounds."

"No. What we can do is use the letter sounds but run them together to make words. That way the sounds are distinctive."

Mike thought for a moment. "That's brilliant! Let me see the circuit diagrams you've got so far."

After about ten minutes, Mike sighed, "Delbert, you've reached a level of sophistication that makes my review redundant. Do you mind if I get them built and try it out with the scanner?"

"Great. I'm at the Martin's for another week and a half if you have any questions."

"Won't get far with it in a week and a half. I've got a ton of exam papers to mark in the next week or so. Wouldn't like to help out in your spare time, would you?"

"No thanks."

~~~

The two weeks went fast. Pillage's Dawn Patrol still existed but participation was down from the year before. Charlie expected it to die out within a year or two. Still, it caused a stir when Delbert showed up the first morning back and word spread through their ranks that he was the original Pillage.

The graduation ceremony was too big and cumbersome to enjoy. Parties afterwards were a different matter and seeing old classmates was fun. They wanted to know what he was up to and could hardly believe he actually flew the Avro Arrow.

~~~

The Comox base commander turned out to be an offi-cious type sporting a moustache and pipe in an effort to look like a World War II ace.

"Come in Pillage. Sit down. Care for a whiskey?"

"No thank you Sir."

"You flew the Arrow? How was it?"

"It was a great airplane Sir."

"There's a rumor going around that one was hidden somewhere. Know anything about that?"

"Looked to me like they destroyed everything in sight Sir. It was horrible to watch."

"Daresay, daresay...well, old Bentwing says you can teach our boys a thing or two about flying that they don't already know. Bit skeptical myself. We've got a skilled team here. But for Bentwing's sake we'll give you a chance to show your stuff. Want you to go up against one of our best boys. My wing commander will ride in your rear seat and report back to me on how it goes."

"Yes Sir."

"Dismissed."

"Yes Sir."

Delbert left wishing the pompous old fool had decided to ride with him instead. Guess he's too smart for that.

~~~

They took off mid-morning. It was set up like a wrestling match, with one person on the other's tail and the object was to break free of the trailing plane. For the first test, Delbert was in the rear position. It was child's play for him to stick with the other airplane no matter what maneuver was tried. In fact, he flew so close the wing commander squirmed in his seat. When it became obvious the lead airplane would never break free, the wing commander stopped the exercise and called for them to reverse positions.

Delbert performed a couple of simple evasive maneuvers to start with, then suddenly pulled his jet up into sharp turning climb until it stalled, kicked it into a spin, pulled it out behind the other airplane and closed fast with afterburner blasting.

"Holy Christ man, are you trying to get us killed?"

"No Sir, the airplane's good for a lot more than that. It's a matter of knowing exactly what these things can do, rather than what the manuals claim they can do."

"We'll try one more. This time don't stall the airplane."

"If you say so, Sir. We'll pull quite a few g's Sir. Will you be able to handle that Sir?"

"Of course."

This time Delbert pushed the nose down with the airplane in a sharp turn, then hit the afterburner and pulled up into a tight loop, tighter than the other pilot was able to fly. As he came into the inverted position, Delbert banked to ninety degrees and pulled the airplane into a tighter turn than the wing commander ever dreamed of flying. The other pilot gamely tried to bring his airplane around but Delbert was now inside his turn and soon on his tail again.

In spite of his fading vision, the wing commander knew he had seen enough. "Take us home."

The next day, Bentwing got a call from the base commander.

"Is this some kind of joke, Bentwing? That kid's a maniac. Damn near pranged his jet with my wing commander on board."

"You decided to test him, didn't you Harry? Wouldn't take my word for the value his methods bring. I know Pillage. Your wing commander's precious ass was safe the whole time. His course will make your best pilots capable of doing what he probably showed your guys."

"Don't think we need that kind of madness."

"You do if you want to keep up with the other squadrons across the country. Unless you want to become the old folks home for flyboys."

"That's a cheap shot, Bentwing, we can hold our heads up with the best of them."

"Not any more, Harry. Look, you probably saw the final product demonstrated. Let him work with some of your pilots. He'll bring them along gradually and there won't be any danger involved. Then, let's see where you stand."

"Well, we'll give it a shot but I'll monitor it closely."

"Great, you'll see the advantage first hand."

Delbert spent the next four weeks with four of their best pilots. Per his recommendation, each was given the option to drop out after the second and third weeks. None did. Within two weeks they realized they were onto something special. After four weeks, they were Pillagers with the insignia to prove it. Other pilots requested the course. A humbler base commander called Bentwing.

"Say, Bentwing, have to eat a little crow here. Your boy's been quite a hit with my pilots. Seems a bunch more want to go through that class. Won't stand in the way of a man who wants to improve his skills. What say we keep young Pillage on for another class?"

Bentwing refrained from an "I told you so" and merely said, "Sure Harry. Have Pillage call me when he's done. Oh, by the way, don't be alarmed if some of the pilots wash out.

Not all our pilots can master this kind of thing. In a way, that's good because it gives a measure of prestige to the successful ones."

Delbert didn't mind another month in Comox. Evenings spent on the water salmon fishing brought a peace of mind like none other. Seagulls bobbed on gentle waves, seals appeared beside kelp beds and killer whales occasionally surfaced suddenly beside the boat. This and the sun setting behind the mountains, all made him feel the majesty of nature. It let him escape to a world far from jet noise and the smell of burnt kerosene.

To actually catch a salmon was merely a side benefit for him. He preferred to simply soak up the scenery and meditate. Did people of other ages, two thousand years ago, twenty thousand years ago, stare at the world around them and wonder why they were lucky enough to live in their times? Or are we truly fortunate to live at the peak time for the human race? Or will people two thousand years from now think the same thing? Can we continue to grow or are we sliding over the crest?

Where in the world we happen to appear is another dimension. I could have been born in squalor, maybe never survived childhood, killed by starvation, sickness, predators, enemies or even parents. I might have lived the pampered life of the rich or a life of terror through a war. Where and when one is born is pure chance. I'm lucky to be born a human in an age of humans, in a civilized society not burdened with hand to mouth existence.

We're the grand prize winners in a lottery that stretches over twenty billion years since the Big Bang started our universe on its present course. And was that really the start? I can't concede that the universe is a one shot thing. A tiny ball of infinitely compressed matter suddenly appears and explodes to create our universe which expands eventually into nothingness.

There must be forces which we have yet to discover which will combine with gravity to eventually slow the expansion and in a much longer time bring about a contraction back once again to the tiny ball that restarts the process. Of course that doesn't help answer how or why it all started. We can't go back beyond the Big Bang because relativity says time started over then. One thing's for sure. Our window of existence in the universe is infinitesimally small and the best we can do is make the most of it.

This turned his thoughts to Sylvia. Is she making the most of her life? I never will make the most of mine without her. If only I could locate her. Talk to her. Know she is the happiest she can be. Why won't they let me contact her? What harm would there be in that?

He returned to the universe riddle to drag himself back from a chasm of self-pity. It seems fruitless to spend more time in a quest to pull a magic force out of the mathematics that describe our expanding universe. The theoretical physicists are welcome to the problem. I prefer to design a digital processor which will open doors for the blind.

~~~

Within three days of arrival in Comox, Delbert had laid out a running track beside a part of the base, along a section of uninhabited beach and back through a forest trail. Every morning he ran it, followed by an exercise regimen patterned after the circuit at UBC.

"What makes you so gung ho?" one of the older pilots asked.

"Exercise keeps my mind alert and builds the muscles needed for high g forces."

That prompted one to join him, than another and another. Inevitably, it became a routine for most of the pilots and many others at the base. The early morning camaraderie soon proved stronger than evening bar social life.

At the end of two months, Delbert left a cadre of twelve Pillagers amongst a number of other jealous pilots. A few had dropped out as predicted. Bentwing felt obligated to develop additional instructor pilots to send out to complete the program, not only at Comox but at all bases across Canada.

CHAPTER FORTY-SEVEN

It was one thing to build pilot skills, another to find pilots who could instruct others. So Delbert spent the Fall and winter with one session after another. Pilots arrived from various bases for the month long course. When he complained that this was a long way from experimental test work, Bentwing sympathized.

"I wish it could be different, son, but we're in a dry spell. Something will come along and when it does, you'll get first crack at it. I really owe you one for what you've made of the Pillager program."

Perhaps what irritated Delbert as much as anything was that instructing took so much of his time. It curtailed his progress with the digital processor design. It was not an issue he could bring up since the design was extracurricular from an Air Force viewpoint. Still he made progress.

Mike told him the circuits to store and retrieve data in memory worked fine. He would use them not only for the scanner signal but also to retrieve instructions used to interpret the data.

After laying out the instruction format, he began to design circuits. Simple integrated circuit chips were now available and he used them where possible. In fact, he soon realized the number of transistors needed without these chips would overwhelm the project. As it was, the design became suspiciously complicated.

Once a character was identified, it would be stored in a separate piece of memory. When the end of a word was detected, either by a signal from the scanner or by a punctuation mark other than an apostrophe, all letters in the word would be burst out by the sound generator.

He took another month to review the design and visualize it in action, sort of a mental lab test. Since he wouldn't be present when the circuits were built and tested, he tried to anticipate what problems might be encountered. In spite of the care taken, he knew problems were inevitable. He could only hope to minimize them.

Finally forced to admit he procrastinated, he mailed a copy of the full design off to Mike. He included his thoughts on circuit board layout and a summary note.

"Mike, I know this will be complicated to build, need a sizeable power supply and require component cooling. As more sophisticated integrated circuit chips become available, we can simplify the design. Perhaps you will find it necessary to wait for that. I hope not. Call me if there are questions."

A week later, he got a call from Mike, "Well Delbert, you outdid yourself this time. I've tried to analyze those circuits and frankly, I can't. Feel like a hog looking at a wristwatch."

"The integrated circuits complicate things since I haven't described what happens inside them. When I get time, I'll put together notes that describe the design."

"I've set up joint mechanical and electronic engineering student teams to develop the processor. It makes a fabulous project for the senior classes. They'll build the circuit boards once we approve the design. After I told them what it's for, they're hot to go and so am I!"

"Great."

"I have a feeling there will be a world of blind people indebted to you for expanding their horizons."

"Or curse me for having to learn another language."

"They already know nothing in life is easy."

CHAPTER FORTY-EIGHT

Three weeks later, Bentwing called Delbert back into his office.

"I've got some flight test work for you. Want you to go down to the McDonnell plant in St Louis and evaluate the Voodoo. The Yanks are tossing us a bone after torpedoing the Arrow. They'll give us a fleet of Voodoos, their best interceptor. I want you to put it through the wringer and see if it will do us any good. The Ottawa powers now concede we still need an interceptor."

"OK, when do I leave?"

"They want you there next Tuesday to go through ground school and simulator training. They'll arrange lodging, etc. for a four week stay. I told them they won't be able to keep you out of the airplane for more than a week and a half. They said the training always takes three weeks. Go easy on them."

"OK, thanks."

"Thank you son, for not bringing up the Arrow again. This bird won't match it but it's the best we'll get."

"I understand."

~~~

Tuesday morning Delbert was in class with a group of USAF pilots. They were polite to his face, merely commenting on his youthful appearance. He sensed that the comments behind his back were more derogatory, probably making fun of the kid from the frozen wastes. By the next Monday morning, he had digested the manuals and spent time out on the flight line.

That afternoon he told the instructor he had learned everything there was to learn from the manuals and asked if he could move on to the simulator.

"No way Sir. We don't let any pilots into the simulator until they pass the ground school."

"Is there a test I can take?"

"Not a single test per se. We evaluate students throughout the two week class and decide if they're ready at the end."

Grin and bear it, he thought, this guy's too proud of his class to ever admit someone might not need two weeks of his brilliant instruction. Towards the end of some sessions, Delbert just had to ask a question about the airplane which the instructor likely couldn't answer. It only seemed fair to make him squirm a little in return.

When he finally reached his first simulator session, the instructor warned him that things would happen awfully fast once the airplane was underway.

"It takes a while to catch up to this bird but don't worry, if you lose control we'll pause the simulator and let you get re-oriented. Any questions before we start?"

"No Sir, I'm ready."

And of course he was. After a perfect takeoff and climb out, he did a series of snap rolls in each direction, then pulled it up into a stall, deliberately kicked it into a spin and recovered from the spin.

"Excuse me Sir," came over the interphone, "that wasn't exactly what we had on the agenda for the first session. It was an impressive demonstration though. Guess you don't need as much air work as we planned. Would like to see some inverted flight, however, and a landing configuration stall."

Delbert flipped the airplane on its back, flew straight and level for a couple of minutes, then made a smooth turn to the left followed by a 360 turn to the right. Straightening out, he hit the afterburners and started an inverted loop, one of the most difficult stunts to perform well. By now, the instructor hoped he would lose it on the way back down. Not a chance. At the top, Delbert brought the thrust back and completed a perfect inverted loop.

Back right side up on the way back to the airport, he performed a landing configuration stall for the instructor. Then he was told to make a series of touch and go's, followed by a full stop at the end of the session.

The instructor began to debrief him, "Mr. Pillage, either you are one hell of a pilot or you've spent some time in a high performance fighter before."

"I flew the Avro Arrow."

"Oh, I see. Well, apparently that gave you a good stepping stone to this bird."

Delbert thought he wouldn't like to learn the step was backward.

"Next session will be a refresher of what we covered today for takeoff and landing, plus we'll look at equipment failures. Any questions?"

"No Sir"

Towards the end of the second session, the instructor had thrown every failure he could think of at Delbert. He even gave him a dual engine failure which forced Delbert to perform a dead stick landing. The instructor shook his head in admiration.

"You do an impressive job. Our next session will concentrate on weapons delivery. You're running through this syllabus at about twice the normal rate. Not sure what we'll use to fill the last three sessions."

"How about the real airplane?"

"They frown on that but I'll see what I can do to shorten the schedule."

"Thanks"

It took two more sessions before the instructor cleared him for flight. They consisted mainly of simulated combat exercises which Delbert enjoyed because they allowed him to stress the simulated airplane to its limits.

"Better not try that in the real bird," was heard more than once. His instructor had spread the word about his ability and told the flight instructor he better strap in tight when he took Delbert up.

The flight instructor took that to mean he would have to deal with a cocky young pilot. But when he came under Delbert's calm and humble scrutiny, he got the opposite impression. He must have meant some other student and got the names mixed up, he thought.

"Pillage, they tell me you're here to evaluate the Voodoo for the Canadian Air Force. You look awful young. Surprised they didn't send one of their more experienced pilots. Not sure if we'll be able to let you fly solo but I can certainly show you what the airplane can do. If you don't mind, I'd like you to ride in the rear seat."

"Unless that's what you do with all your students on the first flight, I do mind. My orders are to wring this airplane out to ensure it will do a good job for the RCAF. Can't do that from the back seat."

"Most of our students have a lot more experience than you can possibly have."

"Don't sell me short before we get off the ground."

Sighing, "OK, you're in the front seat but I'll take us up the first time."

Delbert patiently let him take the jet off, climb to altitude and take them to a practice area.

"OK, kid. It's your airplane. Let's see some smooth turns."

Delbert flew four perfectly coordinated 360 turns, each tighter than the one before. The instructor gained confidence in him so when he rolled the wing up again he was surprised to see Delbert perform a barrel roll, flawlessly. "That wasn't a turn but it certainly was smooth. Want to try a stall?"

"Sure."

And so it went. With each exercise, the instructor became more impressed. Before long they had flown snap rolls, loops, spins and Immelmann's.

"OK son, let's go shoot touch and go's."

Aha, Delbert thought, the magic son word. After four touch and go's, they did a full stop landing to end the session.

"Sorry, Pillage, I totally misjudged you. You're a fine pilot. Guess I learned today not to judge a pilot by his age."

Delbert chuckled, "Old pilots may be safe pilots but even they have to start somewhere."

"Yeah. Look, I want to go up again tomorrow with you on the radio and everything. If that goes as well, the airplane's yours from then on."

"Thank you Sir."

The next day's flight went smoothly. They flew to its published speed and altitude boundaries. Delbert performed a number of simulated combat maneuvers, along with an inverted loop, to finish the air work.

Back on the ground, the instructor said, "I'll clear you for solo flight even though I may get some static. I'll just tell them I can't fly this bird as well as you do already."

"You don't have to go that far."

"Well, it's the truth."

Once on his own, Delbert was free to explore what the airplane could really do. He pushed it to the limits and explored its controllability at those limits. The airplane impressed him. It's no Arrow but it's a good interceptor with the flexibility to handle multiple roles for the RCAF. I'll give it a good recommendation.

He asked for a flight where he could exercise the weapons systems. They agreed but insisted an instructor ride with him to be sure he stayed inside the firing range. That was fine. There were no surprises. All systems performed as advertised. Obviously, there were no nuclear tipped weapons loaded on board but Delbert was convinced they would work equally well.

"Delbert, word's out that you're a pretty special pilot. One of the local air force hot shots wants to challenge you to a dog fight on Thursday. Interested?"

"Sure."

"OK, I'll set it up."

"There's one other area I want to explore before we wrap up the evaluation—low level terrain following. Can you point me to a good location for that."

"Sure, I'll show you on the map and clear the area for tomorrow's flight."

"Thanks. Then we'll wrap up on Thursday."

Impressed with the airplane's controllability in a terrain following environment, he was ready for the contest on Thursday. However, it didn't prove to be much of a contest. The pilot was good but no match for the Pillager maneuvers Delbert demonstrated. When they got together after the flight, the pilot told Delbert he did things with that airplane it wasn't designed to do.

"Apparently it was designed to do them. I think airplane manufacturers always hold something back on us. Afraid we'll give their bread-winners a bad name if too many are lost."

"Well you convinced me. We better start to press the limits, in case we ever get into a war with Canada. Let me buy you a beer."

Delbert spent his last night in St Louis in the company of a bunch of air force pilots. They talked flying and told stories, of which there is no end amongst pilots.

Back home, he submitted a report which declared the Voodoo admirably suited to perform the various interceptor and air superiority roles needed by the RCAF. The report delighted Bentwing, particularly with no mention of how the Arrow would have been a better choice. The kid takes the high road, he thought. He combines all that ability with down to earth practicality. Makes me proud to have him on our team. His pride took another leap the next day when he got a call from his counterpart in St Louis.

"Hey Bentwing, ol' buddy. Where'd you get that hot shot Pillage? Everyone down here's talking about him. You been hybridizing pilots up there or something?"

"He's one in a million, Sam."

"Must be. Did he give the Voodoo a vote of confidence?"

"Sure did. He was very complimentary about it. Thinks it's ideal for the RCAF."

"Great. Well, thanks for exposing us to his talents. If you ever want to let him emigrate to the promised land let me know."

"He's already there, Sam. Thanks for helping us with the evaluation. Good talking to you."

"Later."

CHAPTER FORTY-NINE

A duller routine settled in again. Mike caused a blip of excitement when he reported the circuit boards were built. They were individually tested to find out what power was needed and device temperatures were checked.

"The students did a respectable job, with only a few mid-course corrections. We've also built a box to hold them along with the power supply. I'll send you some photographs."

"Great. I want to see what it looks like. Can we preload the memory with the program instructions or do we need to develop an initialization program to load them?"

"I'll find out."

"Let me know, Mike, and I'll work on it. There's not much to keep me busy here."

"Sure pal, onward and upward."

"Is that an attempt at pilot lingo?"

"Apparently not. See you."

"Right."

Delbert monitored progress with integrated circuits. He hoped for a way to simplify the processor. Every time something surfaced, he incorporated it into a revised design which he intended to dump on Mike once a significant savings was realized.

When the first Voodoos were delivered to the RCAF, Bentwing conscripted Delbert to oversee training. He trained instructors, careful not to make them too aggressive. The first job was to build a team of competent pilots to activate the squadrons formed. There was plenty of time later to bring them to the Pillager level of performance. In fact, he had yet to define what that would be for Voodoos.

With standard training underway, he took time to get re-acquainted with the airplane and explore once again its limits. This led to a Pillager program which he tried out on two of his most trusted seasoned pilots. With a few refinements, he was ready to start the special sessions.

It was inevitable that this would become another full-time job. He realized there would be precious little experimental test flying in Canada over the next few years. In a way, he had to concede that flying the Voodoo to the limits of its capability wasn't a bad substitute for experimental flying. Nevertheless, he missed the interplay with design engineers and the ability to influence designs. Although he never let on to Bentwing, he began to count the days until his Air Force commitment ended.

At least, candidates for Pillager training did not include pilots who washed out before. Still, it was a full-time job. Pilots rotated in from each of the squadrons across the country. Well, all but one. The pompous commander at Comox still held out for special treatment. This meant they were last to be trained.

Eventually, Delbert was sent out to Comox. It took three months, which was fine with him. He still loved the island with all it had to offer in scenery and recreation. Its laid-back culture resembled what he grew up with on Saltspring Island.

The proximity to Vancouver allowed him to talk more frequently to Mike and together they got the scanner functional. It read characters successfully, combined them into words and generated what Mike now called the "music of the words". Occasional errors resulted in a few misspelled words much like what happens in visual reading.

A trial group of blind readers was exposed to this musical language and made good progress. With practice they recognized more and more words. It took time just as it does for children learning to read in school. They were thrilled by the prospect of being able to pick up any book and start reading. Their horizon was now unlimited.

At the end of scheduled sessions, Delbert asked Bentwing for a week's leave so he could spend some time at home, then three days hiking in the Hurricane Ridge region. Unable to visit the island without dwelling on the loss of Sylvia, it still depressed him. The cold mountain air and communing with nature on strenuous hikes cleared his mind. He felt refreshed.

CHAPTER FIFTY

Delbert's leave ended on Friday and he reported in to the Comox base that morning. He and a rookie pilot were ordered to fly a pair of Voodoo's down to Victoria to be put on display for a week.

Although Delbert was intimately familiar with the Voodoo's quirks, Chuck Lansbury was barely checked out. Like a lot of pilots, his ego gave him an unwarranted confidence in his abilities and he was determined to prove them to the Air Force's top pilot.

"Stay on my wing, Lansbury, and I'll show you some interesting terrain at the lower end of the island."

"Yes Sir. Do your worst. I'll be on your tail like a fly on a cow pie."

Another rookie wants to show he's better than seasoned pilots. Maybe I should take him down a rung or two. So instead of a relaxed scenic tour, he took the jet down to under five hundred feet above the terrain. True to his word, Lansbury stuck with him. North west of the Malahat, Delbert led them through a series of mountain valleys with some fairly sharp turns. On one, Lansbury swung a little too wide and had to climb rapidly to clear a ridge.

Embarrassed by his mistake, he accelerated to catch Delbert. He thinks he lost me but I'll be right back on his ass when he comes around that next ridge. And he was, literally.

Unable to bleed off his speed in time and somewhat hemmed in by the valley walls, he ran right up over the lead jet just as Delbert started to climb to clear the approaching saddle. The aircraft grated into each other and for a moment were locked together.

"For Chrissake pull up Lansbury. Get off my back."

Flustered, Lansbury pulled back on the joystick and hit the afterburners at the same time. Now he was a giant blowtorch burning Delbert's tail off. By the time he broke free, Delbert had no rudder and badly reduced elevator control. His first thought was to eject but now they were out of the mountains into the populated area north of Langford.

I've got to get this thing slowed down. Losing hydraulics. If I eject, it will become a ballistic missile. Could wipe out a lot of people. Have to ride it down. Perhaps I can aim it at Langford Lake and eject. He got the airplane slowed down but realized he would overshoot the lake. With very little maneuverability, the only answer seemed to be to crash land it on the golf course up ahead.

That must be Royal Colwood Golf Course. Well they're in for a royal shock. Hope the golfers see me coming and scatter. Those two fairways line up pretty well and if I can touch down early on the first one there should be enough room to slide to a stop.

With almost no control left, he did a masterful job of bringing it down on the fairway in front of the second green. Players on the green jumped out of their skins when the fighter wooshed over twenty feet above them. Their round ended there.

The foursome behind, still on the tee, took off up the hill when they saw the airplane coming. It plowed a furrow as it went. When Delbert saw that it would have to slide across the paved entry road, he fired the fire extinguisher bottles into the already shut-down engines. As it hurtled over the road, it became airborne again briefly. Still, he estimated it would come to a stop before the first tee, perhaps in the pond in front of it.

That was until he saw the rock that sticks out of the first fairway. With no directional control, he wouldn't get by it unscathed. The right side of the body rode up on the rock which caused the airplane to swerve slightly to the left. Now it headed into a few scattered small oak trees with a rock bluff behind. It slammed into the rock before coming to a stop.

The nose of the fighter pushed back into the cockpit area and sheared his feet off above the ankles. The collision knocked him unconscious. Startled golfers ran towards him, then slowed down when they smelled kerosene from the ruptured fuel tanks. A giant of a man, Elmer Lee, rallied them.

"We got to get him out. One of you run to the Clubhouse and call the fire department and tell them to send an ambulance."

He leaped up on the front of the fighter and tried to pull open the canopy. It was stuck. He found the access panel with the lever used to open the canopy in an emergency. Twisting it caused some bolts to clank but the canopy remained jammed.

"Give me an iron," he yelled. He pounded the canopy. It wouldn't break. He wedged it in a crack on the side and tried to pry it open. When he could get his fingers into the crack, he lifted with all his adrenalin fed strength.

First it creaked, then a gap appeared. Now with more leverage, he wrenched it open. He leaned down, unfastened the pilot's harness, tore off the wires and tubes connected to him and tried to lift him out. His legs were wedged in. Elmer could see he was bleeding badly. It took all his strength to pull him free. It was doing further damage to his body, probably breaking bones, but there was no time for anything else.

"His feet are cut off and he's bleeding bad. Wrap a belt around each leg and pull them tight." Two golfers did.

"Doubt if he can last until we get him to a hospital with all that blood loss. He's white as a sheet. Where the hell's that fire truck?"

"The old clubhouse up above is sort of a hospital. At least it's a priory and there's usually a doc there."

"OK, let's get him up there." Elmer picked him up in his arms like a baby and charged up the hill on the left side of the bluff.

"Should I bring his feet?" someone asked.

"No asshole. He'll never walk on them again."

Elmer had to carry him almost to the road before he could get around the fence and into the priory. The nun just inside the door jumped when he charged in. She recovered quickly and immediately led him to the small operating room.

"Get Doctor Wallace!" she yelled.

The doctor took one look at him and started a plasma intravenous drip. He clamped the arteries and removed the belts, gently removed his helmet and checked him over. His legs are broken and certainly there are internal injuries, he thought. Damn, there's no reaction in his legs, must be a back injury. Wish they hadn't carried him in without immobilizing it. Can't blame them though, with that blood loss. Doc Wallace looked up to see the Mother Superior enter the make-shift operating room.

"We need blood to save him. O-negative blood, damn it—sorry Mother."

Ignoring the apology, "Only Sister Maria has O-negative blood here in the priory. I'll talk to her."

"Hurry, Mother."

Half running to Sister Maria's room, she called ahead, "Sister Maria, Sister Maria!"

"What is it, Mother?", the nun replied anxiously flying through the door.

"The injured flier they brought in has suffered a grievous loss of blood and he's O-negative."

"I'll come with you."

The two raced back to the infirmary. "Can you give blood?", asked Doc.

"Of course."

"He has almost no blood of his own and we can only do so much with plasma. When did you last give blood."

"I don't know. Three or four months ago. It doesn't matter."

"Thank you Sister. Sister Theresa, can you get me a pint bottle for the blood?

"Yes of course. We have a supply in the clinic."

"Bring two," said Sister Maria.

"You can't give two," Doc responded.

"What would happen to me?"

"You would get very weak, probably pass out, it would take days to recover."

"That's a small price to pay, Doctor."

Within minutes she lay on a bed, a needle in her arm, a stick to hold on to and blood filling the first bottle. When full, the doctor looked questioningly at her. She nodded vigorously so he started the second bottle. As it filled she did feel lightheaded but was determined to see it full. At last it was. She relaxed and immediately fainted.

~~~

A day later she regained sufficient strength to resume normal duties. Curious to learn the flier's status, she found time to visit his ward that afternoon.

"How is he?" she asked the nun on duty.

"Very weak. It's touch and go. Sadly, his back is injured, paralyzed from the waist down. And his brain was without sufficient blood so long it may not function properly again. They say he had a brilliant mind. What a pity."

A tremor of fear pulsed through Sister Maria as she stepped closer to look at the patient. The blood drained from her face. She looked at his name bracelet to confirm what she already knew and staggered from the room. The nun watched her in consternation and then turned back to the patient.

In the days that followed, Sister Maria spent every spare moment in the ward with him. She watched for any sign of life. Prayed for him. Even though he breathed on his own, he was deathly weak and still apparently in a coma.

On the third day, he looked near death. The Mother Superior administered the last rites. After she left, Sister Maria came in and stood near the bed, a tear trickled down her cheek. His eyes were open, staring at the ceiling. Slowly they moved for the first time, to look at her face.

In almost a whisper, she said "Delbert".

He stared at her for many long minutes. Slowly, his hand slid from under the blankets and he placed it on her waist. The exquisite curve from waist to hips was still there. His fingers rested in the curve. A tear formed in one eye and began to slide down the side of his face. She reached up and gently brushed it away.

"Delbert, fight to live! Please darling, I need you to live. Don't leave me like I left you. Please Delbert." She gently moved his hand and gripped it firmly in both of hers.

"Please fight Delbert, please..."

He closed his eyes and seemed to lose consciousness again. After a few minutes, she moved his hand back under the covers and began to remove hers. She felt him grip her hand a little tighter to hold on to it and knew immediately he had begun to fight. When he finally slept, she took a small, worn wooden carving from her habit and placed it in his hand. Mother Superior watched her as she turned to leave.

"This is the man you lost when you joined the sisterhood, isn't it?"

"Yes, Mother."

"Spend as much time with him as you want, my child. Others will take care of your duties."

"Thank you, Mother."

As she watched her go, the Mother Superior said under her breath, "Father, you are not our beneficent Lord this day but rather a jealous suitor who has brought her earthly love back in pieces to tear out her heart a second time—just to test her loyalty to you? Surely you know she has selflessly devoted herself to your service. Please Lord, redeem yourself and mend what you have torn asunder. Give them a second chance."

~~~

Whenever Delbert regained consciousness, Sister Maria was beside him. On the second day, he pulled the little wooden figure from under the covers and asked in a barely audible voice, "Why did you keep this?"

"To keep something of you near me. I held it each day when I prayed for you. Now I want you to hold it when I'm not here to remind you I'm nearby."

"You are always nearby in my mind."

~~~

Each day he got a little stronger. After a week, the doctor decided he was stable enough to be taken to Jubilee Hospital in Victoria where he could get better treatment.

"Sister Maria, you should be called Saint Maria, you've worked a miracle with him."

The Mother Superior thought he had a point, although the Pope might like additional proof.

"May I see you in my office Sister, when you can break free?"

A little later in her office, "It's very apparent my child that you two share a strong love. I've talked to Mother Agnes in Victoria and she tells me that Delbert hounded her incessantly to be allowed to contact you. She fended him off in the belief it was up to you to initiate any contact. Now it seems that Our Father has taken matters into his own hands."

"I do love him, Mother. I forced the separation so that he would make a life with someone more worthy, someone who could give him children."

"Perhaps that should have been his decision. Perhaps he would agree with me that there is likely no one more worthy than you. In any case, it appears his ability to have children is lost. Now he needs someone strong to bring him back to as normal and productive a life as possible."

"Yes Mother."

"As you know, we make no demands on you. You're free to follow your heart. In a day or two, he will be moved to Victoria. If your calling is now to go with him, you can renounce your vows and go with our blessing."

"Thank you, Mother. In many ways, the sisterhood saved my life. But Delbert needs me now and I want to help him."

"Then go my child, with our prayers for your happiness."

CHAPTER FIFTY-ONE

When Delbert awoke the next morning, he looked for Sister Maria and found Sylvia instead. Without her habit and hair flowing free, she was a vision to behold. Delbert smiled through tears as he reached for her hand.

"Does this mean you can go with me to Victoria?"

"I can go anywhere you go and will if you let me."

She rode in the ambulance with him. During the next week he went through a battery of examinations. The doctors decided to operate on his back to fuse together the damaged vertebrae. They told him his spinal cord had been badly damaged and there was little likelihood he would recover any feeling below the waist. He took the news stoically, even managed a little sick humor.

"Maybe now Charlie will let me retire from soccer."

"That and running are the only things you can retire from," Sylvia rejoined.

"How long can you tolerate being nurse maid to a cripple?"

"Delbert, once you asked me to marry you and I said yes. Things have changed tremendously for both of us since then but that's still my answer. Now the question is will you marry me?"

"How can I burden you with a lifetime of taking care of me and being limited by me in what you can do?"

"Over the past three years I have longed to be with you. It never went away and I came to realize I made three bad mistakes; failing to avoid the rape, botching the abortion and, most important in hindsight, not letting you decide your own course of action. It's wrong to make other people's decisions for them. When a man proposes to a woman he has already made his decision. All that remains is for her to accept or reject the proposal. I'm proposing to you Delbert, will you marry me?"

"... Yes."

She leaned over and kissed him. "Thank you, darling."

~~~

Bentwing paid a surprise visit the next afternoon.

"How are you, son? You look a little frail. They feeding you OK?"

"Sure Bentwing. Can't say I'll be back on my feet soon but I'm getting stronger all the time. Thanks to my fiancée. Bentwing, this is Sylvia Cairns. Sylvia, Bentwing Carson is in charge of Air Force training."

"What a pleasure to meet you, Sylvia. How long have you two known each other?"

"Since we were six years old."

"So you're the girl I stole Delbert from each summer. I'm surprised he ever came east."

"I couldn't compete with the thrill of flying jets," she said with a smile.

"That reminds me, I've taken the liberty to apply for a disability retirement for you. It means you'll get your regular monthly income. I've also put you in for a medal. You put your life at risk and paid the penalty by riding the airplane down rather than eject. Who knows how many lives would have been lost if it had crashed in that populated area."

"The pension will help until I can find a new way to earn a living. I'm not sure a medal is warranted."

"That's not your decision, son."

"Guess I still can't argue with you. By the way, how's Lansbury doing?"

"He hasn't flown since the accident. He feels like a pariah and he'll probably wash out of fighter training."

"Bentwing, will you grant me two favors, only two."

"Sure, son. Name them."

"I want you to force Lansbury to come and visit me, whether an order is enough or it requires brute force. Second, I want you to talk to the Comox pilots. Tell them it was purely an accident and that I beg them to accept him back into the fraternity when he returns."

"You sure you want to see him?"

"Yes."

"OK."

~~~

Late in the morning two days later, Chuck Lansbury gingerly poked his head into the ward.

"Come in Chuck, good to see you."

"I—I wanted to come and see you earlier to apologize but was afraid it would upset you. God, I'm sorry Delbert, I can't tell you how sorry!"

"It was an accident, Chuck."

"I caused it. I'll never fly again. I can't even face the guys knowing I took down the best pilot in the service."

"Listen to me, Chuck. It was an accident. If anything, it was my fault. I never should have taken you into those mountains. You weren't trained for that. I succumbed to a stupid urge to humble you a little. I should have known better. Can you forgive me?"

"Forgive you? You're lying there paralyzed and you want me to forgive you?"

"Yes."

"Delbert, I—" He stopped, choked up, the words wouldn't come.

"Look Chuck, if it makes you feel better, we can share a little guilt for decreasing the RCAF inventory by one Voodoo. But don't feel guilty on my account. You did me a favor. You helped to give me back the woman I love. There's another favor I want to ask of you."

"Name it Delbert, I'll do anything humanly possible for you."

"Start flying again. You've got a lot of talent that right now goes to waste."

"I think they're about to wash me out and I don't know if I can face the guys again."

"No they're not. I've talked to Bentwing and they want to give you a chance to get back in the saddle again. And he promised to explain to the Comox pilots how it was purely an accident and insist they not hold you responsible for what happened. Will you do it for me?"

Chuck grabbed Delbert's hand. With tears in his eyes, he nodded and choked out, "Thanks, Delbert, you're a hell of a man!"

"Show me your Pillager insignia when you get it."

Sylvia entered as Chuck left. "Who was that?"

"Chuck Lansbury. The pilot who helped bring us together again."

"I should thank him."

"I already did."

"That's probably why he was crying when he left. I bet you lifted a heavy load of guilt off his shoulders, dear."

"Hope so. Sylvia, you somehow manage with no source of income and perhaps impose on the generosity of the convent. I've got an unused salary and a lot of back pay in the bank. I want you to find a place for when we're married and move in now. And I'll change the bank account to a joint one shared with you so you can use it to cover expenses."

"Are you sure?"

"Everything I have is yours. A marriage ceremony only legalizes it. I want you able to buy clothes and all the things you want. If you put us in debt—or buy me short pants—we will have to reconsider the arrangement."

"If you talk like that, maybe I'll buy you a used wheelchair so I can spend more on myself," she said laughing.

"Don't care if it's used as long as it has a turbocharger."

"You're looking at the turbocharger."

"And it's giving me a charge."

She hugged him. Then asked, "with all that's gone on, do you think we could get married on the Island? I told my parents we were engaged. After the initial shock, my mother asked if we would get married there."

"Don't see why not, if that's what you want too."

"Wish I knew how people on the Island feel about me. I left in disgrace but a lot of them are probably sympathetic towards my problem."

"You didn't leave in disgrace. You were a victim."

"I don't know if the abortion changed that."

"Perhaps for a few pious Catholics but not for Islanders in general. I'll tell my parents too and see if they know of any reason why we shouldn't get married there."

As it turned out, both families were excited about the prospect, although Phil had some misgivings about a service in the Catholic church.

"Reckon there must be somethin' wrong with a service when it's got to be given in a foreign language."

CHAPTER FIFTY-TWO

Sylvia rented a ground floor apartment. Two weeks later, Delbert could leave the hospital and they moved in. Buying necessities to live in the apartment and looking after Delbert ran her ragged yet left her happier than she had been in years.

True to his nature, Delbert worked hard to rebuild his strength and master the difficulties of life in and out of a wheelchair. He wanted to minimize the burden placed on Sylvia and regain as much independence as possible. Between exercise and hugs, he had no time to feel sorry for himself. Nor had he any inclination. They were like honeymooners getting to know each other again.

~~~

Two weeks into their life together Delbert had a phone call from Dan.

"Your parents gave me your new phone number, how are you?"

After a guilty pang, "OK from the waist up. Actually, I feel no pain and get stronger each day."

"Delbert, tell me if I'm out of line here and I won't mention it again. Are you interested in going flying with me?"

Shocked, "Well, yes that sounds like a good idea. Can I get my hands on the controls?"

"Sure."

"You'd have to work the rudder pedals and brakes. Think you can keep the turns coordinated?"

"You are better. Can Sylvia bring you out to the airport to meet me next Tuesday morning at ten?"

"Ten hundred hours on Tuesday. Can Sylvia come with us? I promised to show her what Saltspring Island looks like from the air years ago and this would be a good time."

"Great! I was about to suggest she join us."

~~~

Tuesday morning found them at the terminal when Dan taxied in, with a very pregnant Virginia in the right seat. It took all three of them to get Delbert into the left seat. Then they climbed in and buckled up.

"Good to see you, Virginia, turns out you were Virgin for short after all."

They both laughed this time. Virginia and Sylvia were friends from the moment they met.

Delbert called for the pre-start checklist and Dan humbly obliged. It irritated Delbert to realize he couldn't taxi the airplane nor keep it aligned with the runway until they were airborne. But other than that, he could control it with a minor amount of help from Dan on the rudder pedals. He felt again the joy of flight and gave Sylvia a spirited commentary as they circled Saltspring Island.

"Remember your first cross country? I want you to fly it backwards up to Comox and show the girls the east coast of Vancouver Island. We'll land there and grab some lunch."

When they were on final approach, Delbert's vision gave away the secret. The whole base was turned out on the tarmac in full dress uniform, flanked by the base band. In the center, a giant banner read "WELCOME PILLAGER ONE".

As they taxied up, Bentwing came to meet them with a wheelchair and a grin from ear to ear. Two burly servicemen lifted him out and into the wheelchair. Sylvia pushed him to the dais as the band struck up "Captains Of The Clouds", the RCAF's unofficial anthem, followed by "The Maple Leaf Forever".

Everyone saluted as he passed.

They turned in front of the dais and faced the crowd, Sylvia behind, Dan and Virginia on either side. The band played the national anthem. Everyone sang. Then Bentwing stepped to the microphone.

"It gives me great pleasure to introduce the best pilot I've ever had the honour to know, Delbert Pillage." Wild applause.

He then introduced the Lieutenant Governor who presented Delbert with a Distinguished Flying Cross. There was a chant of "Pillage, Pillage, Pillage" and the Lieutenant Governor asked if he would like to say a few words.

Delbert took the microphone, "I must first apologize for showing up out of uniform but seeing you on final represented the first inkling I had of this affair. Dan is a master of subterfuge. However, I am forever in his debt since he taught me to fly." Applause. "With Dan is Virginia Martin, his daughter-in-law and behind me is my fiancée, Sylvia Cairns." More applause and whistles.

"When Bentwing condescended to take me back to Malton for jet training, my Mother was apprehensive. 'It sounds dangerous', she said. I said, 'No, it's safe as long as you're careful and take a conscientious approach', which I assured her I would. And for ninety-nine point nine percent of my flying career I did...let that be a lesson for you. The last time I used my feet it was to hike up Hurricane Ridge over there. My feet couldn't think of a better way to go. Please keep your feet on the ground and your heart in the skies. Thank you for coming out today." He saluted them and they gave him a rousing cheer.

Bentwing approached Delbert and said quietly, "Son, there's a Silver Star fueled and raring to go if you want one last flight in it." Delbert looked at Sylvia, she nodded. He turned back to Bentwing, "front seat or back?"

"I'll ride in back." The base watched in silent anticipation as Bentwing wheeled him to the jet trainer. The two servicemen appeared again to lift him up and into the jet. They both buckled up and soon taxied to the end of the runway, turned and took off. They flew out over the water in a sweeping turn to line up once again with the runway.

On approach to the far end, Delbert rolled the jet over on its back and flew towards them at two hundred feet. The crowd gasped. Someone said, "he's flying his own fallen pilot salute." A hushed crowd saluted as Delbert came by inverted, controlling the jet with his left hand and returning the salute with his right. Choked up, no one could speak as they watched him pull up, roll upright and circle again to land.

Over the interphone came, "Should have known you'd pull a stunt like that, son. It brought tears to my eyes, can't remember that ever happening before."

Once parked, Delbert pulled himself up out of the seat to sit on the cockpit sidewall. He felt the emotion of the silent crowd. Saw tears on many faces. To break the spell, he smiled and pumped his fist. A smattering of smiles appeared. In true Anglo-American military fashion, the base commander led a three cheer salute.

"Hip, hip" and the crowd roared "HOORAY!

"Hip, hip", "HOORAY!"

"Hip, hip", "HOORAY!"

Applause followed and people started to talk again.

With Delbert returned to the wheelchair, Sylvia pushed him back towards the dais. She leaned over to whisper, "I hope you can feel the tremendous affection and admiration these people have for you. What a far cry from our early school years."

All he could get out was, "I do."

The base personnel crowded around to congratulate him, shake hands or just pat him on the shoulder. When Chuck Lansbury appeared in front of him, he reached out and pulled him into a hug. A wonderful symbol of closure. Spirits soared.

~~~

On the anticlimactic flight back to Victoria, Delbert thanked Dan two or three times. Both men enjoyed the elation of the day's events.

"You know Dan, I think it might be possible to replace the throttle with a joystick. You could rotate it to operate the rudder, push it forward to control power and pull it back to apply brakes. Differential braking would be tied into the rudder operation. It would be fly-by-wire on the rudder and brakes but we know how to do that now."

Dan laughed. "Nothing can hold you down long."

Sylvia and Virginia chattered away in the back seat. Near Victoria, Sylvia pointed out that all of her female friends in recent years were nuns. She wondered if Virginia would be her maid of honour. Virginia said she would be delighted, especially since Charlie would be best man. So it was settled.

CHAPTER FIFTY-THREE

The wedding set for August eighth, invitations went out to their closest friends. However, with only two weeks to go, it became obvious that the little church in Ganges would never hold the crowd. They would have to move it outside. When both sets of parents approached a state of panic, the Harbour House Hotel stepped in.

Apprised of the situation by a timely word from the priest, they offered to host the ceremony on their flower bordered lawn. In addition, they insisted on providing food and refreshments after the ceremony. They wanted to be a part of the welcome home for the Island's hero. Every hotel, motel and B & B on the island was reserved and Captain Maude agreed to keep the ferry running to Shwartz Bay as long as there were visitors in need of a ride back.

The day arrived, clear and sunny. In addition to family, the Martins, Mike Medane, Dean Calder and many UBC classmates attended. Bentwing and a large contingent of Pillagers came along with Jan Rakowski and Peter Copel. Many nuns were there. The bulk of the attendees, however, were Islanders.

At the appointed time, Charlie wheeled Delbert to the makeshift altar, where they were flanked by Paul and Barry as ushers. Virginia led Sylvia in and the wedding ceremony proceeded without a hitch. When Sylvia and Delbert kissed and turned to face the crowd, a tenor saxophone began playing. Hal Lundquist stepped onto the far end of the lawn, appropriately lubricated. After an introductory chorus, Phil stood up as the two pre-arranged and sang in his rich baritone voice:

We are children playing in his world
    Like puppets on a string
To some he gives a special role
    Like fighters in a ring.

He tests and tests these special ones
    With obstacles severe
And then rejoices in their strength
    When they can persevere.

As he sang, Sylvia reached for Virginia's hand who reached for Barry's. Noticing, Delbert reached for Charlie's who reached for Paul's. Paul and Barry beckoned the parents. The hand joining spread like wild fire. In moments everyone was standing and the chain of hands wound through the crowd.

For they have built a special bond
That none can break apart,
Well tempered by adversity
And love from heart to heart.

Looking at a radiant bride and groom, everyone felt the song was created expressly for them. Emotion surged through their hands.

He blasts them with repeated woes
    That most could never bear,
With trials and tribulations far
    Beyond the normal share.

He smiles when they come through at last
    His searing test of fire,
And saves for them a gift of life
    On the path that they desire.

For they have built a special bond
That none can break apart,
Well tempered by adversity
And love from heart to heart.

As she surveyed the crowd, Sylvia knew they were both accepted fully back into the Island culture. Phil's words captivated them all as he repeated the final chorus.

Can love endure? Can love endure?
We know their's can for sure.

For they have built a special bond
That none can break apart,
Well tempered by adversity
And love from heart to heart.
...Well tempered by adversity
And love...from heart...to heart.

~~~

Nine miles away a very old cow raised her head, sniffed the breeze, let out a soft and mellow moo, then bent again to the grass.